Leslie Charteris

Leslie Charteris was born in Singapore on 12 May 1907. In 1919 he moved to England with his mother and brother and attended Rossall School in Lancashire before moving on to Cambridge University. His studies there came to a halt when a publisher accepted his first novel. His third book, entitled *Meet – The Tiger!*, was written when he was twenty years old and published in 1928. It introduced the world to Simon Templar, a.k.a. the Saint.

He continued to write about the Saint up until 1983, when the last book, *Salvage for the Saint*, was published by Hodder & Stoughton. The books, which have been translated into over twenty languages, have sold over 40 million copies around the world. They've inspired fifteen feature films, three TV series, ten radio series and a comic strip that was written by Charteris and syndicated around the world for over a decade.

Leslie Charteris enjoyed travelling, but settled for long periods in Hollywood, Florida, and finally in Surrey, England. In 1992 he was awarded the Cartier Diamond Dagger in recognition of a lifetime of achievement. He died the following year.

LESLIE CHARTERIS

The Saint In Miami

Series Editor: Ian Dickerson

First published in Great Britain in 1941 by Hodder & Stoughton

This paperback edition first published in 2013 by Mulholland Books
An imprint of Hodder & Stoughton
An Hachette UK company

1

Cover artwork by Andrew Howard
www.andrewhoward.co.uk

A CIP catalogue record for this title is available from the British Library

Paperback ISBN 978 1 444 76628 8
eBook ISBN 978 1 444 76629 5

Printed and bound by Clays Ltd, St Ives plc

Hodder & Stoughton policy is to use papers that are natural, renewable and recyclable products and made from wood grown in sustainable forests. The logging and manufacturing processes are expected to conform to the environmental regulations of the country of origin.

Hodder & Stoughton Ltd
338 Euston Road
London NW1 3BH

www.hodder.co.uk

To Baynard H. Kendrick
because he introduced me to so many of
the scenes in this story

CONTENTS

INTRODUCTION

When I was a teenager back in the 1960s, I worked as a volunteer at the little public library in our town, which had been founded only a few years earlier and stocked with donations from the community. Donations continued to be the main source of the library's books for several years after that, and one of my jobs was to sort and process them so we could get them on the shelves.

One day I came in and found two folding tables pushed together and piled high with books someone had given to the library. It was the largest single donation I recall. As I began to work my way through them, I realized that most of the books were mysteries, my favorite choice of reading matter at the time. One of them, a rather cheap-looking green hardback, intrigued me. It had a drawing on the front of a jaunty stick figure with a halo. The author was someone I'd never heard of: Leslie Charteris. And the title was intriguing, too. *The Saint in Miami.*

Because I was a volunteer at the library, I didn't get paid. But one of the perks of the job was that I got to take home any of those donated books I wanted to and read them before they were ever put on the shelves. I took *The Saint in Miami* home with me, sat down, opened it and started to read . . . and nothing was the same after that. Almost immediately, I was a Saint fan for life.

There were several more Saint books in that same donation, and I read them right away and began looking for more.

I found a paperback copy of *The Avenging Saint*, published by the Fiction Publishing Company, and I ordered more of those editions through the mail. The big public library in the county seat had a copy of *The First Saint Omnibus*, a treasure trove of novellas that kept me happily occupied for a couple of weeks. I scoured other libraries in the area as well as used bookstores, and over the next few decades I managed to read, as best I recall, every book in the series.

When I was asked to write an introduction for one of the Saint re-issues, I didn't hesitate to say yes or to ask if I could write the one for *The Saint in Miami*, the book that started it all for me. I wanted to reread it first, of course, and while I have at least one paperback edition of the novel around here somewhere, I thought it would be nice if I read the same edition I did back in the Sixties. Not the same exact copy, of course. The library got rid of it in a book sale a long time ago. Sold it to me, in fact, for a quarter, but that copy was lost in a fire in 2008. But I knew it was published by Triangle Books, a line of cheap hardback reprints published in the Forties, and when I checked on-line I found that copies of that edition were available for a reasonable price. So in due course, one arrived in the mail, I sat down, opened it, and began to read . . .

Revisiting any favorite thing from our youth is a dangerous proposition. This seems to be especially true with books. Inevitably, when you reread things that almost magically thrilled and enthralled you when you were young, you're going to encounter some of them that make you think, 'Wait a minute. Did I actually *like* this when I was a kid?' So it was with a slight sense of trepidation that I tackled *The Saint in Miami*. I had reread it before, but even that was more than thirty years ago. Would it hold up now? Would it be as exciting, as amusing, as just plain good now as it was then?

In a word, yes.

Since you're about to read the book, quite possibly for the first time, I won't say much about the plot. In the tense days shortly before the United States becomes involved in World War II, Simon Templar, his beautiful long-time girlfriend Patricia Holm, their stalwart friend Peter Quentin, and the colorful and none-too-bright former gangster Hoppy Uniatz, who has become sort of the group's mascot, arrive in Miami Beach in response to a letter from one of Patricia's friends asking for help. When they get there, they find that Pat's friend and her father are missing, and shortly after that a ship is torpedoed and blown up right in front of their eyes. A dead body washes ashore at Simon's feet.

Well, naturally, that's too much temptation for even a Saint to withstand. Simon has to get to the bottom of the whole sinister affair, which launches a fast-paced adventure that climaxes in one of the most suspenseful scenes I've ever read. *The Saint in Miami* truly defines edge-of-the-seat entertainment, and it's told in Charteris's breezy, finely polished prose that manages to be funny, hardboiled, and exciting all at the same time.

I didn't have to worry about this book not holding up. It might as well have been written yesterday by a master author at the top of his game. In fact, it was even better than I thought it would be, as the bishop said to the actress. But you're about to discover that for yourself, because . . . The Saint is back.

James Reasoner

FOREWORD

Readers will get their bearings in this story more quickly if they are forewarned that it was written, and takes place, during the precarious year after Europe came to grips with Hitler in the war which was at first dubbed 'phony' and the year before Pearl Harbor brought America off the sidelines and made it global.

It is another of those books which I sometimes wonder now whether I should have written, because from being highly topical they so quickly become out-dated and so comparatively soon thereafter have become quaintly pseudo-historical – which is great stuff if you are writing about anything from Napoleon on back, but can be embarrassing when your hero is supposed to be still spry and on the job today.

I can only try to assure an incredulous younger section of the audience that there actually are quite a few survivors of those days around, including this author, who are not yet fossilized or even decrepit. And I hope that when they reach our ripe old age, after an exhausting youth of cheering for their favourite football team and watching their pet paladins brawling on TV, they will be able to say the same.

Leslie Charteris

The Saint in Miami

INTRODUCTION BY LESLIE CHARTERIS[1]

. . . I am reminded by a clipping which has just reached me from the Miami Herald, in which Mr Ferman Wilson devotes half his Real Estate column to sniping at me for an error I committed in *The Saint in Miami.*

I first visited Miami in 1935 and stayed there three weeks. I didn't write the book until 1940, by which time my memory had become a little dim about some details, although not about the size of my hotel bill. I had especially forgotten some important facts about Flagler Street, which is one of the main thoroughfares of that city. Of course I had not had the privilege of knowing Flagler Street since the fabulous 20s, as Mr Wilson doubtless remembers it, when many blocks of it were consecrated to real estate offices in which acres of swamp were changing hands several times a day at increasingly astronomical prices. I do not know if Flagler Street was a one way street at that time, although it would have seemed like a good idea, keeping the traffic flowing in a uniform manner past the seething marts of the sub-dividers; but it is certainly a one way street now, and I had forgotten it, and I committed the appalling crime in Mr Wilson's eyes of making the Saint turn west on it.

I also made a mistake in describing the Miami policeman's uniform, which may have been a hangover from Nassau; and it seems that a little later the Saint and his party

[1] From *A Letter from the Saint*, 12th September 1946

caught sight of the Tamiami Canal from a place where Mr Wilson says they couldn't see it.

These of course are very serious offenses and should probably force the book to be withdrawn from circulation. Unfortunately I am still making money out of it, and I need all of this for the fund I am saving for another visit to refresh my geography. After 1935 it only took me seven years to get my overdraft into shape for a return trip to Florida, so if Mr Wilson will let me go on selling my book I may be able to make it again by 1949.

I

How Simon Templar dealt with Phantoms, and Hoppy Uniatz clung Strictly to Facts

1

Simon Templar lay stretched out on the sands in front of Lawrence Gilbeck's modest twenty-five-room bungalow, and allowed the cottony breakers pushing their way in from the Atlantic to lull him with the gentle roar of their disintegration on the slope at his feet.

Although it was an hour after a late dinner, the sand was still warm from the day's sun. Overhead, the celebrated Miami moon, by kind permission of the Chamber of Commerce and the Department of Public Relations, floated among the stars like a piece of luminous cheese, looking more like the product of one of Earl Carroll's electricians than a manifestation of nature. The moon dripped down a silvery opalescence which left black shadows in the areas it missed. The shadows deepened the tiny indentations beside Simon's nose, and for a moment gave an entirely false suggestion of care and worry to his face as he looked at Patricia Holm.

That the appearance of care was false, Patricia knew. Commonplace care was a disease of modern existence which was incapable of infecting the exuberant life of that amazing modern buccaneer who was better known to most of the world by his queer nickname of 'The Saint' than by the names which were recorded on his birth certificate. Worry he might cause to the plodding members of many police forces throughout the world; worry he certainly had caused, in lavish and sometimes even fatal doses, to very many members of that loosely knit fraternity which is popularly referred to as the Underworld, even when it lives in much greater luxury than most respectable people; but the worry stopped there. It was something quite external to the Saint. If it ever touched him at all, it was in the form of a perverse and irresponsible worry – a small irking worry that life might one day become dull, that the gods of gay and perilous adventure who had blessed him so extravagantly through all his life so far might one day desert him, leaving nothing but the humdrum uneventfulness which ordinary mortals accept as a substitute for living . . .

He reached out a brown hand and trickled sand through his fingers on to the arm which Patricia was using as a pillow for her spun-gold hair.

'You know such fascinating people, darling,' he said. 'These Gilbecks must be specially good samples. I suppose it's that open-handed New World hospitality I've read about. Turn your house over to a gang of strangers, and just leave them to it. I expect it has a lot of good points, too. Your guests don't have a chance to get on your nerves. Probably they'll send us a wire in a month or two from Honolulu or somewhere. "So nice to have had you with us. Do come again." '

Patricia moved her rounded arm to ward off the trickle of sand which threatened her hair.

'Something must have happened,' she said seriously. 'Justine wouldn't write me that she was in trouble and then go away.'

'But she did,' Simon insisted. ' "Come," she writes you. "All is not well. My father is moping about the house, bowed down with some mysterious grief and woe. Something Sinister is Going On." So what do we do?'

'I remember,' said Patricia. 'But keep on talking if it amuses you.'

'On the contrary,' said the Saint, 'it hurts me. It scarifies my sensitive soul . . . We gird up our loins and fly out here to the rescue of the beauteous Justine and her distraught papa. And are they here?'

He formed a human question mark by pulling up his knees and looking at them.

Patricia supplied the answer: 'No, they aren't here.'

'Exactly,' Simon agreed. 'They aren't here. Instead of finding them on the doorstep, waiting to welcome us with stuffed tarpon, potted coco-nuts, and poi, we are met by nothing more convivial than a Filipino houseboy with a cold. He informs us in a hoarse gust of germs that Comrade Gilbeck and this voluptuous daughter you've described so lushly have hoisted the anchor on their yacht, which I think is most appropriately named the *Mirage*, and departed for ports unknown.'

'You make a good story of it.'

'I have to. Otherwise I'd be weeping over it. The whole mushy business depresses me. I'm afraid our hosts have taken a powder, as Hoppy would say.'

'Well,' protested Patricia, 'you can't blame me for it.'

'Furthermore,' Simon continued, 'I don't believe there even was any reason for Justine to send for you. Probably Papa had just taken a flier in Consolidated Toothpicks, and then some dentist proclaimed that toothpicks destroy the teeth, and the bottom fell out of the market. After she wrote that letter another dentist came back and said that toothpicks not only prevent decay but also cure cancer, nervous B.O., and athlete's foot. The market boomed again, Pappy rejoiced, and they climbed into their canoe and paddled happily away to celebrate, forgetting all about us.'

'Maybe that's what happened.'

Simon sat up, with a shrug of his wide shoulders, and brushed the sand impatiently from his long legs.

He looked at her, and almost forgot everything else. A trick of that musical-comedy moon made her seem scarcely real. She was part of his life, the most enduring keystone of his happiness, unchanging as the stars; yet at that moment she seemed to have blended into the warm magic of the Florida night, become remote and doubly beautiful, like some cast-up fantasy of moonbeams and mother of pearl. The banter began to die out of his blue eyes. He touched her, and so felt the detachment of her mind which had helped the illusion.

'You really think something has happened, don't you?' he said soberly.

'I'm sure of it.'

A breeze sprang up from the ocean and danced inland, stirring the palm fronds behind them. It seemed to touch the Saint with a chill; and yet he knew there was no chill in the wind. He had felt this other kind of chill so many times before, like the points of a million spectral needles, frozen and feathery-thin, probing every pore with a touch as light as a cobweb. In the past it had led him into the shadow of death more often than he could remember; and yet even more often than that its same impartial touch had warned him of danger in time to escape the falling shadow. It was the chill of adventure – the stirring of a ghostly prescience that was for ever rooted in his uncanny attunement to the whispering wave-lengths of battle and sudden death. And he felt it then, as he gazed out at the shimmering vagueness of the sea.

'Look.' He slid an arm behind Patricia's shoulders and helped her to sit up. 'There's quite a big ship out there. I've been watching it. And it seems to be heading in. I could see the port light a few minutes ago, and now the starboard light's visible too. We must be looking directly at her bow.'

'Perhaps the Gilbecks are coming back, after all,' she said.

'It's much too big for them,' he said quietly. 'But why would a ship that size be heading straight for the shore – as close as that?'

Patricia stared at it.

Out on the ocean, a beam of silver light streamed out suddenly from a searchlight on the vessel's forepeak. It held steady for a second, then turned erratically as if it were hunting for something. The ray swung downwards, struck the water close to the cobbled pathway of moonlight, and swept quickly over the sea, lancing the surface like a scalpel of pure luminance. Leaking rays caught the figures of men behind it and silhouetted them against the whiteness of the superstructure.

Not until then did Simon realise that the ship was even closer to the shore than he had thought. He stood up and raised Patricia to her feet.

'You've felt that there was something wrong all evening,' he said, 'and I guess your hunch was right. There's something wrong out there.'

'It looks as if someone had fallen overboard,' she said, 'and they're trying to pick them up.'

'I wonder,' said the Saint.

He didn't know; but his answer came instantly. Even as he spoke, things happened as if his words had cued them. The searchlight went out, and with it the porthole and deck lights. Black as a collier, the vessel slid into the dappled lane of reflected moonlight.

A finger of intense radiance appeared suddenly on one of her sides, unfolded upwards with a swift blossoming, and pointed into the sky with a burst of glare that momentarily erased the brilliance of the moon. Answering that splash of fire, the entire ship heaved as though a cyclopean hand had struck it from below. For an instant the blaze wrapped it from stem to stern; and then it seemed to vomit all its insides towards the sky in one black and scarlet shower.

The clap of thunder that started from that cataclysmic disruption rolled against Simon's eardrums a split second later.

He caught Patricia's hand and dragged her hastily up the sloping beach to where a fringe of palms and a wall of pinkish stone bordered the. lawn. She felt herself lifted effortlessly through the air for an instant, and then he was crouching beside her under the shelter of the wall. For a fleeting, indefinable lull, the world seemed to stand still. On nearby Collins Avenue, automobiles had stopped while their drivers stared curiously out to sea. The breeze had gone rustling away across the flats of Florida, but the air was filled with a new and more frightening roar.

'What is it?' she said.

'A small tidal wave from the explosion. Hold everything,' he said, and then it hit.

The piled-up crest of white hissed deliriously as it drove up the beach. It smashed against the sloping sand, gained height as it ploughed on, and broke in one giant comber against the wall. Simon held her as the water fell on them like an avalanche. There was a moment of cold, crushing confusion; and then the flood was flattened out and harmless, receding down the beach, leaving no mark except a line of rubble on the lawn.

'And there goes that thousand-dollar Schiaparelli model,' said the Saint, surveying the sodden wreckage of her dress as they stood up. 'Just another casualty to this blitzkrieg business . . .'

His eyes ambled grimly over the scene, watching a gabbling rush of figures towards the shore. The nearer sounds of moving traffic had churned into a pulsing immobility, and a long distance away some female screamed stupidly . . . And then he looked down directly at his feet, and stood frozen in half incredulous rigidity.

Not more than a yard from him, a round-faced youth stared up at him unseeingly from the ground. Clad in a blue seaman's uniform, he lay on his back in the sprawled limpness of death. The wave that had hurled him in had left a small pile of seaweed against one twisted arm. The wrist of that arm was tangled in the looped cords of an ordinary lifebelt. Simon leaned down and looked closer. The moonlight was strong enough for him to read the ship's name that was painted on the belt, and as he read it his blood turned cold . . .

It seemed to him that he stared at it for a space of crawling minutes, while the letters charred themselves blackly into his brain. And yet with another unshaken sense he knew that it was actually no more than a few seconds by the clock before he was able to spur himself out of the trance of eerie and unbelieving dread that spelled from that simple name.

When he spoke, his voice was almost abnormally quiet and even. There was nothing but the steely fierceness of his grip on Patricia's arm to hint at the chaos of fantastic doubts and questions that were screaming through his brain.

'Give me a hand, darling,' he said. 'I want to get him into the house before anyone else sees him.'

There was something in his voice that she knew him too well to question. Obediently but uncomprehending, she bent over and tugged at the sailor's feet while Simon put hands under his shoulders. The man was heavy with waterlogged flaccidness.

They were half-way across the lawn with their burden when a shadow moved on the porch of the guest house. Simon let go his end of the load abruptly, and Patricia hurriedly followed his example. The shadow detached itself from the house and stealthily drew nearer.

The moonlight shed itself with pardonable coyness over a pair of white flannels with inch wide stripes surmounted by a five-coloured blazer which might have been tailored for Man Mountain Dean. Above the blazer, and peering at the Saint, was the kind of face which unscientific mothers used to describe when trying to frighten their recalcitrant young.

'Is dat you, boss?' asked the face.

It had a voice that was slightly reminiscent of a Mason with laryngitis, but at that moment Simon found it almost melodious. The face from which it issued, instead of giving him heart failure, seemed like a thing of beauty. From long familiarity with its abstruse code of expressions, he perceived that the deep furrows in the place where Nature had neglected to put a brow, far from foreboding a homicidal attack, were indicative of anxiety.

'Yes, Hoppy,' he said in quick relief. 'This is us. Don't stand there gawping. Come and help.'

Hoppy Uniatz lumbered forward with the gait of a happy bear. It was not his role to criticise or argue. His was the part of blind and joyful obedience. To him, the Saint was a man who worked strange wonders, who plotted gigantic schemes which slid into beautiful fruition with supernatural simplicity, who moved with a godlike nonchalance in those labyrinths of thought and cerebration which to Mr Uniatz were indistinguishable from the paths of purgatory. Thought, to Hoppy Uniatz, was a process involving acute agony in the upper part of the head; and life had really only become worth living to him on that blissful day when he had discovered that the Saint was quite capable of doing all the thinking for both of them. From that moment he had become an uninvited but irremovable attachment, hitching his wagon complacently to that lucky star.

He looked down admiringly at the body on the ground.

'Chees, boss,' he got out after a time. 'I hear de bang when you boin him, but I can't figger out what it is. De nerz almost knocks me off de porch. What new kinda cannon is dat?'

'There are times, Hoppy,' said the Saint, 'when I feel that you and I should get married. As it happens, it was quite a big kind of cannon; only it wasn't mine. Now help me get this stiff inside. Take him into my room and strip the uniform off him, and make sure that none of the servants see you.'

These were orders of a type that Hoppy could understand. They dealt with simple concrete things in a manner to which he was by no means unaccustomed. Without further conversation, he picked the youth up in his arms and returned rapidly into the shadows. The lifebelt still dangled from the corpse's wrist.

Simon turned back to Patricia. She was watching him with a quiet intentness.

'I expect we could do with a drink,' he said.

'I could.'

'You know what happened?'

'I'm getting an idea.'

The lean planes of his face were picked out vividly for a moment as he lighted a cigarette.

'That ship was torpedoed,' he said. 'And you saw the lifebelt?'

'I only read part of it,' she said. 'But I saw the letters H.M.S.'

'That was enough,' he said flatly. 'As a matter of fact, it said H.M.S. *Triton*. And, as you know, that's a British submarine.'

She said shakily: 'It can't be true—'

'We've got to find out.' His face was lighted again in the ripening glow of his cigarette. 'I'm going to borrow Gilbeck's speedboat and take a trip out to sea and find out if there's anything else to pick up where the wreck happened. D'you want to see if you can locate Peter white I get it warmed up? He should have got back by now.'

2

Lawrence Gilbeck's twin-screw speedboat shuddered protestingly as the Saint drove her wide open to the top of an inbound comber. For a moment she hung on the crest with both whirling propellers free; then they clutched the water again, and she dived into the trough like a toboggan racing down a bank of smooth ice. Curtains of spray leapt six feet into the air on each side of her as she settled down to a steady forty knots. The name painted on her counter said *Meteor*, and Simon had to admit that she could live up to it.

From his place on the other side of the boat, crouching behind the slope of the forward windshield, Peter Quentin spoke across Patricia.

'It'll be a great comfort to all the invalids who've come south for the winter,' he said, 'to know that you're here.'

He spoke in a tone of detached resignation, like a martyr who has made up his mind to die bravely so long ago that the tedious details of his execution have become merely an inevitable anti-climax. He hunched his prizefighter's shoulders up around his ears and crinkled his pleasantly pugnacious features in an attempt to penetrate the darkness ahead.

Simon flicked his cigarette-end to leeward, and watched its red spark snap back far beyond the stern in the passing rush of wind.

'After all,' he said, 'the Gilbecks did leave word for us to make ourselves at home. Surely they couldn't object to our taking this old tub out for a spin. She was sitting in the boathouse just rusting away.'

'Their Scotch wasn't rusting away,' Peter remarked, operating skilfully on the bottle clamped between his feet. 'I always understood that it improved with age.'

'Only up to a point,' said the Saint gravely. 'After that it's inclined to become anaemic and waste away. A tragedy which it is the duty of any right-minded citizen to forestall. Hand it over. Pat and I are chilly after our shower bath.'

He examined the label and sipped an approving sample before he handed the bottle to Patricia.

'Mr Peter Dawson's best,' he told her, raising his voice against the roar of the engine as he opened the throttle wider. 'Pass it back to me before Hoppy gets it and we have to consign a dead one to the sea.'

Somewhere within the small globule of protopathic tissue surrounded by Mr Uniatz's skull a glimmer of remote comprehension came to life as the Saint's words drifted back to him. He leaned over from his seat behind.

'Any time you say to t'row him out, boss,' he stated reassuringly, 'I got him ready.'

Through years of association with the palaeolithic machinery which Mr Uniatz's parents had bequeathed to him as a substitute for the racial ability of *homo sapiens* to think and reason, Simon Templar had acquired an impregnable patience with those strange divagations of continuity with which Hoppy was wont to enliven an ordinary conversation. He took a firmer grip on the wheel and said: 'Who have you got ready?'

'De dead one,' said Hoppy, exercising a no less noble degree of patience and restraint in elucidating such a simple and straightforward announcement as he had made. 'De stiff. Any time ya ready, I can t'row him in.'

Simon painfully worked out the association of ideas as the *Meteor* ate up the silver-speckled water.

'I was referring,' he explained kindly, 'to our bottle of Peter Dawson, which will certainly be a dead one two minutes after you get your hands on it.'

'Oh,' said Mr Uniatz, settling back again. 'I t'ought ya was talkin' about de stiff here, I got me feet on him, but he don't bodder me none. Any time ya ready.'

Patricia gave Simon back the bottle.

'I noticed that Hoppy brought a sack down to the boat,' she said, with the slightest of tremors in her voice. 'I wondered if that was what was in it . . . But has it occurred to you that every coastguard boat for a hundred miles will be headed here? We might have a lot of explaining to do if they got curious about Hoppy's footrest.'

Simon didn't argue. Part of what she said was already obvious. Not so far ahead of them, many new lights were rising and falling in the swell, and searchlights were smearing long skinny fingers over the ocean. The Saint had no definite plan yet, but he had seldom used a plan in any adventure. Instinct, impulse, a fluid openness of approach that kept his whole campaign plastic and effortlessly adaptable to almost any unexpected development – those were the only consistent principles in anything he did.

'I brought him along because we couldn't leave him in the house,' he said at length. 'The servants might have found him. We may drop him overboard out here or not – I haven't made up my mind yet.'

'What about the lifebelt?' said Patricia.

'I peeled the name off and burnt it. There's nothing else to identify it. There wasn't any identification in his clothes.'

'What I want to know,' said Peter, 'is how would a single sailor get lost overboard from a submarine at a time like that.'

'How do you know he was the only one?' said Patricia.

Simon put a fresh cigarette between his lips and lighted it, cupping his hands adroitly around the match.

'You're both on the wrong track,' he said. 'What makes you think he came off a submarine?'

'Well—'

'The submarine wasn't sunk, was it?' said the Saint. 'It did the sinking. So why should it have lost any of its crew? Furthermore, he wasn't wearing a British naval uniform

– just ordinary sort of seaman's clothes. He might have come off the ship that was sunk. Or off anything. The only incriminating thing was the lifebelt. A submarine might have lost that. But his wrist was tangled up in the cords in quite a peculiar way. It wasn't at all easy to get it off – and it must have been nearly as difficult to get it on. If he'd just caught hold of it when he was drowning, he wouldn't have tied himself up to it like that. And incidentally, how did he manage to drown so quickly? I could have held my breath from the time the torpedo blew off until I saw him lying at my feet, and not even feel uncomfortable.'

Peter took the bottle out of Patricia's hands and drew a gulp from it.

'Just because Justine Gilbeck wrote a mysterious letter to Pat,' he said, without too much conviction, 'you're determined to find a mystery somewhere.'

'I didn't say that this had anything to do with that. I did say it was a bit queer for us all to come to Miami on a frantic invitation, and then find that the girl who sent the invitation isn't here.'

'Probably somebody told her about your reputation,' Peter said. 'There are a few old-fashioned girls left, although you never seem to meet them.'

'I'll just ask you one other question,' said the Saint. 'Since when has the British Navy adopted the jolly Nazi sport of sinking neutral ships without warning? . . . Now give me another turn with that medicine.'

He took the bottle and tilted it up, feeling the drink forge his blood into a glow. Then, without looking round, he extended his arm backwards and felt the bottle engulfed by Mr Uniatz's ready paw. But the glow remained. Perhaps it had its roots in something even more ethereal than the whisky, but something nevertheless more permanent. He couldn't have told anyone why he felt so sure, and yet he knew that he couldn't possibly be so wrong. The far fantastic bugles of adventure were ringing in his ears, and he knew that they never lied, even though the sounds they made might be confused and incomprehensible for a while. He had lived through all this before . . .

Patricia said: 'You're taking it for granted that there's some connection between these two things.'

'I'm only taking the laws of probability and gravitation for granted,' he said. 'We come here and find one screwy situation. Within twelve hours and practically spitting distance, we run into another screwy situation. It's just a good natural bet that they could raise their hats to each other.'

'You mean that that kid who was washed ashore with the lifebelt was part of some deep dark plot that Gilbeck is mixed up in somehow,' said Peter Quentin.

'That's what I was thinking,' said the Saint.

Patricia Holm stared out at the roving lights that wavered over their bow. She had had even more years than Peter Quentin in which to learn that those wild surmises of the Saint were usually as direct and accurate as if some sixth sense perceived them, as simple and positive as optical vision was to ordinary human beings.

She said: 'Why did you want Peter to check up on this fellow March? What has he got to do with anything?'

'What did Peter find out?' countered the Saint.

'Not much,' Peter said moodily. 'And I know a lot of more amusing ways of wasting an afternoon and evening in this town . . . I found out that he owns one of the islands in Biscayne Bay with one of these cute little shacks like Gilbeck's on it, about the size of the Roney Plaza, with three swimming pools and a private landing field. He also has a yacht in the Bay – a little runabout of two or three hundred tons with twin Diesels and everything else you can think of except torpedo tubes . . . As you suspected, he's the celebrated Randolph

March who inherited all those patent-medicine millions when he was twenty-one. Half a dozen show-girls have retired in luxury on the proceeds of divorcing him, but he didn't even notice it. The ones he doesn't bother to marry do just about as well. It's rumoured that he likes a sprinkle of marijuana in his cigarettes, and the night club owners hang out flags when he's here.'

'Is that all?'

'Well,' Peter admitted reluctantly, 'I did hear something else. Some broker chappie – I ran him down and scraped an acquaintance with him in a bar – said that March had a big load of money in something called the Foreign Investment Pool.'

The Saint smiled.

'In which Lawrence Gilbeck also has plenty of shekels,' he said, 'as I found out by looking through some of the papers in his desk.'

'But that's nothing,' Peter protested. 'It's just an ordinary investment. If they both had their money in General Motors—'

'They didn't,' said the Saint. 'They had it in a Foreign Investment Pool.'

The *Meteor* canted up the side of a long roller, and above the sound of the engine a deep glug floated forward as Mr Uniatz throatily inhaled the last swallow from his bottle. It was followed by a splash as he regretfully tossed the empty bottle far out over the side.

'You still haven't told us why you were interested in March,' said Patricia.

'Because he phoned Gilbeck twice today,' said the Saint simply.

Peter clutched his brow.

'Naturally,' he said, 'that hangs him. Anyone who phones anybody else is always mixed up in some dirty business.'

'Twice,' said the Saint calmly. 'The houseboy took the first call, and told March that Gilbeck was away. March left word to have Gilbeck call him when he got back. Two hours later he phoned again. I took the call. He was very careful to make sure I got his name.'

'A sinister symptom,' Peter agreed, wagging his head gravely. 'Only the most double-dyed villains worry about having their names spelt right.'

'You ass,' said the Saint dispassionately, 'he'd already left his name once. He'd already been told that Gilbeck was away. So why should he go through the routine again?'

'You tell us,' said Peter. 'This is making me seasick.'

Simon drew at his cigarette again.

'Maybe he knew Gilbeck wasn't there, all the time. Maybe he just wanted to impress on that dumb Filipino that Randolph March was trying to get hold of Gilbeck and hadn't seen him.'

'But *why*?' asked Patricia desperately.

'Look at it this way,' said the Saint. 'Lawrence Gilbeck and Justine left unexpectedly this morning, without saying where they were going or when they'd be back. Now suppose Gilbeck was mixed up with Comrade March in some fruity skulduggery, and Comrade March found it necessary to the welfare of several million dollars to get him out of the way. Comrade March would naturally have an alibi to prove he hadn't been anywhere near Gilbeck on the day Gilbeck disappeared, and a little artistic touch like that telephone routine wouldn't do the alibi any harm.'

Peter searched weakly for the second bottle which he had thoughtfully provided.

'I give it up,' he said. 'You ought to write mystery stories and earn an honest living.'

'And still,' said Patricia, 'we're waiting to know why all this should have anything to do with that ship being sunk.'

The Saint gazed ahead, and the clean-cut buccaneering

lines of his face were carved out of the dark in a mask of bronze by the dim glow of the instrument panel. He knew as well as they did that there were many other possible explanations, that he was building a complete edifice of speculation on a mere pinpoint of foundation. But much better than they ever could, he knew that that ghostly tingle in his scalp was more to be trusted than any formal logic. And there was one other thing which had come out of Peter's report, which seemed to tie all the loose fragments of fact together like a nebulous cord.

He pointed.

'That ship,' he said, 'was some sort of Foreign Investment – to somebody.'

3

Red and green dots that marked a floating village of motley craft rushed up to meet them. A trim white fifty-footer, coldly ornate with shining brass, detached itself from the welter of boats, made a tight foaming turn, and cut across their bow. Simon reversed the propellers and stopped the *Meteor* with the smoothness of hydraulic brakes.

The fifty-footer was earmarked with the official dignity of the Law. A spotlight snapped on, washed the *Meteor* in its glare, and revealed a lanky man in a cardigan jacket and a black slouch hat standing in the bow.

The man put a megaphone to his lips and shouted: 'You better get the hell on in – there're too many boats out here now.'

'Why don't you go on in yourself and make room for us?' asked the Saint pleasantly.

'On account of my name's Sheriff Haskins,' came the answer. 'Better do what I tell you, son.'

The simple statement held its own implications for Hoppy Uniatz. It conflicted with all his conditioned reflexes to be using a sacked-up cadaver for a footrest, and to have a policeman, even a policeman as incongruously uniformed as the man on the cruiser, dallying with him at such short range. The only natural method of handling such a situation presented itself to him automatically.

'Boss,' he volunteered raucously, leaning forward on to the Saint's ear, 'I brung my Betsy. I can give him de woiks, an' we can get away easy.'

'Put it away,' snarled the Saint. He was troubled by a feeling that the spotlight on the police boat was holding them just a little too long. To face it out, he looked straight into the light and shouted amiably: 'What happened?'

'A tanker blew up.'

Sheriff Haskins yelled the answer back through the

megaphone, and waved his free hand. Water boiled at the cruiser's stern, and she began to edge nearer. Thirty feet from the *Meteor* she reversed again. Haskins stood silent for a time, leaning across the rail and steadying himself against the police boat's roll. Simon had a physical sensation of the sheriff's scrutiny behind the shield of the adhesive spotlight.

He was prepared for the question when the sheriff asked: 'Haven't I seen you before?'

'You might have,' he said cheerfully. 'I drove around town for a while this afternoon. We're staying with Lawrence Gilbeck at Miami Beach, but we only got here today.'

'Okay,' said Haskins. 'But don't hang around here. There's nothing you can do.'

The spotlight went out, a muffled bell clanged aboard the police launch, and she moved away. Simon eased in the *Meteor's* clutch, let her pick up speed, and headed round in a wide circle.

'I wonder how long it's going to take that lanky sheriff to figure out that you're you,' Peter said meditatively. 'Of course you couldn't help talking back to him so that he'd pay particular attention to you.'

'I didn't know he was the sheriff then,' said the Saint, without worry. 'Anyway, there'd be something wrong with our destiny if we didn't get in an argument with the Law. And don't get soft-hearted and pass that bottle back to Hoppy. He's had his share.'

He settled down more comfortably behind the wheel, and worked the *Meteor's* bow to port until they were running southwards, parallel with the coast. It was the direction in which that single light had moved which he had seen immediately after the explosion, but he didn't know why he should remember it now. On the surface, he was only heading that way because he had enjoyed the outward run, and it seemed too soon to go home.

The ocean was a vast, peaceful rolling plain in which they floated half-way to the stars. Along the shore moved a life of ease and play and exquisite frippery, marked by a million fixed and crawling and flickering lights. Among those lights, invisible at the distance, cavorted the ephemeræ of civilisation, a strange conglomeration of men and women arbitrarily divided into two incommiscible species. There was the class which might have sober interests and responsibilities elsewhere, but in Miami had no time for anything but diversion; and there was the class which might play elsewhere, if it had the chance, but in Miami existed only to minister to the visiting players. There went the politicians and the pimps, the show girls and society matrons, the millionaires and the tycoons and the literati, the prostitutes and the gamblers and the punks. Simon listened to the lulling drone of the *Meteor* and felt as if he had been suddenly taken infinitely far away from that world. It was such a tenuous thing, that culture on which such playgrounds grew like exotic flowers. It was so fragile and easily destroyed, balanced on nothing more tangible than a state of mind. In a twinkling that coastline could be darkened, smudged into an efficient modern blackout more deadly than anything in those days which had once been called the Dark Ages. The best brains in the world had worked for a century to diminish Space; had worked so well that no haven was safe from the roaring wings of impersonal death . . .

Even a few seconds ago, the ocean on either side of them had been coloured with the flat soft hues of a deadened rainbow. It was the same caressing water of the Gulf Stream which day by day lapped the smooth tingling bodies of bathers near the shore. But out there it had been covered with sluggish oil, keeping down the blood of shattered men who would never play any more. It was so much easier to tear down than to build . . .

'Look, boy,' said Patricia suddenly.

The Saint stiffened and came out of his trance as she caught his arm. She was pointing to starboard, and he looked out in the direction where her finger led his eyes with an uncanny crawling sensation creeping up the joints of his spine as if it had been negotiating the rungs of the ladder.

'Chees, boss,' said Mr Uniatz, in a voice of awe, 'it's a sea-soipent!'

For once in a lifetime, Simon was inclined to agree with one of Hoppy Uniatz's spontaneous impressions.

Just above the surface of the water, reflecting the moon-glow with metallic dullness, moving sluggishly and with a deceptive air of slothfulness, drifted a weird phantasm of the sea. No living movement flexed its wave-washed surface, and yet it was indubitably in motion, splashing its way forward with loggy ponderousness. A sort of truncated oval tower rose from its back and ploughed rigidly through its own creaming wash.

Instinctively Simon spun the *Meteor's* wheel; but even before the swift craft could swing around the apparition was gone. A bow wave formed against the conning tower, climbed up it, and engulfed it in a miniature maelstrom. For a few seconds he stared in fascination at the single piece of evidence which told him he had not been dreaming: something like a short stubby pipe which went on driving through the water, trailing a thin white wake behind. While he looked, the top of the periscope moved, turned about, and fixed the *Meteor* with a malevolent mechanical eye. Then even that was gone, and the last trace of the submarine was erased by the smooth-flowing surface of the sea.

Peter Quentin drew a deep breath, and rubbed his eyes.

'I suppose we all saw it,' he said.

'I seen it,' declared Mr Uniatz. 'I could of bopped it, too, if ya hadn't told me to put my Betsy away.'

Simon grinned with his lips.

'The only thing that's any good for bopping those sea-serpents is a depth charge,' he said. 'And I'm afraid that's one thing we forgot to bring with us . . . But did anyone see any markings on it?' None of them answered. The speedboat lifted her bow under his touch on the throttle and ate up the miles towards the shore. Simon said: 'Neither did I.'

He sat quietly, almost lazily, at the wheel; but there was a tension in him that they could feel under his repose. It reached out invisible filaments to grip Peter and Patricia with the Saint's own stillness of half-formed clairvoyance, while their minds struggled to get conscious hold of the chimeras that swam smokily out of the night's memories. The only mind which was quite untroubled by any of these things belonged to Hoppy Uniatz, but it is not yet known whether anything more psychic than a sledge-hammer would have been capable of penetrating the protective shield of armour plate surrounding that embryonic organ.

Peter reopened his reserve bottle.

'We got rid of the name on the lifebelt,' he said hesitantly. 'If we all swore the submarine had swastikas on it, we might gum things up a bit.'

'I had thought of that,' said the Saint. 'But I'm afraid you might gum them the wrong way. Your passport would be against you. There may have been some other lifebelt or another stray clue that we didn't pick up. Then we should just make matters worse. They could say we were just part of a clumsy plot to try and hang it on Hitler. It's too much risk to take . . . Besides which, it wouldn't help us at all with this Gilbeck-March palaver.'

'You're still very sure that they're connected,' said Patricia.

Simon swung the wheel again, and a quartering comber sped them through the inlet into the comparative quiet of Biscayne Bay.

'I'm not quite sure,' he said. 'But I'm going to try and

make sure tonight.'

The plan had begun to shape itself almost subconsciously while they raced over the sea. The outlines of it were still loose and undefined, but the nucleus was more than enough. He knew now what he was going to do with the body of the youth that lay under Hoppy's elephantine brogues, and his forthright mind saw nothing ghoulish in the idea. The owner of the body could have no practical interest any longer in what happened to it: it was an article as impersonal as a leg of mutton, a piece of merchantdise to be used in the most profitable way Simon could see. He knew that the idea that had come to him was crazy, but his best ideas had always been that way. There were immovable boundaries to the world of speculation and theory: beyond those frontiers there was no way to travel except by direct action. And the more straightforward and direct it was, the better he liked it. He had never found any better place to meet trouble than half-way.

Close by the rocks of the County Causeway, bordering the ship channel, he slowed up the *Meteor* and began to edge her in to the treacherous bank.

'Pat, old darling,' he said, 'you and Peter are going ashore. Hoppy and I are going to pay a call on Comrade March.'

She looked at him with troubled blue eyes.

'Why can't we all go?'

'Because we're too big a party for an expedition like this. And because somebody ought to be back at Gilbeck's to hold the fort in case anything turns up there. And lastly because if anything goes wrong, Hoppy and I might need an alibi. Get going, kids.'

The *Meteor* delicately nosed the bank. Peter Quentin jumped out on to the rocks and helped Patricia to follow him. He looked back unwillingly.

'March's place is called Landmark Island,' he said. 'It's

right next to where his yacht's anchored. The yacht is a big grey thing with one funnel, and it's called the *March Hare*. If you're not home in two hours we'll come looking for you.'

Simon waved his hand as the *Meteor* drifted away in the current. Scarcely waiting till they were clear, he stole a notch or two out of the throttle and turned the sleek speedster away in a wide arc. A big passenger ship was crawling up the channel behind him, looming doubly large beside the speeding cars on the Causeway. Its whistle howled piercingly as they crossed under its bow; and the Saint smiled.

'Bellow your head off, brother,' he said softly. 'Maybe you're lucky you didn't sail two hours ago.'

They headed down the bay at a moderate and inconspicuous pace that hardly raised the voice of the engine above a mutter; and Mr Uniatz sat up on the narrow strip of deck behind the Saint and tried to bring the conversation back to fundamentals.

'Boss,' he said, 'do we bump dis guy March?'

'That remains to be seen,' Simon told him. 'Meanwhile you can take the sack off that sailor.'

Mr Uniatz clung with the pride of parenthood to his original idea.

'He's better in de sack, boss, when we t'row him in. I got it weighted down wit' some old iron I find in de garage.'

'Take him out of the sack,' Simon ordered. 'You can throw the sack and the old iron in, but make sure he doesn't go with them.'

He switched off the engine as Hoppy began moodily to obey. Ahead of them loomed the grey hull of the *March Hare*. Besides the riding lights, other subdued lights burned on her, illuminating her deck and superstructure with a friendly glow, and at the same time vouching for the fact that there were still people on board who might not be quite so friendly. But to Simon Templar that was merely an interesting detail.

The delight of his own audacity crept warmingly through his veins as the speedboat drifted silently towards the anchored yacht. The *Meteor* heeled slightly as Hoppy lowered the weighted sack into the bay.

'Now whadda we do?' asked Mr Uniatz hoarsely. 'He ain't got nut'n on but his unnerwear.'

Simon caught the anchor chain and made fast to it, steadying the *Meteor* with deft but heroic strength to ease her against the hull without a sound that might have attracted the attention of the crew. The moon was over the *March Hare's* stern, and it was dark at the bow. His job began to look almost easy.

'I'm going on board,' he said. 'You wait here. When I let down a rope to you, pass up the body.'

He stretched his muscles experimentally, and felt under the cuff of his left sleeve to make sure that the ivory-hilted throwing knife which had pulled him out of so many tight corners nested there snugly in the sheath strapped to his forearm. Over his head, the anchor chain slanted steeply up to the *March Hare's* flaring prow. He gripped the *Meteor's* foredeck with soft-shod feet and jumped for the chain, and hung there above the rippling tide as the speedboat floated under him to the length of the painter. Then he went swarming up the chain with the soundless agility of a monkey.

He reached the hawsehole, and swung both legs up to it. Manœuvring himself gingerly, he was able to get the fingers of one hand over the edge of the deck planking near the bow. With a quick muscular twist he sent the other hand up to join it, and chinned himself cautiously.

With his eyes on a level with his hands, he discerned a deck hand in white ducks leaning over the rail on the opposite side of the bow. Simon lowered himself again, and began to work his way aft with infinite patience, suspended from the edge of the deck by nothing but the grasp of his bent fingers.

When he was almost amidships he chinned himself again. This time the forward end of the deckhouse secured him from the danger of being caught at a disadvantage if the man in white had happened to turn round, and there was no one else to be seen from that angle. He freed one hand and reached up for the lowest bar of the rail. In a few seconds more he was standing on the deck and melting into the nearest pool of shadow.

From the stern of the yacht, soft voices and the tinkle of ice in glasses mingled with the faint music of a low-tuned radio. Motionless against the side of the deckhouse, Simon listened for an envious moment, and discovered that his throat was parched from the salt air and the neat whisky he had swallowed. The melodious sounds of tiny icebergs in cold fluid were almost more than his resolution could resist; but he knew that those amenities had to wait. He started back towards the bow with the flowing stealth of a cat.

The seaman at the rail had not moved, and did not move as Simon crept up to him on noiseless rubber soles. The Saint studied his position scientifically, and tapped him on the shoulder.

The man spun round with a hiccup of startlement. With his mouth hanging open, he had time to glimpse the sheen of a shaded deck light on crisp black hair, the chiselled leanness of devil-may-care lines of cheekbone and jaw, a pair of mocking blue eyes and a reckless mouth that completed the picture of a younger and streamlined reincarnation of the privateers who once knew those coasts as the Spanish Main. It was a face which by no stretch of imagination could have belonged to any ally of his, and the seaman knew it intuitively; but his reactions were much too slow. As he reached defensively for a belaying pin socketed in the rail near by, a fist that seemed to be travelling with the weight and velocity of a power-diving aeroplane struck him accurately on the point of the chin, which he had carefully placed in the exact position where Simon had planned for him to put it.

Simon caught him neatly as he fell.

An open hatch just forward of the deckhouse gave him a view down a narrow companion into a lighted alleyway. Simon hitched the unconscious man on to his shoulder and carried him down.

The alley contained four doors labelled with neatly stencilled letters. The inscription on one door said stores. Open, it revealed a dark locker which exhaled an odour of paint and tar. It took exactly three minutes to truss the victim, gag him with his own socks and handkerchief, and tuck him away inside. After which Simon examined the other resources of that very conveniently located storeroom.

He returned to the deck with a length of rope and a stout piece of wood slotted at each end, known to seafaring persons as a bosun's chair. He moved along the rail until he was directly over the *Meteor*, rigged the chair, and lowered it over the side.

A jacketed steward came out on deck amidships, carrying a tray, and turned aft. Simon crouched like a statue by the rail and watched him go. The steward had not even glanced in that direction when he emerged; but there was some slight difficulty in judging how long he would be gone, and on the return trip he could hardly help noticing Simon's operations at the bow.

Hoppy gave a couple of tugs at the rope to signal that the cargo was ready to load.

There was still no sign of the steward returning.

'Well,' said the Saint, to his guardian angel, 'we've got to take a chance some time.'

He took a fresh grip on the rope and began to haul. The burden swung free at first, then bumped dully against the side as it came higher. The Saint threw all the supple power of his back and shoulders into the task of speeding its ascent, while he breathed a prayer that no member of the crew had been in a position to notice the thud and scrape of its contact. After what seemed like a year, the lolling head of the body came in sight above the edge of the deck.

And then the Saint's tautly vigilant ears caught the scuff of the steward's returning footsteps.

Holding tightly to the rope, Simon stepped rapidly backwards until the deckhouse concealed him. Then he fastened the rope to a handy stanchion with a couple of quick half-hitches.

The steward's footsteps pattered along the deck, slackened hesitantly, and shuffled to a dubious stop. The Saint held his breath. If the steward raised an alarm from where he stood, he might as well take a running dive over the side and hope for the best . . . But the steward's nerves were under phlegmatically good control. His footsteps picked up again, approaching stolidly, as he came on forward to investigate for himself.

Which was an unfortunate error of judgment on his part.

He came past the corner of the deckhouse into Simon's field of vision and stood still, looking down movelessly at the lifeless head of the boy dangling against the bottom of the rail. And Simon stepped up behind him like a phantom and enclosed his neck in the crook of an arm that was no more ghostly than a steel hawser . . .

The steward became gradually limp, carrying his perplexity with him into the land of dreams; and Simon picked him up and transported him over the same route that he had taken with the deck hand. He also treated him in exactly the same way, binding and gagging him and pouring him into the store locker with his still sleeping fellow crewman. The only distinction he made was to remove the steward's trim white jacket first. The Saint's humanitarian instincts made him reflect that the atmosphere of the storeroom might grow warmer later with its increasing population; and furthermore another use for that article of clothing was beginning to suggest itself to him.

It was a little short in the sleeves, but otherwise it fitted him fairly well, he decided as he shrugged himself into it on his way back to the deck.

He had an instant of alarm when he returned towards the dangling body and saw a ham-sized hand groping with very lifelike activity above the level of the deck. A moment later he had identified it. He grasped it, and assisted the perspiring Mr Uniatz to heave himself over the rail.

'I ought to push you back into the drink,' he said severely. 'I thought I told you to wait in the boat.'

'De stiff stops goin' up,' explained Hoppy, 'so I t'ought dey mighta gotcha. Anyhow, dey ain't no more drink. I finish de udder bottle while I'm waitin'.' He became aware of the uniform jacket which was now buttoned tightly over the Saint's torso, and stared at it with dawning comprehension. 'I get it, boss,' he said. 'We're gonna raid de bar an' get some more.'

He beamed at the prospect like an ecstatic votary at the gates of Paradise. Simon Templar had long been aware of the fact that Mr Uniatz's nebulous notions of an ideal after life were composed of something like floating out through eternity in an illimitable sea of celestial alcohol; but for once the condition of his own palate left him without the heart to crush the manifestations of that dream.

'I've heard you bring up a lot of worse ideas, Hoppy,' he admitted. 'But first of all we'd better finish lugging in the stiff, before somebody else comes along.'

A brisk exploration along the starboard side disclosed that the door from which the steward had emerged gave into an alley athwartships from which a lounge opened forward, a dining saloon aft, and a broad stairway descended to the accommodations provided for the owner and his guests. Simon stood at the head of the staircase and listened. No sound came from below. While he stood there, Hoppy Uniatz caught up with him, with the body draped over one herculean shoulder.

Simon beckoned him on.

'We'll take him below,' he said in a low voice. 'Stay far enough behind me so that if anything blows up you'll be in the clear.'

He stepped quietly down to the bottom and inspected the broad alleyway in which he found himself. He felt no particular anxiety at that point. Randolph March would have no reason to suspect that his yacht was in the hands of a boarding party. From the sounds Simon had heard on deck, Mr March was probably engrossed in a pleasant *tête-à-tête* which would effectively distract his attention from all such ideas. And all the crew who had not gone ashore were probably asleep, except the watchman who had already been disposed of, and the steward detailed to attend to Mr March's alcoholic requirements, who had encountered a similar doom but who could at a suitable moment be interestingly replaced . . .

The elements of the idea took firmer hold on his imagination as he tiptoed over the carpet. His shoes sank two inches into the resilient pile. He reached the door of a stateroom, listened for a moment, and opened it. A pencil flashlight from his hip pocket discovered sycamore panelling and the silken covers of a double bed.

'This'll do, Hoppy,' he said, and stood aside while Mr Uniatz brought his burden in.

He closed the door and switched on the lights.

'Put him in the bed and tuck him in,' he said. 'He deserves a bit of comfort now.'

Hairbrushes and other personal toilet gadgets on the dressing-table suggested that the cabin might be in current occupation. Simon looked through a couple of drawers, and found a suit of rainbow silk pyjamas. He threw them on the bed as Hoppy pulled down the covers.

'Fix him up nicely,' he said. 'He's a guest of the management . . .' Another thought crossed his mind, and he went on speaking more to himself than to any audience. 'Maybe he's been here before. And I wonder what he was then . . .'

He stood guard by the door while Hoppy carried out his commission, kindling a cigarette and keeping one ear alertly cocked for any sound of human movement in the alleyway outside. But there was none. So far, the adventure couldn't have gone more smoothly if it had been mounted on roller bearings. He began to feel a glutinous and godless exhilaration rising within him. There was no longer any doubt in his head that this was going to be one of his better evenings . . .

Hoppy Uniatz finished his task, and turned towards him with the air of a man who, having accomplished a worthy but tiresome duty, feels himself entitled to return to more important and more satisfying projects.

'Now, boss,' said Mr Uniatz, 'do we take de bar?'

The Saint rubbed his hands gently together.

'You are a single-minded man devoted to the life of action, Hoppy,' he remarked. 'But there are times when the wisdom of the ages speaks through your rosebud lips. I think we will take the bar.'

The steward had come out on to the deck from the central alleyway. Returning to the head of the stairway, Simon considered the dining saloon which faced him. It seemed the most likely turning point in the trail; and he was not mistaken. When he went in, he found a very artistic glass and chromium bar set back in an alcove half the width of the deckhouse, the other half probably being taken up by the galley.

'Dis is it,' said Mr Uniatz complacently. 'What kind of Scotch have dey got?'

'Control yourself,' said the Saint sternly. 'It's that selfish attitude of yours, Hoppy, which is so discouraging to anyone who is trying to improve your character. Let us try to think first of others, as the good books tell us. We were obliged to remove Mr March's steward. Mr March, by this time, is probably getting quite impatient for his next round of drinks. Clearly it's our duty to substitute our services for his incapacitated factotum and see that he gets his gargle.'

He investigated the selection of supplies with a critical eye, secure in the spell of silence which was guaranteed by Mr Uniatz's anguished efforts to interpret his last speech into words of one syllable. Finally he fixed his choice on a row of bottles whose labels met with his approval, and set them up on a tray. A pair of silver ice-buckets from the back of the bar were indispensable accessories, and a built-in refrigerator provided plentiful supplies of ice.

'Let's go,' said the Saint.

He moved out on to the deck with his accumulation of booty. He no longer felt that there was any call for stealth. Quite boldly and carelessly he walked aft and came around the end of the deckhouse to an open veranda sheltered by white canvas awnings.

Randolph March was there – Simon recognised him at once from pictures he had seen in the tabloids. The pictures had not shown the colouring of the round pink face and straight fair hair, but they had possibly over-emphasised the marks of premature dissipation under the eyes and the essential weakness of the mouth and chin. From the deck chair beside him, a girl with red hair and big violet eyes also looked up with a revelation of complete physical beauty that made Simon's sensitive heart lose its regular rhythm for an instant. She had been listening to something that March had been telling her when Simon came into sight, with an expression of rapt adoration to which any heir to the March millions could legitimately have been held entitled; but a lingering trace of the same expression still clung to her features as she turned, and was responsible for an intervening moment of speechlessness before the Saint could recapture his voice.

Then he recovered himself, and bowed to them both with mildly derisive elegance.

'Good evening, little people,' murmured the Saint.

2

How Mr Uniatz found a Good Use for Empties, and Sheriff Haskins spoke of his Problems

1

It could not be denied that such a transparently expressive face was no handicap at all to anyone so exquisitely modelled as the red-haired girl. From the topmost waves of her softly flaming hair, down through the unbelievable fineness of her features, down through the unworldly perfect proportions of her curving shape, down to the manicured tips of her sandalled toes, there was nothing about her which any connoisseur of human architecture could criticise. The clarity of expression which in any less flawless creature might have been disillusioning, in her was only the last illuminating touch which crowned a masterpiece of orchidic evolution. And it seemed to Simon Templar that the admiration in her eyes, after they rested on him, lasted just a little longer than a hangover from Randolph March's practised charm should have justified.

Perhaps he flattered himself . . . But there was no doubt that Randolph March was conscious of a break in the spell of his own fascination. March was notorious for his appreciation of expensive beauty, and he was acutely cognisant of anything that interrupted beauty's appreciation of himself. There was the petulance of a spoiled brat in his face as he shot a glance at the brimming mint julep in his hand and found the frosty glass still full.

He scowled venomously at the Saint in his steward's jacket.

The captain must have hired new help without consulting him: for the life of him he couldn't remember having seen the man before. Neither could he remember having ordered any champagne. The *March Hare* had a wine list that could be boasted about; but the hazards of war were making good vintages increasingly difficult to obtain, and Randolph March held good vintages in the fanatical reverence which can only be acquired by a man who has developed epicurean tastes with a studious eye for their snob value rather than out of the sheer gusto of superlative living.

Then, other details percolated through the disintegrating aura of his romantic mood as he incredulously counted the forest of bottles bristling on the tray in front of him. The new steward was blithely swinging a couple of silver ice-buckets in one hand like a juggler waiting to go into an act, while a cigarette slanted impudently up between his lips. And while Randolph March stared at the sight, the steward banged the buckets down on the deck and used the hand thus freed to remove Mr March's feet from the extension rest of his deck chair and make room there for the tray.

Randolph March fought down an imminent apoplectic stroke for which his eccentric life would still not normally have qualified him for at least another ten years, and snapped: 'Take that stuff away!'

The steward blew out a cloud of cigarette smoke and plunked bottles into the ice-buckets, giving them a professional twirl which no Parisian *sommelier* could have bettered.

'Don't call it "that stuff",' he said reprovingly. 'A '28 Bollinger deserves a little more respect.'

The girl laughed like a chime of silver bells, and said: 'Oh, do let's have some! I just feel like some champagne.'

'There you are, Randy, old boy,' said the Saint, giving the bottles another twirl. 'The lady wants some. So what have you got to say?'

'You're fired!' March exploded.

The Saint smiled at him tolerantly, as one who humours a fractious child.

'That's all right with me, Randy, old fruit,' he said amiably. 'Now let's all have a drink and talk about something else. I've got a few questions to ask you.'

He selected a bottle, approved its temperature, and popped the cork. Sparkling amber flowed into a row of glasses while March watched in a paralysis of fuming stupefaction. Once March started to rise, but sank back slowly when Simon turned a cool blue eye on him. The Saint's complete and unperturbed effrontery was almost enough to hold anyone immobilised by itself; but there was also an easy air of athletic readiness in the Saint's bantering poise which was an even more subtle discouragement to March's immediate ideas of personal violence.

Simon passed the tray. The red-headed girl took her glass, looking up at him curiously under her long lashes. March hesitated, and Simon pushed the tray closer to him.

'You might as well, Randy,' he said. 'Perhaps you'll need it before I've finished.'

March took the glass, not quite knowing why he did it. Simon looked around for Hoppy, but Mr Uniatz had already taken the precaution of providing for his own simple tastes. A bottle of Scotch was tilted up to his mouth, and his Adam's apple throbbed in a clockwork ecstasy of ingurgitation. The Saint grinned, put down the tray and took a glass for himself.

'You'd better talk fast,' said March. 'I'll give you just five minutes before I turn you over to the police.'

'Five minutes ought to be enough,' said the Saint. 'I want to talk to you about a shipwreck.'

'This is frightfully exciting,' said the girl.

Simon smiled at her and raised his glass.

'I think so too, Ginger,' he drawled. 'You and I ought to get together. Anyway, here's to us.'

'Whatever you want to talk about,' said March, 'doesn't make any difference to me.'

The Saint chose a vacant chair and settled himself luxuriously. He blew a smoke-ring into the still warm air.

'That ought to make everything quite easy,' he remarked. 'Because what you think about it doesn't make any difference to me . . . So about this shipwreck. Not very long ago a tanker loaded with gasoline blew up just a little way off the beach. I saw it happen. It certainly made a very impressive splash. But after the fireworks were over, I saw something else. It looked like the light of a ship sailing away from the wreck. And it kept on sailing away.'

March patted a yawn and said: 'I like your infernal gall, trespassing on my yacht to tell me a story like that.'

'I only did it,' said the Saint mildly, 'because I wondered if by any chance the ship that sailed away might have been yours.'

A glibly modulated voice broke into the softly playing music of the radio and said: 'Here is the latest bulletin on the *Selina*, the tanker which blew up off Miami Beach two hours ago. No survivors have yet been picked up, and it is feared that all hands may have perished in the disaster. The cause of the disaster is not yet known, but the explosion appears to have taken place so suddenly that there would have been no time to launch the boats. Coastguard vessels are still on the scene . . . We now take you back—'

'That's the first I've heard of it,' March said flatly. 'We were out taking an evening cruise, but I didn't see any explosion. I did hear something like a distant clap of thunder, but I didn't think anything of it.'

Simon jumped up suddenly and snatched a napkin from the tray.

'That's too bad, Ginger,' he murmured. 'I hope it won't stain your dress. Let me get you another glass.' He worked over her busily, and went on without looking up: 'Naturally, if you'd had any idea what had happened, you wouldn't have sailed away. You'd have turned round and gone rushing to the rescue.'

'What do you think?' retorted March scornfully.

'I think you're a goddam liar,' said the Saint.

March spluttered: 'Why, you—'

'I think,' Simon proceeded, in the same impersonal and unruffled voice, 'that you were out cruising to see if the tanker really would blow up, and when you were satisfied about that you turned round and came home.'

He was watching March like a hawk then. He knew that his time was measured in seconds, but he hoped there would be enough of them for March's reaction to tell him whether his unformed and fantastic ideas were moving in anything like the right direction. But March's stare had a blankness that might have been rooted in any one of half a dozen totally different responses.

And then March glanced up with a quick change of expression, and Simon heard Hoppy Uniatz's disgusted voice behind him.

'Chees, boss, I couldn't help it. He got de drop on me.'

The Saint sighed.

'I know, Hoppy,' he said. 'I heard him coming.'

He turned unflurriedly and inspected the new arrival on the scene. This was not another steward or a deck hand. It was a man of medium height but square and powerful build, who wore a captain's stripes on the sleeve of his white uniform. The square and slightly prognathous cut of his jaw matched the cubist lines of his shoulders. On either side of a flat-lipped mouth, deep creases like twin brackets ran down from the nostrils of an insignificant nose. Under the shadow of the peak of his cap his heavy-lidded eyes were like dry pebbles. He held a .38 Luger like a man who knew how to use it.

'Ah, Captain,' said March. 'It's lucky you came along.'

The captain stayed far enough away, and kept his Luger aimed midway between Simon and Hoppy, so that he could transfer the full aim to either one of them with a minimum of waste movement.

'I heard some of the things he said, so I thought something must be wrong.' His voice was deep-pitched and yet sibilant, an incongruous combination which jarred the ear to an antagonism as deep as instinct. 'What does he want?'

'I think he's crazy,' said March. 'I don't even know how he got on board.'

'Shall I send for the police and have him removed?'

The Saint selected a fresh cigarette from a jar on the table, and lighted it from the stump of its predecessor. He looked out at the lights of Miami.

'They tell me that the local jail is up in that tower.' He pointed languidly. 'It seems to be a very nice location. You take an elevator up to the twenty-fourth floor. It's a beautiful modern hoosegow with a terrace where the prisoners take their constitutionals every day. I suppose Hoppy and I might get as much as thirty days up there for boarding your yacht without permission. I just wonder how much of that time you'd really feel like gloating over us.'

There was nothing very menacing in his voice, certainly nothing frightening about his smile, but Randolph March fingered a wispy blond growth on his upper lip and shot a glance at the girl.

'Karen, my dear, we may have some trouble with these men,' he said. 'Perhaps you'd better go inside.'

'Oh, please!' she pouted. 'This is much too much fun to miss.'

'That's the spirit, Karen, darling,' murmured the Saint approvingly. 'Don't ever miss any fun. I promise I won't hurt you, and you may have some laughs.'

'Damn your impudence!' March sprang up. He was bolder now that the tough-featured captain had arrived. 'Don't talk to her like that!'

Simon ignored him, and went on: 'In fact, darling, if you like tonight's sample you might call me up tomorrow and we'll see if we can organise something else.'

March took a step forward.

'Damn your impudence,' he began again.

'You repeat yourself, Randy.' Simon cocked a reproachful eyebrow at him. 'Perhaps you're not feeling very well. Do you have a sour stomach, burning pains, nervous irritability, spots before the eyes, a flannel tongue? Take a dose of March's Duodenal Balm, and in a few minutes you'll be mooing like a contented cow . . . Or do you really want to start something now?'

It was curious what a subtle spell his lazy confidence could weave. Even with the added odds of the captain's muscular presence, and the Luger which was really the dominant factor in the scene, there was something about the Saint's soft-voiced recklessness which made Randolph March's natural caution reassert itself. His clenched fists relaxed slowly.

'I don't have to dirty my hands on anyone like you,' he stated loftily, and half turned. 'Captain, call some of the crew and have these men taken away.'

'You'll find a couple of your pirates tied up in the store locker,' the Saint told him helpfully. 'I had to park them there to keep them out of the way, but you can let them out. You can probably wake up a few others. Bring as many as you can, so it'll be interesting . . . And when you call the police, maybe you'd better tell them who they're sending for. You forgot to be inquisitive about that.'

'Why should we be?' The captain's voice had a sudden sharpness.

Simon smiled at him.

'The name is Simon Templar – usually known as the Saint.'

2

So far as Randolph March was concerned, the announcement was a damp squib. A quick pucker passed across his brows, as if the name struck a faintly familiar note and he was wondering for a moment whether it should have meant more.

Simon wasn't sure about the girl Karen. Her glamorous, wide-eyed attitude towards March, he felt certain, was nothing but a very polished pose; but whether the pose sprang from stupidity or cunning he had yet to learn. Since events had begun to occur, she had exhibited an unusual degree of detachment and self-control. She had only moved once, in the last few minutes, and that was to refill her champagne glass. Now she sipped it tranquilly, watching the proceedings like a spectator at a play . . .

Oddly enough, the captain was the only one who gave a satisfactory response. In pure dimension, it was very slight: it only meant that his Luger moved to definitely favour the arc of fire in which the Saint stood. But to Simon Templar, that in itself was almost enough, even without the stony hardening of the pebbly eyes under the shading peak of the cap. It gave Simon a strange creeping sensation in his spine, as if he had come close to the threshold of a discovery that was not yet definite enough to seize.

'What about it?' said March. 'I don't care what your name is.'

The captain said: 'But I know him, Mr March. The Saint is a well-known international criminal. The newspapers call him "the Robin Hood of modern crime". He is a very dangerous man. Dangerous to you and to me and to everyone else.'

'So wouldn't it be very much simpler and safer,' said the Saint, 'not to call the police? Why not go for another evening cruise – take us out to sea and quietly destroy us and sink our boat and let the underwriters write us off as *spurlos versenkt* – like you did with Lawrence Gilbeck and his daughter?'

'The man's a maniac,' said March in a colourless tone.

'I am,' Simon confessed affably, 'completely nuts. I'm loony enough to think that after you've moved us into that elegant penal penthouse, Hoppy and I will just stroll around the roof garden wondering how long it'll be before you join us. I'm daft enough to think that I can send you to the chair for a very fine and fancy collection of murders. Like the murder of Lawrence Gilbeck and his daughter Justine. And some poor kid who was washed up on the beach tonight, with one wrist conveniently tangled into a lifebelt with the name of a British submarine on it. Not to mention a much larger collection of guys who went down with a tanker that got itself torpedoed tonight by a mysterious submarine which I think you could tell us plenty about. Of course, that's just another of my screwy ideas.'

He knew that it was screwy, but he had to say it. He had to find out what sort of response the outrageous accusation would bring.

March sat up, and his eyes narrowed. After a moment he said slowly: 'What's this about a submarine? The radio said the tanker blew up.'

'It did,' said the Saint. 'With assistance. As it happens, I saw the submarine myself. So did three other people who were with me.'

March and the captain exchanged glances.

The captain said: 'That's very interesting. If it's true, you certainly ought to tell the police about it.'

'But why do you think I should know anything about it?' demanded March.

'Maybe on account of the Foreign Investment Pool,' said the Saint.

He was firing all his salvos at once, in the blind hope of hitting something. And it was dawning on him, with a warm glow of deep and radiant joy, that none of them were going altogether wide. Not that there was anything crude and blatant about the way they rang the bell. It was far from making a sonorous and reverberating clang. It was, in fact, no more than an evanescent tinkle so faint that an ear that was the least bit off guard might have doubted whether anything had really happened at all. But the Saint knew. He knew that his farfetched and delirious hunch was coming true. He knew that all the things he had linked together in his mind were linked together in fact somehow, in some profound and intricate way which he had yet to unravel, and that both Randolph March and the captain were vital strands in the skein. He knew also that by talking so much he was putting a price on his own head; but he didn't care. This was adventure again, the wine of life. He knew.

He knew it even when March relaxed and took a cigarette from the jar and lounged back again with a short laugh.

'Very amusing,' said March. 'But it's getting quite late. Captain, you'd better get rid of him while he's still funny.'

'He's a dangerous man,' said the captain again, and this time he said it with only the most delicate shade of added emphasis. 'If I thought he was making a threatening movement, I might have to shoot him.'

'Go ahead,' said March in a bored voice.

He put the cigarette in his mouth and looked for a match. Simon stepped over to him, flicked his lighter, and offered it with an obsequious efficiency which could not possibly have been rivalled by the steward for whom he was deputising. The muscles of his back crawled with anticipation of a bullet, but he had to do it. March stared at him, but he took the light.

'Thank you,' he said and turned his slight puzzled stare to the captain.

Simon surveyed them both.

'You had a chance then,' he remarked. 'I wonder why you didn't take it? Was it because you didn't want to shock Karen?'

He put the lighter back in his pocket with the same studied deliberation. 'Or did it occur to you that if the police had to investigate a shooting on board they might dig out more than you'd want them to?'

'As a matter of fact, Mr March,' said the captain placidly, 'I was wondering how many other people he might have told his ridiculous story to. You wouldn't want to be annoyed with any malicious gossip, no matter how silly it was.'

'Perhaps you'd better find out,' March suggested.

'I'll take him ashore to the house and do that while we're waiting for the police.'

Probably that was the precise mathematical point at which the Saint's last lingering fragments of doubt dissolved, creeping over his scalp with a spectral tingle on their way out before they melted finally into nothingness.

The dialogue was beautifully done. It was exquisitely and economically smooth. There wasn't a ragged tone in it anywhere that should have betrayed anything to the listener who wasn't meant to understand too much – and Simon wondered whether the girl Karen was in that category. But in those few innocuous-sounding words a vital problem had been considered, a plan of solution suggested and discussed, a decision made and agreed on. And Simon knew quite clearly that the scheme which had been approved was not one which promised great benefits to his health. What would happen if they got him safely away into a secluded room in the house, and what that huskily soft-spoken captain's notions might be on the subject of likely methods of finding out things from a reluctant informant, were not the most pleasant prospects in the world to brood about. But he had staged the scene for his own benefit, and now he had to get himself out of it.

Simon knew that not only the fate of that adventure but the fate of all other possible adventures after it hung by a thread; but his eyes were as cool and untroubled as if he had had a platoon of infantry behind him.

'You don't have to worry about me,' he said. 'But Gilbeck left a letter which might be much more of a nuisance to you.'

'Gilbeck?' March repeated. 'What are you talking about?'

'I'm talking about a letter which he thoughtfully left in his house before you kidnapped him.'

'How do you know?'

'Because I happen to be living in his house at the moment.'

The furrow returned between March's brows.

'Are you a friend of Gilbeck's?'

'Bosom to bosom.' Simon refilled his champagne glass. 'I thought he'd have mentioned me.'

March's mouth opened a little and then an expression of hesitant relief came over his face.

'Good Lord!' he exclaimed. He laughed, with what was obviously meant to be a disarming heartiness. 'Why ever didn't you say so before? Then what is all this business – a joke?'

'That depends on your point of view,' said the Saint. 'I don't suppose Lawrence Gilbeck and Justine found it particularly funny.'

March plucked at his upper lip.

'If you really are a friend of theirs,' he said, 'you must have got hold of the wrong end of something. Nothing's happened to them. I talked to the house today.'

'Twice,' said the Saint. 'I took one of the calls.'

'Mr Templar,' said the captain carefully, 'you haven't behaved tonight like one of Mr Gilbeck's friends would behave. May we ask what you're doing in his house while he is away?'

'A fair question, comrade.' Simon raised his glass and barely wetted his lips with the wine. 'Justine asked me to come and be a sort of general nursemaid to the family. I answer the phone and read everybody's personal papers. A great writer of notes and jottings, was Brother Gilbeck.' He turned back to March. 'I haven't ferreted the whole business out yet, Randy, but it certainly does look as if he didn't really trust you.'

'For what reason?' March inquired coldly.

'Well,' said the Saint, 'he left this letter I was telling you about. In a sealed envelope. And there was a note with it which gave instructions that if anything happened to him it was to be sent to the Federal Bureau of Investigation.'

March sat quite still.

The girl lighted a cigarette for herself, watching the Saint with intent and luminous eyes.

March said, in an uneven voice: 'Better put your gun away, Captain. It's nice of Mr Templar to come and tell us this. We ought to know more about it. Perhaps we can clear up some misunderstandings.'

'Pardon me, sir.' The captain was perfectly deferential, but he kept his gun exactly where it was. 'We should be more certain of Mr Templar first.' He turned his dry stony eyes on the Saint. 'Mr Templar, since you seem to be so sure that something has happened to Mr Gilbeck, did you carry out his instructions and mail that letter?'

Simon allowed his glance to shift with a subtle hint of nervousness.

'Not yet. But—'

'Ah, then where is the letter?'

'I've still got it.'

'Where?'

'At the house.'

'It would be so much better if you could produce it to Mr March and prove that you're telling the truth.' The captain's eyes were as hard and flickerless as agates. 'Perhaps you didn't really leave it at home. Perhaps you still have it with you.'

He took one step closer.

The Saint's left hand stirred involuntarily towards his breast pocket. At least, the movement looked involuntary – a defensive gesture that was checked almost as soon as it began. But the captain saw it, and interpreted it as he was meant to interpret it. He took two more steps, and reached towards the pocket. Which was exactly what Simon had been arranging for him to do.

A lot of things happened all at once, with the speed and efficiency of a highly specialised juggling routine. They can only be catalogued laboriously here, but their actual sequence was so swift that it defeated the eye.

The Saint made a half turn and a neat flick of his right wrist which jarred the bubbling contents of his champagne glass squarely into the captain's eyes. Simultaneously the fingers of the Saint's left hand closed like spring-steel clamps on the wrist behind the captain's Luger. Meanwhile, all the unexpected physical agility which justified Hoppy Uniatz's professional name, and compensated with such liberality for the primeval sluggishness of his intellect, surged into volcanic activity. One of his massive feet swung up from the rear in a dropkick arc which terminated explosively on the base of the captain's spine; and almost immediately, as if the kick had only been timed to elevate the captain to meet it, the top of the captain's skull served as a landing field for the whisky bottle for which by this time Mr Uniatz had no further practical use. The captain lay down on the deck in a disinterested manner, and Simon Templar turned his Luger in the direction of Randolph March's slackly drooping jaw.

'I'm sorry we can't stay now,' he murmured. 'But I'm afraid your skipper had some unsociable ideas. Also it's getting to be time for Hoppy's Beauty sleep. But we'll be seeing you again – especially if Lawrence Gilbeck and Justine don't show up very soon. Try not to forget that, Randy . . .'

His voice was very gentle, but his eyes were no softer than frozen sapphires. And then, as quickly and elusively as it had come, the chill fell away from him as he turned to smile at the girl, who had not moved at all in those last hectic seconds.

'You'll remember, won't you?' he said. 'Any time you feel like some more fun, you know where to find me.'

She didn't answer, any more than March, but the recollection of her raptly contemplative gaze stayed in his mind all the way home and until he fell asleep.

3

He was breakfasting heartily on fried chicken and waffles served under the shade of a gaudily striped umbrella when Peter Quentin and Patricia joined him on the patio.

'You must have been tired.' Patricia slipped her bath robe back from her brown shoulders, and draped slender tanned legs and sandalled feet along the length of a cane chair. 'Peter and I have been swimming for two hours. We thought you were going to sleep all day.'

'If we hadn't heard you snoring,' said Peter, 'we could have hoped you were dead.'

The Saint's white teeth denuded a chicken bone.

'Early rising is the burden of the proletariat and the affectation of millionaires,' he said. 'Being neither, I try to achieve a very happy mean.' Holding the bone in one hand, he used it as a pointer to indicate the retreating form of a billowy negress who was waddling away into the background with a tray: 'Where did the Black Narcissus come from? She wasn't here yesterday. She says her name's Desdemona, and I find it hard to believe.'

'Don't talk with your mouth full,' Patricia told him. 'She showed up this morning with a coloured chauffeur named Eben. It was their day off yesterday.'

'That's interesting.' Simon stirred his coffee. 'And the Filipino houseboy was down town on some errand. So nobody actually saw how Gilbeck and Justine left.'

'They phoned,' she said; and he nodded.

'I've helped people to make phone calls myself, in my day.'

Peter Quentin hoisted his powerful trunk-clad form on to a sunwarmed coping, and swung his sandy feet.

'If the Gilbecks don't show up today, skipper, do we just stick around?'

Simon leaned back and glanced around contentedly at the

semi-tropical scene. The house sprawled out around him, cool and spacious under the roof of Cuban tile. A riot of poinsettias, hibiscus, and azaleas bordered the inner wall of the estate and overflowed into the patio. On the other side of the house, a palm-lined driveway swept in a horseshoe towards Collins Avenue. The heightened colours drawn in flashing sunwashed lines made a picture-book setting for the ocean's incredible blue.

'I like the place,' said the Saint. 'Gilbeck or no Gilbeck, I think I'll stay. Even without the succulent Justine. Desdemona cooks with the thistledown touch of a fairy queen. It's true that she sometimes looks at me with what a more sensitive man might think was black disapproval, but I feel I can win her. I'm sure that she'll learn to love me before we part.'

'It'll be one of your biggest and blackest failures if she doesn't,' said Patricia.

Simon ignored her scathingly and lighted a cigarette.

'Here in the midst of this epicurean if somewhat decadent Paradise,' he said, 'we can exist in sumptuous and sybaritic splendour at Comrade Gilbeck's expense, even though we may have to deny ourselves such British luxuries as bubble-and-squeak and toad-in-the-hole. It's a beautiful place to live. Also it's full of fascinating people.'

'You haven't tried the restaurant where I had dinner last night, when I was out sleuthing for you,' said Peter Quentin. 'They served me a very fat pork chop fried in peanut oil, and coffee with canned milk which turned it a disappointed grey. There was also a plate of grass and other vegetable matter, garnished with a mayonnaise compounded of machine oil and soap flakes.'

'The fascinating people are the principal attraction,' Patricia explained. 'Particularly the one with red hair.'

The Saint half closed his eyes.

'Darling, I'm afraid our one and only Hoppy must have been embroidering the story. I told you last night exactly what happened. The whole thing was most casual. Somehow she has fallen under the baleful spell of March's Gastric Ambrosia, but naturally my superior beauty impressed her. I judged her to be a demure little thing, unversed in the ways of the world and unskilled in duplicity.'

'And shy,' said Patricia.

'Perhaps. But certainly not lacking – at least in several major points which a crude man might find attractive in that particular type of girl.'

'I suppose that's why you offered to find some more fun for her.'

'So long as she has her fun,' Peter observed, 'it can't really matter if you get us all bumped off.'

Simon created a perfect smoke-ring.

'We don't have to worry about that for the present. I think our murders will be temporarily postponed on account of the hitch which I contrived last night.'

'You mean that letter you invented?'

Simon refrained from answering while Desdemona hove alongside to collect the dishes. When the last of them was on the tray supported by her ample arm, she asked stoically:

'When is you-all goin' away?'

The Saint flipped a half dollar in the air, caught it, and placed it on the edge of the laden tray.

'That was one of the best breakfasts I ever ate, Desdemona,' he told her. 'I think we'll wait until Mr Gilbeck gets back.' He added deliberately: 'Are you sure they didn't give you any idea how long they'd be away?'

' 'Deed they didn't.' Desdemona's eyes grew round as they moved from Simon to the shiny coin. 'Sometimes they's gone a week acruisin'. Sometimes 'taint moh than foh a day.'

She departed stolidly on that enlightening note, and Peter grinned.

'You'd better try some folding money next time,' he suggested. 'She doesn't seem to thaw for silver.'

'All artists are temperamental.' Simon stretched his legs and took up from where he had been interrupted. 'Yes, I was talking about that letter which I was clever enough to invent.'

'What makes you think they believe in it any more?'

'Perhaps they don't. But on the other hand, they don't know for certain. That's the catch. And even if they've decided that I really didn't have a letter last night, the idea's been put into their head. There might be a letter. I might even write one myself, having seen how they reacted to the idea. It's a discouraging risk. So they won't bump us off until they're quite sure about it.'

'How nice,' Peter said glumly. 'So instead of being bumped off without any mess, we can look forward to being tortured until they find out just where they do stand.'

Patricia straightened suddenly.

Simon looked at her, and saw that her cheeks had gone pale under the golden tan.

'Then,' she said slowly, 'if Gilbeck and Justine haven't been murdered – if they've only been kidnapped—'

'Go on,' said the Saint steadily.

She stared at him from a masklike face that mirrored unthinkable things.

'If you're right about all these things you've guessed – if March really is up to the neck in dirty business, and he's afraid of Gilbeck giving him away—'

One distraught hand rumpled her corngold hair. 'If Gilbeck and Justine are prisoners somewhere, this gang will do anything to make them talk.'

'They wouldn't need to do much,' said the Saint. 'Gilbeck would have to talk, to save Justine.'

'After which jolly interlude,' Peter said woodenly, 'he can allow himself to be slaughtered in ineffable peace, secure in the knowledge that March and Company have nothing but affection for his fatherless little girl.'

'But they'd never believe him now,' Patricia said, shakily. 'When he says he doesn't know anything about any such letter, they'll think that that's just what he would say. They'll torture him horribly, perhaps Justine too. They'll go on and on, trying to find out something he can't possibly tell them!'

The Saint shook his head. He stood up restlessly, but his face was quite calm.

'I think you're both wrong,' he said quietly. 'If Lawrence Gilbeck and Justine are still alive, I think that letter will be their insurance policy. While he believes in it, March won't dare have them killed. And he won't need to torture them. Directly he asks about it . . . well, Gilbeck didn't make all his money by being slow on the trigger. He'll know at once that we're on the job. He'll catch on to the possibilities at once. He'll say, sure, he left a letter, and what are they going to do about it? Isn't that what you'd do? And what *are* they going to do about it? There's no use torturing anyone who's ready to tell you anything you want to hear. Gilbeck hasn't got any secret information that they want.'

'How do you know?' asked Peter.

'I don't,' Simon admitted. 'But it isn't probable. My theory is perfectly straightforward. Gilbeck just went into March's Foreign Investment Pool. He was ready to overlook a few minor irregularities, as a lot of big business men would be. You don't make millions by splitting ethical hairs. Then Gilbeck got in deeper and found that some of the irregularities weren't so minor. He got cold feet, and wanted to back out. But he was in too deep by that time – they couldn't let him go. Now, our strategy is that he knew there'd be trouble, so he left a protective letter. All right. So there's a letter, and I've got it.'

Patricia kept looking down, moving one hand mechanically over the contour of her knee.

'If only you had got it,' she said.

'It might help us a lot. But as it is, the myth is a pretty useful substitute. Unwittingly, we've put Gilbeck in balk. March has got to believe in the letter. I was firing a lot of shots in the dark, but they hit things. He won't be able to figure where I got all my information, unless it was out of this imaginary letter. Which means that he's got to take care of me before he can touch Gilbeck. And he's got to be awfully cautious about that, until he's quite sure what angles I'm playing.'

'I'll have to order some wool,' said Peter. 'It sounds like a winter of sitting around and knitting while March's outfit are sinking ships and wondering about you in their spare time.'

Simon crushed out his cigarette and took another one from the packet on the table. He sat down again and put his feet up.

'I read the morning papers in bed,' he said. 'They've picked up a few bodies from that tanker, but no live ones. The way it happened, it wasn't likely that there'd be any. The cause of the explosion is still an official mystery. There was no mention of a submarine, or any other clues. So perhaps we gummed up the plot when we caught that lifebelt.'

'It's not so easy now to believe that we really saw a submarine,' said Patricia. 'If we told anyone else, they'd probably say we'd been drinking.'

'We had,' answered the Saint imperturbably. 'But I don't know that we want to tell anyone else – yet. I'd rather find the submarine first.'

Peter leaned against a pillar and massaged his toes.

'I see,' he soliloquised moodily. 'Now I take up diving. I

tramp all over the sea's bottom with my head in a tin gold-fish-bowl, looking for a stray submarine. Probably I'll find Gilbeck and Justine as well, tucked into the torpedo tubes.'

'There are less unlikely things,' said the Saint. 'The sub must have a base on shore, which has got to be well hidden. And if it's so well hidden, that's where we'd be likely to find prisoners.'

'Which makes everything childishly easy,' Peter remarked. 'There are approximately nine thousand, two hundred, and forty-seven unmapped islands in the Florida Keys, according to the guidebook, and they only stretch for about a hundred miles.'

'They wouldn't be any good. A good base wouldn't be too easy to hide from the air, and the regular plane service to Havana flies over the Keys several times a day.'

'Maybe it has a mother ship feeding it at sea,' Patricia ventured.

Simon nodded.

'Maybe. We'll find out eventually.'

'Maybe you'd better call in the Navy,' said Peter. 'That's what they're for.'

The Saint grinned irreverently.

'But it would make things so dull for us. I thought of a much more exciting way of invoking the Law. I called the sheriff's office in the middle of the night and told them that they could find a dead body on the *March Hare*. I hope it gave Randy a lot of fast explaining to do.'

'I hope you've got plenty of fast explanations yourself,' Peter said dampeningly, and pointed with one finger.

Simon looked round towards the driveway.

White dust swirled around the wheels of an approaching car. It disappeared behind the corner of the house. A minute later, Desdemona plodded heavily towards them across the patio. She came to anchor in front of the Saint,

'I think,' said Patricia, getting to her feet, 'that Peter and I will let you amuse him while we have another swim.'

Simon waved them away.

'If you see me being taken off in the wagon,' he said, 'don't bother to wait lunch.'

A couple of moments after they had gone, the official presence of Sheriff Newton Haskins cast its long shadow into the cheery courtyard.

Seen in the bright light of day, the officer who had hailed them from the police boat appeared even thinner and more lugubrious than he had the night before. He was dressed in funereal black, defying the thermometer. His broadcloth coat was pushed open behind pocketed hands, disclosing a strip of spotless white shirt topped by a narrow and unfashionable black bow tie. He might very easily have been mistaken for an undertaker paying a business call on the bereaved – except for the width of the cartridge belt at his waist, which sagged to the right under the weight of a holstered gun.

His approach was leisurely. Hands in pockets, he watched Patricia's and Peter's retreat to the beach, studied the flowers, and cast an appraising glance up at the cloudless sky. Only after he had apparently satisfied himself that the heavens were still in place did he condescend to notice the Saint.

Extended backwards in his chair, with his ankles crossed on the table, Simon greeted him with a smile of carefree cordiality.

'Well, well, well – if it isn't our old friend Sheriff Haskins! Sit down, laddie. All my life I've heard of this southern hospitality, but I didn't think a busy officer like you would have time to come and welcome a mere tourist like me.'

Hands still in his pockets, Newt Haskins seated himself slowly in a metal garden chair with an exhibition of perfect muscular control He began a survey at the Saint's bare feet, enumerated his legs, reviewed his blue gabardine shorts and the rainbow pattern of his beach robe, and ended up gazing dispassionately into the Saint's mocking eyes.

'You'd be surprised, son, how many crooks I've welcomed to Miami in the past ten years.'

'Crooks, Sheriff?' Simon's brows lifted in faint inquiry. 'Do I misunderstand you, or is that meant to refer to me?'

Haskins's left hand crawled out of its pocket like a turtle, bearing with it a plug of black tobacco. His deep-set, sharp grey eyes sank farther into his Indian brown face as he bit off a chew. Holding the remainder of the plug, his hand crawled back into its hole again. Watching the methodical working of the muscles along his lean jaws, Simon had an irresistible nostalgic memory of another officer of the Law with whose habits he was much more familiar – the gum-chewing Chief Inspector Claud Eustace Teal of Scotland Yard.

'You, son? Now, there shuah ain't no use leapin' to conclusions thataway.' Haskins's speech, when he was not shouting through a megaphone, lagged naturally into the native Floridian's drawl. 'Actually, I come on a jaunt out heah to have a few words with Mr Gilbeck. Seein' he warn't around, I thought I might make myself sociable-like an' pass the time o' day.'

'A very noble impulse,' said the Saint reservedly. 'But you have an ambiguous line of conversational gambits.'

The sheriff's otter-trap lips pursed themselves, and for one tense moment Simon feared that a stream of tobacco juice was destined to desecrate the virgin whiteness of the stucco wall. The crisis passed when Haskins swallowed, moving his larynx pensively up and down.

'Listen, son,' he said. 'Every tout, grifter, dip, gambler, yegg, land shark, and mobster, from Al Capone down to any lush-rolling prostitute, hits this city sooner or later, and we find 'em sunnin' their bottoms along our shore.'

The Saint fluttered his eyelids and said: 'But how poetical you are, daddy. Please tell sonny more.'

Haskins's face remained glum, except for a passing glint in the depths of his lethargic grey eyes which might equally well have come either from anger or amusement.

'Big and little, man and woman, killers an' punks,' he said, 'I've met 'em all. They don't none of 'em scare me.'

'That takes a great load off my mind,' said the Saint, with the same dulcet challenge.

'I thought it might do you good to know.'

'Well,' drawled the Saint, with dangerous camaraderie. 'Neighbour, that shuah is white of you. Ah ain't met sech a speerit o' kindheartedness sence mah ole gramppaw had his whiskers et plumb off by General Beauregard's horse in the Civil Wah.'

Haskins rounded out a cavernous cheek with his cud of tobacco.

'Simon Templar,' he said, without heat, 'you may think that's a southern accent, but it stinks of Oxford to me.' He leaned back in his chair and stared skywards. 'Modern police methods are makin' it awful tough for the boys, son. I sent a cable to Scotland Yard last night, an' I got an answer just before I come out heah.'

'Give me one guess and I'll tell you who answered you.' A joyful smile began to dawn on the Saint's face. 'Is it possible – No, this is too good! . . . But is it possible that it could have been signed with the name of Teal?'

The sheriff crossed his legs and fanned the air with a number eleven toe.

'I wonder if you'll be so infernally happy when you know what he had to say.'

'But I know what he had to say. That's what makes me so happy. If you'd only come to me in the first place, I could have saved you the cost of your wire. Let's see – it would have been something like this . . . He told you that I'd run the gamut of crime from burglary to murder – he thinks. That I dine on blackmail and arson seasoned with assault and battery – he suspects. That every time a body is found under the Chief Commissioner's breakfast table, or somebody puts a home-made shilling into a cigarette machine, the whole C.I.D. spews itself into prowl cars and dashes off to arrest me – they hope. Was that it?'

'It didn't have all those fancy touches,' Haskins allowed, 'but that's about how it read.'

Simon trickled blue smoke through insolent and delighted lips.

'There's only one thing wrong with your reading,' he murmured. 'You must have got so excited over the first part that you didn't stop to read through to the end.'

'An' what might that have done for me?'

'You might have found out that all the first part was really nothing but the foam on poor old Teal's fevered brain. You might have discovered that none of those things have ever been proved, that I've never been convicted of any of them or even brought to trial, that there isn't the single ghost of a charge he could bring against me today, and that I'm known to be getting pretty damn tired of having every dumb cop in creation ringing my doorbell and making me listen to a lot of addlepated blather that he can't prove.'

Haskins's left hand sought daylight again without the plug of tobacco, and its blunt thumbnail made a test for stubble around the deep cleft of his chin.

'Son,' he said, 'I've been compared to everything from the disappearin' view of a racehorse at Tropical Park to havin' my maw never find out what my paw's last name was. It ain't never got a rise out of me. I don't aim to change my tactics now. You and your friends are guests in a prominent citizen's home, an' I'm treatin' you as such. But as sheriff of this county I've got a few questions to ask you, and I expect you to answer 'em.'

It was a rare event for Simon Templar to feel admiration for any professional enforcer of the Law. But admiration for any cool, unflustered opponent who could meet him in his own field and exchange parry and riposte without vindictiveness but with a blade sharp enough to match his own, was a tribute which none of his instincts could refuse. He drew at his cigarette again, and over his fingers his eyes twinkled calculatingly blue but with all malice wiped out of them.

'I suppose that anything I say can be used as evidence against me,' he remarked cheerfully.

'If you're fool enough to tell me anything incriminatin',' said Haskins, 'that's true. Don't blame me for it.'

'Shoot,' said the Saint.

Haskins considered him.

'I saw you scootin' around in Gilbeck's speedboat last night, and I sort of wondered at the time why he wasn't along with you.'

'I sort of wondered myself. You see, we came here on a special invitation to visit him. And as you've already found out, he isn't here.'

Haskins took the rather long end of his nose between thumb and forefinger and wiggled it around.

'You mean they warn't here to welcome you, so you just thought you'd move in an' wait for 'em.'

Simon nodded.

'Sort of *noblesse oblige* not to leave without seeing your hosts.'

The sheriff took off his black hat and fanned himself thoughtfully.

'Where did you go last night after I chased you away?'

'We took a little spin. The moonlight kind of got me.'

'It used to do that to me when I was your age. So you took a little spin an' came back ashore.'

'That's right.'

'Here?'

'But of course.'

'There was a lot of funny goin's-on around Miami last night,' said Haskins, with an air of perplexity. 'They don't make sense to me. Some time in the small hours of the mawnin', my office got a call that Randolph March was carryin' an unreported body around on his yacht. Silly sort of thing, wasn't it?'

'Was it?' Simon asked innocently.

'Well, it turned out to be not so silly, at that.' Haskins uncrossed his long legs languorously. 'I took a jaunt out there, and it seems there *was* a body. The captain said they'd been out that evening, an' the lad fell overboard an' drowned before they could find him again.'

'Who was he?'

'One o' the crew. Some kid they picked up in Newport News. They didn't even know where his home was or if he had any family. Don't suppose nobody ever will. There's lots of kids like that on the waterfronts . . . But the funny thing was, nobody on the *March Hare* had called me. They were just wonderin' whether they ought to when I got there.'

'It all sounds most mysterious,' Simon agreed sympathetically.

Haskins stood up and mopped his brow.

'It shuah does. Heah's all hell apoppin' just a few hours after you land in town. You're known from heah to Shanghai as a troublemaker, although I ain't sayin' you deserve it. But if you're as clever as they say you are you naturally wouldn't have any convictions – yet. But you can't blame me for wonderin' about you.'

'Brother,' said the Saint, with the silkiest possible undertone of warning, 'you're beginning to sound just a little too much like Chief Inspector Teal. You remember what I told you? Just because a few queer things happen here, and I'm in Miami at the time, you come charging after me—'

'When I charge you, son, I'll have something.' Haskins scuffed along the floor of the patio with a phlegmatic toe. 'You look at what's been bustin' loose. A tanker blows up, for no reason. I get a mysterious phone call that nobody can account for, about a body. An' then it seems Gilbeck an' his daughter ain't heah, but you are, an' nobody knows where they've gone.'

'So,' said the Saint, 'I must be mixed up with sinking ships and kidnapping millionaires as well.'

Haskins's eyes were flinty mist.

'Son,' he said, 'I don't know what you're mixed up with.'

His right hand snaked suddenly out of his pocket and flattened out in front of Simon Templar. The Saint gazed down at the oblong slip of paper held in its palm. Written on it in plain capitals were the words:

LAWRENCE GILBECK:
YOU CAN'T GET AWAY WITH IT ALL THE TIME.
I'M COMING TO PUT AN END TO YOUR TROUBLES.

The thin linear figure drawn as a signature at the lower right-hand corner wore a halo slightly askew.

Simon stared at it for just three seconds.

And then, progressively, he began to laugh.

It started as a tentative chuckle, grew up into a louder richness that became tinged with the overtones of hysteria, and ended in a culmination of wild hilarity that mere words could scarcely choke their way through. The whole rounded gorgeousness of the business was almost too shattering to endure.

The full magnificence of it had to work itself into his

system by degrees. The March Combine had taken the hurdle of the planted body neatly enough – he had realised that. But in their impromptu comeback they had unsuspectingly sown the seeds of a supernal fizzle of which history might never see the like again.

'Of course,' sobbed the Saint weakly. 'Of course I wrote it. What about it?'

The sheriff scratched his long stringy neck.

'That sort of note only means one sort of thing to me.'

'But you don't know the background.' The Saint wiped his streaming eyes. 'Justine Gilbeck wrote us weeks ago that papa was behaving like a moulting rooster: he seemed to be in trouble of some sort, but he wouldn't tell her about it. She was worried stiff. She asked us to come here and try to find out what it was and help him. I can show you her letter. Let me get it for you.'

3

How Simon Templar made a Pleasure of Necessity, and Patricia Holm was not Impressed

1

Sheriff Haskins's equine face seemed to grow longer and gloomier as he completed a patient reading of the letter. Then he referred again to the note signed with the Saint's emblem.

' "*You can't get away with it all the time*," ' he read off it. 'What would that mean?'

'Oh, I was always kidding him that you can't make millions honestly,' Simon replied easily. 'I always told him that one day his sins would catch up with him and he'd go to jail. It was a standing rib. So of course when Justine said he was worried I had to make a crack like that.'

Haskins shifted his cud.

' "*I'm coming to put an end to your troubles*." That would be sort of double meanin', hunh?'

'Yes.'

'On account of what we'll call this fictitious reputation of yours.'

'Naturally.' The Saint was still a little shaky with laughter. 'Now wouldn't it be fair to tell me where you got that note from?'

'I dunno yet.' Haskins gazed at it abstractedly for a moment longer, and put it back in his pocket. He returned his attention to Justine Gilbeck's letter. He said, as if he were making a comment on the weather: 'I guess there's plenty of this letterhead in the house.'

'And we're all master forgers,' Simon assured him blandly. 'Signatures are just baby stuff to us. We think nothing of four whole pages of handwriting.'

Haskins put the letter back in its envelope and studied the postmark. He tapped it on his front teeth.

'Mind if I keep this a while?'

'Not a bit,' said the Saint. 'There must be a bank in town that knows her writing, and they've probably got other friends here as well. Check up on it all you like. And then come back and apologise to me.'

Haskins put on his hat and turned his head in the manner of a buzzard seeking sustenance. Finding a spot which suited his fancy, he scored a nicotine bull's-eye at the roots of an unoffending lily, and said: 'Maybe you better not leave town just yet, in case I might want to do that.'

A suitable remise was shaping itself on the Saint's tongue when it was abruptly cut off by the arrival of another car. It was a very different proposition from the sheriff's well-worn but serviceable jalopy. This was an enormous cream-coloured custom-built Packard, which whirled into the driveway and whipped around the front of the house with an effortless speed that made Simon tip an imaginary hat to the skill of the driver. Above the side of the roadster he had time to catch a glimpse of a jacket of Lincoln green and a mane of tawny hair tossed in the wind, and abruptly changed his mind about making a barbed retort.

He made a starting movement towards the house.

'All right,' he said amiably. 'I'll be expecting you.'

Haskins held his ground, absorbing the scenery with his seamed poker face.

'I don't get much pleasure out of life, son,' he explained, 'and while I'm right respectably married, red-heads have always been a weakness of mine. When I get a chance like this, I sorta hesitate to hurry off.'

'Then by all means don't hurry,' said the Saint hospitably; but his brain tightened into preparedness, tinged with a certain malevolence of which Haskins was the sole beneficiary.

It might well have suited the devious purposes of March and his captain to say nothing about his unconventional visit to the *March Hare*, but the girl's attitude was much less predictable. By trying to get rid of her during their exchange of backchat the night before, March had suggested that she wasn't entirely in his confidence; but Simon was not yet ready to attribute her prompt response to his invitation to nothing but the fascination which his beauty and charm had been able to exert on her during an interview in which his attention had been mostly elsewhere. She was a very uncertain quantity still, and the Saint wasn't anxious for Haskins to find out about that visit to the *March Hare* too soon. It was a situation that demanded active management . . .

Stimulated by the arrival of a lady, Haskins sought a nearby flower-bed and in more or less gentlemanly fashion disposed of his chew. Simon took advantage of the disgorgement to cross the patio alone and greet the girl as she came out.

By night she had been beautiful; but so were many girls whose glamour vanished with the dawn. She was not one of them. Under the sunlight she took on a flaming vividness that matched the heady colours in the courtyard. The setting took her into its composition and framed her with perfect rightness, as if its exotic blooms took life from her and she from them . . . What the Saint had to do was an attractive task.

'Karen darling!'

His voice was warm and eager. And before she could speak, he had wrapped her in his arms, holding her tightly against him and covering her lips with his own.

'The scarecrow in black's the sheriff,' he said in an urgent *sotto-voce*, and went on aloud: 'This is wonderful! Why haven't I seen you for so many years?'

The first rigidity of her supple body gave him a bad moment. But he had to give her a clue, and this seemed to be the only way. If she still didn't want to play, it was the will of Allah . . . He kept her in an embrace of iron, and kissed her again for luck.

Her strength was pent up against him; and then suddenly it wasn't. He loosed her, and she smiled, and he felt a breathlessness which could not be wholly put down to the suspense.

'It's lovely to see you, dear.' Her voice was cool and self-possessed. 'I heard this morning that you were here, and I rushed right over.' She turned towards Haskins as he shuffled up. 'Why, hullo, Sheriff. I didn't expect to see *you* again today.'

'It's an unexpected pleasure for me, Miss Leith.'

'The sheriff was out on Randy's yacht last night, Simon,' she explained quickly. 'Oh, I forgot – you don't know Randy, do you? You must meet him. Randolph March. Anyway, he has this yacht, and we were out last night, and a poor boy fell overboard and got drowned, and the sheriff had to come out and see about it.'

Haskins's eyes had a birdlike brightness.

'Why, miss,' he said, with an air of persuasive surprise, 'wasn't it Mr March who told you Mr Templar was heah?'

'Oh, no! Mr March would be frightfully jealous if he knew I'd come here. You *will* be an old dear and not say a word about it, won't you?' She took his enslavement for granted with a glance of saccharine seduction, and turned away again to twine fingers with the Saint. 'Sally wrote me from New York.'

'I hoped she would,' said the Saint happily.

The shadow of great gloom fell back over Haskins's face. The brightness went out of his eyes, to be replaced by a look of dour resignation. He said: 'Well, folks, I don't like to interrupt the meetin' of old friends. I guess I'll be moseyin' along.'

'Won't you even stay for a drink?' Simon invited halfheartedly.

'No, son.' Haskins raised his hat to the girl. 'You'll have lots of private things to talk about, I'm sure. I'll be seein' you both again 'fore long.'

'Bring your bloodhounds,' said the Saint, as he escorted the funereal figure towards the house. 'Maybe we can put something up a tree.'

He watched the sheriff's departure with mixed feelings. It was a remarkably difficult thing to divine exactly what Mr Haskins was thinking or believing at any given time. He had a disturbing faculty for shaping phrases that could hold as much or as little as the hearer's conscience wanted to read into them.

But there was a much more pleasant, if no less problematical, factor to be dealt with immediately; and Simon Templar temporarily dismissed the less alluring enigma with a shrug as he went back to the patio.

She had sat down on the footrest of a deck chair, and she was using a mirror and lipstick to repair the damage he had done to her mouth. He wondered if she also had felt any of the unaccountable breathlessness which had caught him during the infliction of the damage; but if she had, she was a good dissembler. She made him wait until her full lips were again flawless enough for her satisfaction.

Then she said calmly: 'You like very direct methods, don't you?'

'It was the only thing I could think of,' he said, matching her for calm. 'I didn't know you'd met him, and I had to make sure you wouldn't drop any bricks.'

'What made you think I'd respond to your kind of hint?'

'I just hoped.'

'You don't hate yourself very much.'

'Anyone can hope. But I'm not asking you to excuse me.

I'd do the same thing again, even if I knew it was hopeless. I found out it was worth it.'

'I'm glad you were satisfied.'

She was packing lipstick and mirror carefully back in her bag.

He regarded her thoughtfully, digging a package of cigarettes out of the pocket of his robe.

'Now,' he said, 'let's ask why you came here.'

'You told me to look you up if I wanted some fun,' she said innocently. 'Well, I've always liked fun. But perhaps our ideas of fun aren't quite the same.'

'Did March send you?'

'Did you think I was lying to that sheriif? March would be mad as hell if he knew I'd been here.'

'You lied about that drowned boy.'

Her eyes were big with ingenuous astonishment.

'I only repeated what Randy told me. I suppose the boy just fell overboard and I didn't notice it. Perhaps they didn't want to tell me about it at the time because it would have spoiled the trip. And if it wasn't true, how else could the body have got there?'

Simon tightened his lips on an unlighted cigarette.

'You lied about me.'

Colour touched her cheeks.

'Wasn't that what you wanted me to do?'

'Of course. But why did you do it?'

'Because I like you.'

'How much?'

'Enough.'

'So you liked Randy enough too, before I arrived. And when somebody better than me comes along, I can move back into the same museum. It must be a life full of variety.'

'I'm sorry.' Her slim fingers drummed on her knee. 'If you'd be more at home with a Bible Class, I can always go.'

The Saint struck a match.

'I have a sort of weakness,' he explained apologetically, 'for knowing what's going on. A lot of weird things have been happening lately, and a guy can't be too careful. My dear old grannie always told me that. If you really want me to believe that you just came following me in search of fun, I'll be a little gentleman and stop arguing – out loud. But you seemed to be pretty well in with Randy last night, and you may have gathered that there is some unfinished business between him and me. So I'm going to ask a lot of questions about your change of heart, whether you like it or not. On the other hand, if you've got something else on your mind, let's quit stalling and have it out.'

'Suppose I came here to tell you something?'

'To warn me off?' he said quizzically. 'I've been warned off before.'

'Damn you!' she flashed. 'You wouldn't have to tell me you couldn't be warned. Anyone would know it. You're the Saint – the King of Crime – the magnificent infallible hero! You couldn't be told that you were meddling with something too tough for you. I wouldn't waste my time.'

'Then what?' he inquired equably.

She mastered the temper that went so well with her proud fiery head.

'I might be able to tell you where Haskins found the note that brought him here. I might—'

A whining sound like that of a magnified malignant mosquito zipping between them cut her off. From the direction of a driveway a rifle cracked, sending its echo bouncing out to sea. Frozenly she turned her head and stared at the scar where a mushroom bullet had excavated its own grave in the stucco wall.

Bushes crashed at the base of the palms along the driveway. Simon saw the fluttering movement of the foliage, and heard a squeal reminiscent of a frightened rat, and the sound of a heavy fall. Instinctively he reached for Karen Leith, and was ready to swing her out of the way of whatever might be developing. With her soft figure in the curve of his arm, he stood warily watching the shrubbery.

'You can always find some excuse for this sort of thing, can't you?' she remarked, with commendable sangfroid.

'It's a knack I have,' he said, without a shift of his keen blue eyes.

The nearer oleanders began to sway. They parted, making way for the passage of Hoppy Uniatz's pithecanthropoid physique.

Mr Uniatz clutched a rifle in one hand, and the neck of a denim-clad figure in the other. His homely face was beatific with the consciousness of work well done as he ploughed towards the patio with both his burdens at trail. The worn heels of the lanky captive in his right hand bumped limply along behind him, kicking up little spurts of dust.

He waded through an intervening bed of assorted petunias, leaving a wide swath of destruction behind him, and dumped his prize at Simon's feet with the pleased and playful air of a spaniel bringing in a bird.

'Dis is de lug,' he said. 'He shoots at ya once before I can get to him.'

He swung his foot at the offender broodingly.

'Before you boot him to death,' Simon intervened, 'let's find out if he's got anything to say.'

He released the girl, and inspected the catch with interest.

The man was breathing noisily, sucking in gobs of air to

replenish the supply which had been temporarily cut off by the clutch of Hoppy's ungentle hand. He stared back up at Simon with sunken rabbit eyes which formed reddish beads in a face of a million lines. The wrinkles converged on loose-hung lips drawn back over snaggly yellow teeth. Topping the face was a dirty thatch of unkempt hair.

'A very pretty creature,' said the Saint, and turned to Karen. 'Is he a friend of yours?'

Her red lips tightened.

'Thanks for the flattery.'

'Well, have you ever seen him before?'

'Thank God, no. Why should I have?'

'I just wondered,' said the Saint carelessly, 'who he was aiming at.'

From behind them, Patricia asked anxiously: 'What happened, boy? We heard the shot from the beach.'

The red-haired girl whirled round and stared at her with detached appraisal. Peter Quentin came up on the run and stopped beside Pat, and did his own staring. As between expert inventories, there was nothing much in it for either side to claim an edge.

'Friends of mine,' said the Saint. 'Miss Holm and Mr Quentin.' He pointed to the bullet hole in the wall. 'Miss Leith very kindly came here to tell me something, and she was about to do it when our little playmate took a pot at us.'

'I warn't shootin' at nobody,' the man broke out in a sullen whine.

'Get up,' ordered the Saint coldly.

The man hesitated, and Hoppy prodded him in the stomach with the muzzle of the rifle.

'Giddap, youse! You hoid what de boss said.' The man scrambled to his feet, and Hoppy turned to Simon. 'Lemme woik him over a bit, boss. I can break him down.'

'In the rumpus room,' said the Saint.

Mr Uniatz took hold of the prisoner's collar and moved him off, encouraging his progress by goosing him briskly in the stern with the rifle barrel. Simon followed, and was not surprised to find the others silently entering the playroom after him.

He waved them to chairs, and carefully closed the door. The room was spacious and rather bare, an admirable venue for some mildly athletic cross-examination. Best of all, it was well soundproofed with an eye to its normal function; but that feature was equally convenient for other things. Mr Uniatz pushed the scowling captive into a seat, and then became aware that in addition to its other advantages the room also contained a bar. It seemed to him that this was a last refining touch of architectural genius. Satisfied that the situation was now under the Saint's adequate command, he eased away on a voyage of exploration . . .

Simon straddled a chair, leaned on his folded arms, and scrutinised the specimen for dissection for a leisured period which was intended to give it every opportunity to realise its predicament.

'You can make it just as tough as you like, brother,' he announced at length. 'What were you shooting at us for?'

The man glared back at him with stubborn animosity, wriggling uneasily on the edge of the hard seat which Hoppy had chosen for him. The overalls he wore were a shade too small. An ungainly stretch of sockless ankle showed white above the tops of his shoes.

'What's your name?' asked the Saint patiently.

The red eyes squinted.

'None of your goddam—'

The rest of the speech was cut off with a clunking sound as Mr Uniatz tapped him moderatingly on the side of the head with the bottle of Peter Dawson which he had just opened.

'I can make him come t'ru, boss,' he volunteered. 'I know a guy once in Brooklyn I have to ask questions about some dough he is holdin' out. He talks for two hours straight when I hold matches under his toes.'

'You see, brother,' Simon explained, 'Hoppy gets homesick for the good old days every now and again and wants to play, and I simply haven't the heart to refuse him.'

The man's gnarled fingers clasped and unclasped nervously. He ran one hand up the leg of his overalls to remove sweat from the palm.

'My name's Lafe Jennet,' he said sulkily. 'I was shootin' at a bird. You ain't goin' to kill nobody and you ain't goin' to hurt nobody, and I ain't aimin' to talk none to you.'

'Boss,' pleaded Mr Uniatz, warming to the flow of inspiration and Scotch whisky, 'I got anudder idea. You get some pliers outa de car an' take hold of de guy's toenails—'

'We may have time to try both,' said the Saint cheeringly. 'Take off his shoe.'

He rose and turned his back and strolled towards a window. He heard Hoppy's frightening voice.

'Stick out ya foot or I'll kick ya shins in.'

'The other one,' Simon said without looking round. 'Not the one he stuck out. Take off his other shoe.'

'It don't make no difference, boss. It woiks de same.'

'The other shoe, Hoppy.'

He gazed out at the sunlit scene outside, and waited. The sound of a brief scuffle ended in a grunt of pain.

'It's off, boss. Which ja wanna try foist?'

Karen Leith crushed out her cigarette and gave a tiny sigh.

'Take a look at his ankle and tell me what you see,' Simon instructed.

'Chees, boss, he's got ringwoim,' Hoppy exclaimed admiringly. 'Howja know dat?'

'It's the gall of a leg-iron.' Simon turned from the window

and strode back towards the prisoner. 'You've been towing around a ball in a chain gang, Lafe. You ought to have blown yourself to a pair of socks. The mark shows.'

'You're pretty damn smart, ain't you?' Jennet spat out. 'Well, I been in a chain gang an' I served my time. So what's it to you?'

Simon stepped back a pace and surveyed the calloused ankle.

'You escaped, Lafe,' he stated impassively. 'You hung it on the limb. Somebody knocked that shackle off you with a sledgehammer. Your ankle's still black and blue. Of course, if you'd rather talk to Sheriff Haskins than to me, we can always send for him.'

Jennet's bloodshot eyes swivelled from left to right, as if in search of a way of escape that was not there. He sat erect for an instant, a picture of deadly hatred; then he slumped back and gripped his hands about one knee.

'I'll talk to you, mister.'

'That's splendid.' Simon drew his cigarette into a glow. 'Who hired you to shoot at us?'

'I don't know.'

The Saint raised his eyebrows.

'Hoppy—'

'I told you, I don't know. That is, I don't know nuthin' except his name – Jesse Rogers.'

Behind him, Simon heard the quick grating creak of a wicker chair. For some reason it made his mind flash back to the night before, when Karen Leith had spilled her champagne.

He turned quickly. She was lighting a cigarette with a tremorless hand. She had taken the match from a box on a table beside her – her shift of position in reaching for the light accounted for the sound.

Simon resumed his interrogation with a sheepish feeling that for once his nerves had played him false.

'Where does this guy live?'

'I don't know.'

'I suppose you don't know nothing except his address.'

'See here,' Jennet snarled. 'I said I'd talk, an' I'm talkin'. I lammed from the gang a week ago from a road camp near Olustee. I got a friend owns a barge near heah. I done somethin' for him once, so he done somethin' for me. He hid me out.'

'What's his name?'

'A Greek called Gallipolis. This Rogers comes in to do a little gamblin'. Somehow he got on to me. He come out there early this mornin'. It was a case of you or me. Either I did the job or he sent me back to the gang. I never saw him before, an' I don't know nuthin' about him.'

'Are you sure,' said the Saint, 'that you weren't hired to kill a girl? A red-haired girl?' He pointed to Karen. 'Like this one?'

'No, mister. It was you.'

'You must be a lousy shot.'

'I'm the best danged—'

Jennet broke off raggedly.

The Saint looked at him peacefully and said: 'Oh, are you? Then under those humble and somewhat smelly overalls you must hide a kind heart after all.'

'Mister, I never tried. If I'd tried, you wouldn't be standin' up now. I never could shoot a man in cold blood.'

The Saint took a meditative saunter up and down the room. Nobody else moved. Aside from the almost inaudible pad of his bare footsteps, the only thing that intruded into the stillness was the sedative gurgle of good Scotch laving the appreciative palate of Mr Uniatz.

Finally he faced Jennet again, with his decision made.

'I'm going to give you a chance to prove your story,' he said. 'I want to meet this guy Rogers.'

Jennet's face crinkled with a touch of fear.

'What good does that do me?'

'If your story's true,' Simon told him, 'I might forget my legal duty and not give you back to Sheriff Haskins.'

'How do I know?'

'You don't,' said the Saint unhelpfully. 'You'll just have to take a chance. You're going to lead me to that barge after lunch . . . Hoppy, give him his shoes back and tie him up. I'll have some food sent over, but don't let Desdemona in. She might be a little startled. Take the tray at the door. I'm going to put on some clothes and get a drink.'

As they crossed the patio, Karen Leith looked at her watch.

'I'm afraid I'll have to go,' she said.

'Must you?'

'I've stayed too long already.' She turned to Peter and Patricia. 'It's so nice to have met you.'

'You must come again,' said Patricia, in a voice of arsenical sweetness.

Simon's lips twitched impenitently as he took the red-haired girl's arm and led her around the house.

'Did you change your mind about what you were going to tell me?'

'I'll exchange it for something else.'

'Another catch?'

'You don't have to trade if you don't want to.'

'Suppose you ask first.'

She played with a bracelet on her wrist.

'I wanted to be here before Haskins arrived. I came as soon as I knew. Since I was late, I'd give anything to know how you were able to satisfy him.'

The Saint laughed, softly and rapturously, like a small boy.

'That's making it too easy. I wanted you to know. I'd have told you anyway. I even wish I could be sure you'd go back to March and tell him. It's too good to lose.'

'Why?'

'Because it was the best thing that could have ever happened. I didn't have to deny anything. I admitted that I wrote that note.'

'But—'

'I know I didn't. But I might have. It fitted perfectly. You see, Justine Gilbeck wrote us a letter and begged us to come here, because her father was in some sort of mysterious trouble and she thought we might be able to help. I'd kept the letter. So I just had hysterics, and showed it to Haskins.'

Her face showed a mixture of reactions too complex to analyse. Red lips and deep violet eyes were both as elusive as the reflections in rippling water; but he felt the involuntary stirring of firm muscles in her rounded arm.

'Now, Ginger,' he said, 'where did that note come from?'

'From the *Mirage*.' Her voice at least was completely matter-of-fact. 'It was found this morning, abandoned at Wildcat Key. There was no trace of the Gilbecks or their crew.'

He walked a few steps in silence, trying to find a niche for this new knowledge.

'Where is this Wildcat Key?' he asked evenly.

'It's just outside of Card Sound, south of Old Rhodes Key.' They had reached the cream-coloured Packard. 'We could run down there on a fishing trip tomorrow – if your blonde girl friend wouldn't object.'

He opened the car door.

'Let's have dinner tonight and talk it over – if you can get away from Randy again.'

She settled herself on the maroon leather upholstery. The starter whirred, twisting the motor into a throaty purr.

'What else is there to talk over?'

'I still haven't asked you the most important question?'

'What's that?'

'What is your place in this picnic?'

His hand was still on the car door, and for a moment her fingers rested lightly on his.

'Ask me tonight,' she said. And then she was gone, and he was crinkling his eyes into the dust of her departure.

3

Simon Templar poured gin and French vermouth into a tall crystal mixer, added a shot of Angostura, and swizzled the mixture with a long spoon. Then he poured some of it over the olives in three cocktail glasses and passed them around.

'In spite of your lack of sex appeal,' Peter Quentin said frowningly, 'Patricia and I have been getting attached to you. We're going to miss you when you're gone.'

'Gone where?' Simon inquired.

Peter flourished a hand which seemed to push back the walls of the house and patio and encompass the world outside.

'Out to the Great Beyond,' he said sombrely. 'When you start for that barge this afternoon, you might wear a target over your heart. It'll give March's snipers something to aim at, and save a lot of messy bracketing.'

Simon regarded him compassionately, and tested his concoction.

'You're worrying about nothing. You heard Lafe Jennet boast about how he could shoot, and I believe him. That bloodshot eye was hatched out behind a rifle sight. He could knock an ant out of a palm top, shooting against the sun.'

'Then what was he trying to do – knock down the wall?'

'The trouble with your peanut brain,' said the Saint disparagingly, 'is that you're putting the March Combine in the same class as Hoppy – bop 'em quick, and the hell with where they fall. You've forgotten our mythical protective letter, and other such complications. If Jennet could have popped me if he'd wanted to, which I believe, then his orders only were to scare me. And the organiser of the scheme expected that we'd catch him. And the organiser also expected Jennet to squeal when things started to look too tough. And Jennet did. He squealed all he knew, which was exactly what he was meant to squeal, and did it much better that way than if they'd tried to coach him in a part. The idea being to make me think I've been pretty clever, and send me rushing out to this barge like a snorting warhorse.'

'And that's just what you mean to do, so everybody ought to be happy.' Peter finished his Martini and ate the olive. 'Whatever they've arranged for you there goes through according to schedule, and you end up at the bottom of the Tamiami Canal, weighted down with a couple of tons of coal.'

He went back to the portable bar for a refill.

'His red-headed heart-throb won't look so luscious in black,' said Patricia troubledly.

'Believe it or not,' said the Saint, 'she came here to tell me something.'

'I notice you're doing your listening with your mouth these days,' Peter remarked. 'You shouldn't have washed off her lipstick – it suited you.'

Simon sprawled himself out in a chair and gazed at them affectionately.

'Do you two comedians want to listen?' he inquired. 'Or would you rather go on rehearsing your new vaudeville act?'

He told them everything that had happened from the arrival of Haskins to the capture of Lafe Jennet. They didn't find the affair of the note so wildly hilarious as he had done, being more practically concerned with the miraculous good fortune that had deflated it; but when he came to his parting conversation with Karen Leith, they sat up, and then pondered it silently for several seconds.

'Wouldn't it be more likely,' Peter said at last, 'that Karen's visit was timed to find out whether the note business had worked?'

'But she covered me up for Haskins.'

'She covered up your visit to March,' Patricia corrected. 'March wouldn't want that brought in, anyway.'

'And then, if the note had misfired somehow, she was there

to put the finger on him for Jennet.' Peter was developing his theory with growing conviction. 'And when Jennet missed, she could report back that you were on your way out to this gambling barge—'

'And if you get out of that alive,' said Patricia, 'she'll have another chance on your date tonight—'

'And if he still accidentally happens to be alive in the morning,' Peter concluded, 'there's a fishing trip down to Wildcat Key on which anything can happen . . . It all hangs together, Chief. They've got about half a dozen covering bets, and your luck can't hold for ever. They haven't missed a loophole.'

The Saint nodded.

'You may be absolutely right,' he said soberly. 'But there's still no way out of it for me. If we want to get anywhere, we can't barricade ourselves in the house and refuse to budge. I've got to follow the only trail there is. Because any place where there's a trap there may be a clue. You know that from boxing. You can't lead without opening up. I'm going with my eyes open – but I'm going.'

They argued with him through lunch, but it would have been more useful to argue with the moon. The Saint knew that he was right in his own way; and that was the only way he had ever been able to handle an adventure. He had no use for conniving and tortuous stratagems: they were for the ungodly. For him, there was nothing like the direct approach – with the eyes open. So long as he was prepared for pitfalls, they merely formed the rungs of a ladder, leading through step after step of additional discovery to the main objective. They might be treacherous, but there could be no adventure without risk.

When it was ultimately plain that his determination was immovable, Peter demanded the right to take the risk with him. But the Saint shook his head just as firmly.

'Somebody has to stay here with Pat,' he pointed out. 'Certainly she can't come. And I'd rather leave you, because you're brighter than Hoppy. If there's so much cunning at work, the whole scheme might be to get me out of the way for a raid on this place.'

It was impossible to argue with that, either.

And yet, as the Saint sped by the waters of Indian Creek and crossed it at 41st Street, he had few doubts that for the present he himself was the main centre of attraction to the ungodly. Later it might be otherwise; but for the present he was satisfied that the ungodly would regard his entourage as small fry to be mopped up at leisure after he had been disposed of.

The open 16-cylinder Cadillac which he had chosen from the selection in the well-stocked garage purred past the golf course and held a steady fifty to the Venetian Causeway. The islands of Rivo Alto, Di Lido, and San Marino, splashed with multi-hued homes of luxury, slid past them like a moving diorama. The Saint stole a glance at Lafe Jennet, who was packed like a blue sardine between himself and Hoppy on the front seat.

'When we hit Biscayne Boulevard, Sunshine,' he said, 'which way do we turn?'

'For all of me,' Jennet said viciously, 'you can run yourself into the bay—'

The last word expired in a painful involuntary exhalation caused by the pulverising entrance of Mr Uniatz's elbow into the speaker's ribs.

'De boss astcha a question,' said Mr Uniatz magisterially. 'Or woujja like a crack on de nose?'

'Turn left, an' go west on Flagler,' said Jennet, and shut his mouth more tightly than before.

A phalanx of skyscrapers swept by, towering reminders of the perverted Florida boom. A magic city with no more than four or five million acres to spread out in had had to drive its fingers of commerce into the sky.

At Flagler Street they had to slow down. A traffic policeman, picturesque in pith helmet, white belt, and sky-blue uniform, gazed at them without special interest while he held them up. But Hoppy Uniatz put one hand in his coat pocket and crowded the pocket inconspicuously into Jennet's waist, and Jennet crouched down and made no movement. The policeman released their line, and they drove on.

They had to crawl for some blocks – first through the better shops, whose windows reproachfully displayed their most stylish variety of clothing to a throng of sidewalk strollers whose ambition appeared to be to wear as few clothes as the Law would let them; then further westward past barkers, photo shops, fortune tellers, and curio vendors with despondent-looking families of tame Seminole Indians squatting in their doors. A newsboy with his papers and racing forms hopped on the running-board, and Simon noticed a card of cheap sunglasses pinned to his shirt. He bought a pair, and stuck them on Jennet's nose.

'We don't want some bright cop to recognise that sour puss of yours while you're with us,' he said.

Eventually the traffic thinned out, and Simon opened the big car up again. They whispered past the Kennel Club and golf course, and Jennet spoke again as they came in sight of the Tamiami Canal.

'You turn left here. Go right on Eighth Street. Then you turn off again just before you hit the Tamiami Trail. You'll have to leave the car there, whether you like it or not. There ain't no way but walkin' to reach that barge.'

The relics of abandoned subdivisions grew less frequent. Flatwoods crept close to the highway. Thrust back by the hand of man, curbed but impossible to tame, the wilderness of Florida inched inexorably back and waited with primeval patience to reclaim its own.

Jennet said: 'You'd better slow down. T'ain't far, now.'

They had gone several blocks without passing another car when he indicated a dim trail leading to the right. Simon pulled the wheel over and nursed the big car skilfully over the rutted track carpeted with brownish pine needles. When the track petered out he eased the Cadillac into a thicket of pines which formed a natural screen against the outside world, and stopped the engine. He climbed out, and Hoppy Uniatz yanked Jennet out on the other side.

'I never said Rogers would be here now,' Jennet growled sulkily. 'What happens after this ain't nuth'n to do with me.'

'I'll take a chance on it,' said the Saint. 'All you have to do is to lead me on.'

He was ready for the chance by then, ready with every trained and seasoned sense of muscle and nerve and eye. This was the first point at which ambushes might begin, and even though all his movements seemed easy and careless he was overlooking no possibilities. Under lazily drooping lids, his hawk-sharp blue eyes never for an instant ceased their restless scanning of the terrain. This was the kind of hunting at which he was most adept, in which he had mastered all the tricks of both woodsman and wild animal before he learned simple algebraic equations. And something that lay dormant in his blood through all city excitements awoke here to unfathomable exhilaration . . .

The flatwoods ended suddenly, cut off in a sharp edge by encroaching grass and palmettos. Still in the shelter of the trees, he redoubled his caution and halted Hoppy and Jennet with a word.

He stared out over a far-flung panorama of flatness baked to a crusty brown by years of relentless sun. A covey of quail zoomed up out of the bushes ahead with a loud whirr of wings, and were specks along the edge of the trees before the startled Hoppy could reach for his gun.

A narrow footpath wound away through the palmettos. The Saint's eyes traced its crooked course to where the unpainted square bulk of a two-storied houseboat broke the emptiness of the barren plain. Boards covered the windows on the side towards him, but a flash of reflected light from the upper deck showed that at least one window remained unboarded at the stern. The palmettos hid any sign of water, giving an illusion that the houseboat rested on land.

Lafe Jennet said: 'Come on.'

The Saint's arm barred his way.

'Will Gallipolis be there now?'

'He's always there. Most time durin' the afternoon he runs a game.'

Simon tramped out his cigarette, conscious of the revealing smoke.

'Keep him here,' he instructed Hoppy. 'Don't come any closer unless I call for you, or you hear too many guns going off. Keep well hidden. And if I don't get back by dark, give him the works, will you?'

He moved off like a shadow through the trees to a point where the flatwoods bellied out closest to the barge. The rest of it was not going to be so easy, for even that shortened stretch was at least a quarter of a mile without any obvious cover. Evidently Mr Gallipolis had chosen his location with a prevision of unannounced attack that would have done credit to a potential general. A single marksman could have picked off a dozen men between the trees and the boat, even though the invading forces took it at a run; while suitable preparations for any less vigorous visitor could be made on board long before he came within hailing distance.

Simon stopped again at the point of the wood, and slapped a mosquito on his neck. A squirrel chatted rowdily in a nearby tree, protesting against the Saint's intrusion. The sudden noise made the patterned landscape of glaring light and eccentric shadow seem unconsciously still.

He leaned against a tree and let a rapid newsreel of the events of the day run through his mind, trying to pick out of it some guiding inkling of March's campaign; but it was not a profitable delay. He could always appreciate the finer points of an adversary's inventiveness, but the introduction of Lafe Jennet and Gallipolis and the thus far legendary Jesse Rogers formed a kaleidoscope that was hard to fit in to any preconceived pattern. The only apparently comprehensive theory was the one which Peter Quentin had propounded, and yet even that still had one vital flaw. It did not take into account the protective letter with which March must credit him with having covered his exposed flank. He couldn't believe that the ungodly would have him killed without first having dealt with that contingency. And yet there was very little sense left in any supposition which could make his projected call on Mr Gallipolis seem foolproof.

The Saint shrugged defeatedly. After all, there was still only one positive way to find out.

He tested the freeness of his gun in his shoulder holster, dropped to the ground, and began to crawl.

4

The palmetto bushes made a barrier that jabbed stinging points through his light clothing. Saw-edged grass rasped smartingly against his face and neck. His shirt was soaked with perspiration before he had gone fifty yards; and he was cursing artistically under his breath by the time the sandy ground pitched sharply up, barring his way with the dredged-out bank of the canal.

The bank was bare of vegetation. He lay flat and wriggled his way to the top of the ten-foot rise of sand and clay. Working one eye warily over the summit, he took stock again of the houseboat twenty paces away. The boarded windows stared blankly back at him. Except for a pair of grey socks dangling limply from a line on the top deck near the bow, the ancient craft might have been abandoned for years.

A foot from his head, something moved; and the dampness of his shirt turned cold.

It was something that had been so still, blending so well into the baked desolation of its background, that without the movement he might have missed it entirely. The movement brought it to life in mosaic coils of deadly beauty, while he lay rigid and felt his muscles tautening like shrinking leather. Black unwinking eyes stared impersonally into his, making the skin of his face creep as if cobwebs had touched it. Then the coils straightened fluidly out, and a five-foot cottonmouth moccasin slithered gracefully away.

The Saint used his forearm to wipe clammy dew from his brow. There might not actually be any sniper waiting on the barge for him to show himself, but the dangers of his present method of approach had been unmistakably demonstrated.

In any case, the decision to abandon them was now virtually taken out of his hands. Between the point he had reached, and the sluggish water where the barge floated, there was literally no cover at all. The space had to be crossed and the only way was to do it quickly.

He raised himself up on to his toes and fingertips, and took off over the top like a sprinter. Bent low to the ground, he shot across those few perilous yards with the sure-footed soundlessness of a fiddler crab scooting for its hole, and boarded the stern with no more uproar than a fragment of rising mist.

There was no shot.

He stood with his back to the bulkhead and got his breath, listening to a clink of chips and a mumble of voices that were audible through a torn screen door. But it seemed that the sounds came from some distance away amidship, and he opened the door and sidled through into dimness. As his eyes adjusted themselves to the gloom, he saw an oil stove, racked-up dishes, a sink, and a stained table. Across from him was another door, and beyond that he found a narrow hall. The voices came from an open door which made a rectangle of light in the dark passage. A game seemed to be unconcernedly in progress, and there were no other symptoms at all of an alarm. Unless the stage had been very carefully set for him, his entrance seemed to have been achieved without a hitch.

And once again there was only one way to find out.

He sauntered noiselessly down the hall and walked into the open room.

Five men sat around a baize-covered table. A tired-looking man in a green eyeshade sat with his back to a window dealing stud. An even more tired-looking cigarette drooped from his lower lip. As he called the bets in a tired monotone, the cigarette wobbled up and down. The five men raised their heads from the cards as the Saint came in. One of them looked horsey; the other three were in shirtsleeves and seemed about as menacing as book-keepers on a holiday.

The dealer flipped up five cards and said: 'King bets.' He lowered his eyeshade again and continued in his breath-saving tone: 'Five dollar limit stud. The house kitty's fifty cents out of each pot over five dollars. It's an open game. Don't stand around watching. If you want to play, take a chair.'

He shoved one out beside him with some pedal jugglery, while he dealt the second round, and Simon sat down because the chair faced the door.

The dealer pushed chips in front of him.

'The yellow are five, the blues one, the reds a half, and the whites a quarter. Fifty bucks, and you pay now.'

Simon peeled money off his roll, and looked over the room while the hand was finished. There was nothing much to it. A double gasoline lantern hung over the table. The light from the window, which was on the water side of the barge and open, cut a square shaft of light through a fog of cigarette and cigar smoke. The walls had two or three petty drawings tacked up on them.

The dealer ladled chips towards a winner, gathered up cards, and shuffled them with the speed of a boy's stick rattling along a picket fence. He dealt once around face down, and a second round face up. The Saint was high with a queen.

'Queen bets.' The cigarette moved up and down.

The Saint squeezed his hole card up, peeped at it, and flattened it down. He had a pair, back to back, and he didn't like to start that well in a game.

'A buck,' he said, and tossed a blue chip in.

The dealer stayed on a ten. Two of the book-keepers dropped out, but the horsey man with a nine and the other book-keeper with a seven spot stayed in. More cards fluttered from the dealer's agile hand, and finished up by leaving him a second ten.

'Pair of tens bets,' he droned, and pushed out a yellow chip with a finger stained with nicotine to match it.

The horsey man said: 'Nuts!' and rid himself of his cards. The surviving book-keeper with a seven and a jack showing spent five dollars. Simon figured him for a pair of jacks, and looked down at his own visible queen which had gotten married to a king.

'Let's make it expensive,' he said, and flipped two yellows in.

The dealer stayed, but the book-keeper folded up with a sigh. Simon got another king. The dealer gave himself an ace of spades. He removed the stub of his cigarette and said: 'You bet, friend.'

'The works,' said Simon with an angelic smile, and used both hands to shove in his entire pile.

'Don't clown, brother.' The dealer ran his thumb along the edge of the pack and snapped it with a flourish. 'I told you there's a five buck limit on this game.'

Simon's eyebrows rose in an arch of sanctimonious perplexity.

'What game?'

'Don't be funny,' the dealer advised. 'The game you're in now.'

'Oh,' said the Saint in a voice of silk and honey, 'I wasn't betting on the game. I just want all the money back for my chips.'

'See here,' said the dealer dangerously, 'what sort of a place do you think this is?'

The invisible coldness of angry men waiting for an explanation slid down like an avalanching glacier and crystallised the atmosphere of the room; but the Saint was utterly at ease. He leaned back in his chair and favoured the dealer with his most benevolent and carefree smile.

'I think,' he said, 'that it's the sort of place where ugly little runts like you give suckers a nice game with a marked deck.' He sat up again; and suddenly, without warning, he snatched the pack out of the dealer's hand and smeared it in front of the other players. 'Look for yourselves, boys. It's all done in the veins of the leaf in the left-hand corner. Nothing to notice if you aren't looking for it, but as plain as a bill-board when you know the code. It's nice work, but it gives the house too much of an edge for my money.'

The horsey man picked up some cards with a grin which held nothing but trouble.

'If you're right about this, guy, there's more coming to me than I've lost here today.'

'Use your eyes,' said the Saint cynically. 'I don't know how many of you are in with him, but the rest of you can see it. You might like to do something about it. Personally, I'll have my dough back and talk to the manager.'

'You'll do that,' muttered the dealer.

There was the sound of one padding step in the alleyway outside, and a new man showed in the doorway with a sub-machine-gun covering the room.

The Saint knew an instant of frozen expectancy when all the other close calls he had ever had passed in review before the immutable knowledge that some day somewhere there must be a call too close to dodge, and he thought: 'This is it.' For a flash the whole set-up seemed entirely rational and obvious. A gambling barge, a quarrel over a card game, a few shots, and the whole thing might be settled in a way in which Randolph March couldn't possibly be implicated. Only a supreme combination of intuition and will-power kept his right hand from starting a hopeless dive for the butt of the Luger under his arm. It was a more than human feat to sit there without movement and expect the tearing shock of lead; but he thought: 'That's what they're waiting for. They want to be able to say I fired first. I won't give them that break, anyway.' But there were goose-pimples all over his body.

The horsey man forced a laugh that clicked his teeth

together, and stammered: 'G-good God, Gallipolis, what's the ripper for?'

There was still no shooting, and it seemed to Simon that he had stopped breathing for a long time. In a detached but still partly incredulous way he began to take in the details of the prospective gunner.

Any co-operative reader who has been herded along the paths of romance and adventure by well-trained authors before, knows that a Greek must be fat, swarthy, and apparently freshly rubbed down with oil. It is this chronicler's discouraging task to try to convince such an audience that Mr Gallipolis most inconsiderately declined to conform to these simple requirements. His figure was svelte, almost feminine. Limpid eyes showed tar-black in a sunburnt face crowned with crisp black curls. He wore a pink polo shirt open at the neck, khaki pants, and very clean white tennis shoes. He leaned against the door jamb and exhibited flawless white teeth in a grin. His hands on the double grips of the Thompson gun were as slender as a girl's.

He didn't even seem to pay any special attention to the Saint. His eyes enfolded the dealer in a melting embrace.

'Why did you push the buzzer, Frank?' he inquired liquidly. 'There's no stick-up here.'

'That's what you think,' said Frank. 'This cheapskate you let in here was trying to pull a fast one and welsh on us.'

The Greek said: 'So?' and his eyes wrapped themselves around Simon. 'Who the hell are you and how did you get on board? I never saw you before.'

'I came in the back door,' said the Saint. 'I sat in the game and accused your dealer of cheating, that's all.'

Gallipolis's face grew long with melancholy.

'Were you cheating, Frank?'

'Hell, no! He was getting in too deep, so he tried to start something.'

'That's a lot of malarkey!' said one of the book-keepers boldly. 'He didn't start anything. He said these cards were crooked, and they are. We've seen 'em.'

Gallipolis looked amused.

'I have a hell of a time with dealers,' he told the Saint. 'How much you got coming?'

'Fifty dollars.'

'Give him his money, Frank.'

'I'll be—'

'Give him his money,' repeated Gallipolis, with a broadening smile.

The dealer produced a ten and two twenties and slapped them on the table. Gallipolis stepped aside and spoke to the Saint again.

'Come on, mister. You must have something on your mind or you wouldn't have come in the back door. We can talk it over in the bar.'

Simon took his money and stood up, admiring the way Gallipolis handled his gun. As Simon walked around the table, the Greek edged along the wall to keep the other players out of the line of fire. He was behind Simon when the Saint reached the door.

'Take it easy,' he recommended as the Saint stepped outside. 'If you start running I can drop you before you make the end of the hall.' He turned back to the other players. 'See what you can get out of Frank, boys. If you're still short anything, see me before you go.'

As Gallipolis left the room, the horsey man said: 'Did you ever eat a pack of cards, Quickfingers?' and left the table to close the door.

The bar furniture comprised a simple pinewood counter and three kitchen tables flanked with chairs. The Saint, walking with a circumspect negation of haste, reached it alive, which he had at no time taken for granted. He discovered that the landward windows were shuttered to conceal an inside coating of thin sheet steel. A square hole provided an outlook from the window at one end of the bar, and would also, Simon decided, have served very well for a gun port.

Gallipolis rested the machine-gun on the counter and nodded Simon to a chair. He studied the Saint with his ever-present grin.

'Well, you're on board. So what? You don't look like a heist man. What are you, a Sam?' He answered his own question with a shake of his curly head. 'No, you don't look like the Law. Give, friend, give. Who are you, and what do you want?'

4

How Mr Gallipolis became Hospitable, and Karen Leith kept her Date

1

'I'm Simon Templar.' The Saint locked hands around his knee.

Curtains veiled the Greek's swimming eyes.

'So? The Saint? I heard you were in the southlands.'

'Who told you?'

Gallipolis shrugged.

'News leaks out fast to a boat like this. I thought you were big time – the biggest of the lot. What the hell's the idea of picking on me?'

Muffled noises came from the poker room, followed by curses and a groan. The Saint said: 'I'm afraid your customers really are feeding that pack of cards to Frank. I wonder if he's got a good digestion.'

'He had it coming,' said Gallipolis, still grinning. 'But you didn't come out here just for that. What else have I got that you want?'

The Saint found a smoke, thumbed his lighter, and inhaled pensively.

'I'm looking for a guy named Jesse Rogers.'

The Greek's face remained pleasantly receptive, with just a faint upward movement of his strongly-marked black eyebrows. Simon could picture his expression staying exactly the same right up until his forefinger squeezed a trigger.

'So?'

'Do you know him?'

'Sure.'

It was a spine-tickling sensation, having to take all the initiative while growing more firmly convinced that Gallipolis would give no illuminating facial reaction until something fatal was said, and then fatal would be the only word for it.

'Do you want to tell me anything about him?'

'Why not?' The Greek's candour seemed engagingly unfeigned. 'He's an entertainer – sings smutty songs at the piano. He plays here sometimes.'

'When?'

'Oh, not professionally. I mean he gambles. He works every night at a dive uptown called the Palmleaf Fan. You could have found him there. Why did you have to come and make trouble here?'

Simon decided that he couldn't be any worse off if he played a line of equally calculated frankness.

'I never heard of him until this morning, or you either,' he said. 'Not until a friend of yours who calls himself Lafe Jennet took a shot at me and missed me by about three inches.'

'You're wrong both ways, Mr Saint.' Gallipolis was still grinning, but mechanically. 'Jennet isn't a friend of mine; and he didn't take a shot at you, or he'd have hit you. He could put a bullet up the rear end of a southbound flea.'

'I wouldn't be less excited,' said the Saint, 'if he could pop a bedbug in the starboard eye. The point is that I hate being shot at, even in fun. So I told Lafe that I'd have to send him back to the chain-gang where he belongs, after playing a few other games with him, unless he told me where he got this humorous idea. He told me that someone he met out on this barge blackmailed him into it.'

Gallipolis considered his machine-gun and said: 'Meaning me?'

'No – this fellow Rogers. He said he didn't know anything

about him except that he often hung out around here. So I thought I'd drop out and see.'

'You could have come to the door and asked.'

'How did I know you weren't in on it?'

The houseboat was silent except for the sounds of breaking furniture and a body bumping up and down on the floor.

'The bear came over the mountain,' said Gallipolis eventually, 'to see what he could see. It's a good story, anyhow. Where's Jennet now?'

'He's waiting in the woods with a friend of mine.'

'That's a good story, too.'

'How do you think I found this boat if Jennet didn't show me?' Simon asked patiently.

'You want to fetch him in?'

The question was almost casual; but Simon knew that it was a challenge, and might become more than that. Gallipolis still had him guessing.

But he had to balance the situation entirely by his own system of accountancy. It had seemed like a good idea at first to leave Jennet behind, not knowing what might be waiting on the barge. But he had found out more about that since – at least, enough for the present. He was a prisoner under the nozzle of a sub-machine-gun, which was an irrevocable temporary fact, regardless of what anyone was thinking or whatever other scheming might be going on. He had no further use for Mr Jennet. And he had told Hoppy to come after him if he hadn't returned by nightfall; but Jennet would be a handicap to that, and in any event Hoppy could have been knocked off with ease, being no Indian fighter, before he had moved his own length into the open . . . It didn't seem as if ceding the point could make anything much worse, and it might even make some things clearer.

'If you want him badly enough,' said the Saint; and he had

covered all those points in such a lightning survey that his hesitation could barely have been timed with a stop-watch.

'I just want to know if all this is on the up-and-up,' said Gallipolis, and he might even have been telling the truth. 'You'd better take your gun out first and slide it across the floor. If you want to try shooting it out okay, but you're making a mistake. A Tommy gun is better than an automatic, no matter how good you are.'

Simon obeyed, cautiously. The gun he was giving up meant nothing to him, being the one he had taken from March's captain, and Gallipolis handled his weapon as if he had wielded it before.

The Greek leaned against the lengthwise end of the bar, and it slid creakingly sideways, disclosing a good-sized hole in the floor under it. He toed the Luger into the hole, and said: 'Stand up and turn around. I want to see if you've got any more.'

Simon stood still with outstretched arms while Gallipolis explored him. The Greek's touch was quick and thorough. He ended the frisking by patting Simon inside of each thigh.

'Don't get me wrong,' he said, 'but I've got a bullet hole in my shoulder from a fellow I thought I'd disarmed. He was wearing a crotch gun, and when I turned around he pulled it on me by zipping open his fly.'

The Saint said: 'Gosh, what fun!' and forbore to mention the knife strapped to his forearm.

'Come along,' said Gallipolis, backing into the passage. 'But don't get too close.'

He stopped outside the poker room and rapped on the door. Still keeping Simon covered, he said through the panels: 'You fellows stay inside until I say it's clear. We're having visitors. If you want to work on Frank some more, keep him on the table. He makes a noise when he hits the floor.'

He motioned Simon in the opposite direction.

At the other end of the hallway, facing the kitchen entrance, another door gave into a sort of reception room which covered the forward end of the barge. They had to zigzag around a counter which practically bisected it and at the same time provided an effective barrier against any too rapid entry or exit. On the other side of the counter was another screen door.

'You go out and call 'em,' said Gallipolis. 'I can watch you from here.'

Simon stepped out on to the short cramped foredeck and semaphored with his arms. After a while he saw Mr Uniatz step out of cover, herding Lafe Jennet ahead of him.

'I just wouldn't shoot too quickly, comrade,' Simon said, in a tone of moderate counsel. 'Some other friends of mine know where I am, and if I don't get home they might pay you a call and ask questions.'

'Some of your fairy tales seem to be true,' Gallipolis acknowledged impersonally. 'We'll see what happens. I never shoot till I have to.' He was watching the approaching duo at an edgewise angle through the door. 'If this big baboon belongs to you, tell him to put his gun away before he comes in.'

'I'll tell him,' said the Saint, 'but you'd better play down the ukelele. Hoppy is kind of sensitive about some things. If you wave that chopper in his face the wrong way, he might try to shoot it out regardless. You'd do much better to be sociable. Welcome him with liquor, and he'll drink out of your hand.'

He spoke idly, but his nonchalance was mostly simulated. Behind it, he was trying to make sense out of an absurd idea that had been gathering strength in his subconscious.

The barge was authentic – a cheap hangout where cheap gamblers could lose their money breaking a grandmotherly law. But with that there went an enforced deduction that the Greek also might be authentic. And if Gallipolis was genuine, and Jennet was likewise, within their limitations, then there was nothing left but the absurd idea that they were only carefully placed stepping-stones to something else. And an idea like that did a superlative job of making everything meaningless and chaotic . . . It made it difficult even for such an actor as the Saint to throw off all artificiality as he watched Hoppy and Lafe Jennet reach the bank of the canal.

'Hi, boss.' Mr Uniatz used the back of one hand to clear trickling sweat from his eyes. Patches of damp under the arms of his blazer testified further to his discomfort. 'What makes out?'

'Come on in,' said the Saint encouragingly. 'They've got a bar.'

'A bar!' Mr Uniatz's face grew slowly radiant from within, as he appeared to gradually comprehend the all-foreseeing beneficence of a Providence which had not neglected to mitigate the horrors of even such a God-forsaken spot as that with Elysian springs of distilled consolation. Gathering new strength from the thought, he speeded the hesitant Mr Jennet up the rickety gangplank with his knee. 'Gwan, youse,' said Mr Uniatz. 'Whaddaya waitin' for?'

'Put your gun away,' said the Saint. 'You won't need it.'

'But—'

'Put it away,' said the Saint.

Gallipolis spoke softly and said: 'You come in now.'

Simon complied, and cleared the doorway. Jennet came in next, boosted by Mr Uniatz's ready knee. Mr Uniatz followed, and saw the Thompson gun. His hand started to move, and nothing but the Saint's steady nerves and ancient familiarity with Mr Uniatz's reflexes could have stopped the movement short of disaster. But the Saint said, exactly at the critical moment, in a voice of level confidence: 'Don't be scared, Hoppy. It's just a house custom.'

In spite of which he felt hollow in the pit of his stomach for an instant, until Hoppy's arm relaxed. All the theories in the world would have little bearing on the subject if Gallipolis had cause to get nervous.

'Okay, boss.' Mr Uniatz had been in houses with unusual customs before. 'Where is dis bar?'

'Through there,' said Gallipolis.

They all went through. Gallipolis came last, heeling the door shut behind him. He crossed to behind the bar and laid the weight of his gun on the counter. He reached behind him, without averting his eyes, and hitched over a bottle. With a repetition of the same movement he brought over four glasses, wearing them on his fingers like outsized thimbles, and plunked them on the bar beside the bottle.

'Help yourselves,' he said, 'and let's hear more about this.'

It was the merest chance that Simon happened to be standing in a position which gave him a direct sight through the shutter peephole on to a lone black shape that was stalking across the waste outside. It was an additional accident of eyesight and observation which identified the figure to him with instant certainty, even at that distance, and even though the identification left him windmilling on the brink of the ultimate chaos whose possibility he had barely divined three minutes ago.

Very deliberately he uncorked the bottle and poured himself out a glass.

'Before we do that,' he said, 'maybe you'd better put the thunder iron away.'

'For why?' The Greek's voice had a delicate edge of invitation.

'Because, literally, we're all in the same boat,' Simon remarked conversationally. 'You've taken away my gun, but Hoppy still has a concealed arsenal. And you can't even conceal yours. It might make it awkward to explain things to the sheriff – and I just happened to see him ambling over this way.'

Gallipolis turned back from a quick stare through the peep-hole, and Simon had an uneasy feeling that the crisis would have no amusing features at all if the Greek failed to grasp his cue.

Gallipolis said, in a low and rapid monotone: 'What sort of a plant is this? There's more men hidden in the trees. I saw them move. I've a notion to drill you, you dirty stool!'

Oddly, his surprise seemed as sincere as his anger. But there was no time to puzzle out nuances like that. The Saint said: 'Drilling me won't get you anywhere. And if you don't know how Haskins got here, I don't either.'

'Talk fast,' said Gallipolis, 'and don't lie. The sheriff never spotted this barge. Who tipped him off?'

'On my word of honour,' said the Saint steadily. 'I wish I knew.'

Over the bar, Gallipolis gazed at him with relentless penetration. The slender fingers of his right hand twined with deceptive laxness about the pistol grip of his weapon. The liquid eyes roved through impenetrable fancies, as though he were working out lyrics for a ballad entitled 'Death Comes to the Houseboat,' or something else equally delightful. But when he grinned again, he looked exactly the same as he had before.

'Look, master mind,' he said. 'The sheriff is your problem. You brought Jennet here. Nobody can prove I ever saw him before. If this is a plant, it stinks. If it isn't, you find a way out of it.'

'We can both find a way out of it, if you'll give me a chance. But get rid of the typewriter, or you're in deeper than anyone.'

Gallipolis digested the thought, and seemed to make his choice.

'This is a hell of a way to make a living,' he remarked, and gave a tired sigh. The hole in the floor under the bar was still exposed. He deposited the sub-machine-gun tenderly in it, and slid the bar back, and said: 'I may be a sucker, but I just wish I knew when you were levelling. There's something screwy going on, but I don't get it.'

'Neither do I,' said the Saint, and his manner was almost friendly.

Gallipolis looked hopeful.

'If you want to scram now, you've still got time.'

'I think I'll stay.'

'I was afraid so,' said Gallipolis sadly.

It was at that moment that another sound made itself heard.

It was a raucous and rasping sound, a primitive ululation that seemed to bear little relation to any vocal effort that might have been wrung from the diaphragm of an articulate human being. An experienced African hunter might have associated it with some of the more hideous rumblings of the wild such as the howl of an enraged rhinoceros, or the baffled bellow of a water-buffalo which has arrived at its favourite wallow only to find it parched and dry. This doughty hunter would have been pardonably deceived. The sound did have a human origin, if Mr Uniatz can be broadly classified as human. It was his rendition of a groan.

Simon turned and looked at him.

For perhaps the first time in his life Mr Uniatz stood gazing at a bottle without making any attempt to assimilate its contents, gripped in a kind of horripilant torpor like a rabbit fascinated by a snake.

'What's the matter?' Simon demanded with real alarm.

Mr Uniatz tried to speak, only to find himself impeded by the bulk of a painfully dust-caked tongue. Mutely he pointed with a trembling finger, which indicated the contents of the bottle better than words. In a shaft of afternoon sunlight through the gun port, the liquid gleamed with the translucent clarity of a draught from the backyard pump – refreshing, innocuous, unsullied, colourless, and clear. A shudder of abhorrence jarred his gargantuan frame. To one who in his opulent days had quaffed the finest and most potent liquors on the market, such an offering was an affront. To one who in less prosperous times had uncomplainingly got by with snacks of rubbing alcohol, lemon extract, jamaica ginger, or bay rum, this disgusting fluid promised to titillate his palate about as much as a feather would tickle an armadillo.

'It's a bottle of dat stinkin' Florida water, boss,' Hoppy got out miserably. 'I smelled dat stuff before. Dis ain't no bar – it's a washroom.'

Gallipolis turned insultedly from staring through the window.

'That's the hottest water you ever tasted, big boy. It comes fresh from a local spring. Why don't you try it?' He filled his own glass, grinned at Simon, and said: 'Here's to crime!'

The Saint sniffed his portion experimentally. It didn't seem at first as if Hoppy could be entirely wrong. The bad-egg bouquet brought back memories of sulphur springs flowing through fetid swamps. But Hoppy had to be given a lesson in good manners.

Simon closed his eyes and drank the liquor down.

He realised the gravity of his error before the sabre-toothed distillation of pine knots and turpentine was half through making scar tissue of his tongue. But by that time it was far too late. He tried to gasp out 'Water!' but the descending decoction had temporarily cauterised his throat in one clean searing tonsillectomy. Smouldering vocal cavities excavated into strange shapes by the toxic stream sent out the request in an impotent whisper. Tear ducts dilated in salty sympathy. He propped himself feebly against the bar, believing that the power of speech was lost to him for ever.

Through a watery haze he watched Hoppy Uniatz, reassured, lift up the bottle, tilt back his head to the position of a baying wolf, and lower the contents by three full inches before he straightened his neck again.

'Chees, boss . . .'

Mr Uniatz momentarily released his lips from the bottle with the partly satiated air of a suckling baby. He stared at it with a slightly blank expression. Then, as if to batter his incredulous senses into conviction, he raised the bottle a second time. The level had dropped another four inches when he set it down again, and even Lafe Jennet's graven scowl softened in compulsive admiration.

'Chees, boss,' said Mr Uniatz, 'if dat's de local spring water I ain't drinkin' nut'n else from now on!'

The Saint wiped his scorched lips with his handkerchief, and looked at it as if he expected to find brown holes in the cloth. He was even incapable of paying much attention to the entrance of Sheriff Haskins into the bar. He breathed with his mouth open, ventilating his anguished mucous tissues, while Haskins draped himself against the door and said: 'Hullo, son.'

'Hullo, Daddy.' The Saint valiantly tried to coax his voice back into operation. 'It's nice to see you again so soon. You know Mr Gallipolis? – Sheriff Haskins.'

'Shuah, I know him.' Haskins chewed ruminatively. 'He's a smart young fellow. Runs a nice quiet juke we've knowed about for a yeah or more. I figgured to raid it one o' these days, but I gave up the idea.' He nodded tolerantly towards the reddening Greek. 'He ain't big enough to use that much gas on. I'd have no time for anythin' else if I started knockin' off every ten-cent joint around Miami that runs a poker game an' sells a bad brand o' shine.'

Gallipolis leaned his elbows on the bar.

'Then what did you come for, Sheriff?'

'This.'

Haskins moved like a striking rattler, snatching off the dark glasses that Simon had bought for Jennet.

Jennet snarled like a dog, and snatched at the bottle on the bar. It must always be in doubt whether Hoppy Uniatz's even faster response was the automatic action of a co-operative citizen or the functioning of a no less reflex instinct to retain possession of his newly discovered elixir. But no matter what his motivation might have been, the result was adequate. One of his iron paws grabbed Jennet's wrist, and the other wrenched the bottle away. There was a click of metal as Haskins deftly handcuffed the struggling convict.

'Thanks,' said the sheriff dryly, giving Hoppy the benefit of the doubt, and at the same time giving Mr Uniatz his first and only accolade from the Law. 'You're wanted up near Olustee, Lafe, to do some road work you ain't never finished. Might think you were a tourist, the way you were ridin' around town.'

'I was kidnapped,' Jennet whined. 'Why don't you arrest them, too?' His manacled hands indicated the Saint and Hoppy. 'They drug me out here at the point of a gun.'

'Now, that's right interestin',' said Haskins.

He turned his back on Jennet and walked to a place beside Simon at the bar. He moved his left thumb, and Gallipolis produced another bottle of shine, Hoppy having cautiously taken the first bottle out of range of further accidents. Haskins refilled the Saint's glass and poured himself a liberal drink.

Simon Templar contemplated the repeat order of nectar unenthusiastically. The stuff had an inexhaustible range of effects. At the moment, the first dose was still with him: his throat was cooling a little, but his stomach now felt as if he had swallowed an ingot of molten lead. Besides which, he wanted to think quickly. If there were going to be a lot of questions to answer, he had to decide on his answering line.

And disintegrating as the idea might seem, he simply couldn't perceive any line more straightforward, more obvious, more foolproof, more unchallengeable, more secure against further complications, and more utterly disarming, than the strict and irrefutable truth – so far as it went. It was a strange conclusion to come to, but he knew that subterfuge was a burden that was only worth sustaining when its objective was clearly seen, and for the life of him he couldn't see any objective now. So he watched in silent awe while the sheriff filtered his four ounces of sulphuretted hydrochloric acid past his uvula without disturbing his chew.

'Gawd A'mighty,' Haskins exclaimed huskily, eyeing his glass in wild astonishment. 'Must have squeezed that out of a panther. Did you come all the way out here to get a drink of that scorpion's milk? Give me an answer, son.'

'I'm glad somebody else thinks it's powerful,' said the Saint relievedly. 'Actually, Sheriff, I came out here looking for a man.'

Haskins found a place between vest and pants, and scratched himself over the belt of his gun.

'I'll feel a sight better, son, if you tell me more.'

'There's nothing much to hide.' Simon felt even more certain of the tightness of his decision. 'A few minutes after you left this morning, Jennet took a shot at me from the bushes. If you want to, we can drive back in and you can dig his mushroom bullet out of the Gilbeck's wall.'

The sheriff pushed back his hat, found a wisp of hair, twisted it into a point, and said: 'Well, now!'

'My friend Hoppy Uniatz – that's him over there, under the bottle – caught Jennet. We also got a rifle with his fingerprints on it – it must have 'em, because he wasn't wearing gloves. You can have that too, if you want to come back for it and prove that it fired the bullet in the wall.'

Haskins's shrewd grey eyes stayed on the Saint's face.

'Guess you wouldn't be so keen for me to prove it, son, if it warn't true,' he conceded. 'So I'll save myself the trouble. But it still don't say what you're doin' with Lafe out here.'

'After we caught him,' said the Saint, 'we worked on him a little. Nothing really rough, of course – he didn't make us go that far. But we persuaded him to talk. I didn't have the least idea why he or anybody else should be shooting at me. He told me he was forced to do it by a guy named Jesse Rogers who knew he was a lamster; and he said he met this Rogers out here. So we just naturally came out for a looksee.'

'That's a lie,' said Gallipolis. 'Jennet was just playing for time. He hasn't been here since he was sent up, and you can't prove anything else.'

'That was only what he told me,' Simon confessed.

Haskins replaced his corkscrewed forelock.

'I shuah am bein' offered a lot of easy provin' to do,' he observed morosely. 'What I want is the things you-all ain't so ready to show me. How about this guy Rogers?'

'He comes here,' said Gallipolis. 'But he's been coming on and off for two years.'

'Know anythin' about him?'

'No more than anybody else who comes here. I know what he looks like and how much he spends.'

The Greek's limpid-eyed sincerity was as transparent as it had been when he told Simon quite a different story.

Haskins ambled over to a corner and ejected his chew with off-hand accuracy into a convenient cuspidor.

'This business is gettin' so danged tangled up,' he announced as he came back, 'it's like watchin' a snake eatin' its own tail. If it keeps on long enough there won't be nuth'n left at all.'

'Perhaps,' Simon advanced mildly, 'you'd save yourself a lot of headaches if you took Lafe back to your office and saw what you could get out of him there.'

The sheriff was troubled. He searched beyond the Saint's serious tone for some justification of his feeling of being taken for a ride. It was difficult to define the glint in the Saint's scapegrace blue eyes as one of open mockery; and yet . . .

'An' where will you be,' he asked, 'while that's goin' on?'

'I might see if I can get a line on this Rogers bird,' said the Saint. 'But you know where to get in touch with me if you need me again.'

'Look, son.' Haskins's long nose moved closer, backed by a narrowing stare. 'Whether or not you know it, you've done me a right smart good turn today. Lafe's meaner 'n gar broth, an' wanted bad. I'll be plenty happy to see him tucked away. But I don't want no more trouble on account o' you. Suppose now we all go back to town peaceable like, an' you leave the findin' of this Rogers to me.'

Simon took out a pack of cigarettes and meditatively selected one.

He felt even more uncannily as if he were a puppet that was being taken through some conspicuous but meaningless part of a complex choreography, while the real *motif* was still running in incomprehensible counterpoint. Too many people seemed to be too completely genuine to too little purpose.

There was, of course, the girl Karen, who might be classed as an unknown quantity. But it was impossible to visualise the pickle-pussed Lafe Jennet, no matter what his status as a marksman might be, as an embryo Machiavelli. Gallipolis had displayed several paradoxical characteristics, but the Saint felt ridiculously and unreasonably certain that among all of them there was a perplexity which contradicted the part of a conspirator. And there could be no doubt at all about the sheriff. Newt Haskins might speak with a drawl and chew tobacco and move slothfully under the southern sun, but his slothfulness was that of a lizard which could wake into lightning swiftness. He had quite unmistakably the rare gem-like clarity of character of a man whom no fear or fortune could ever swerve from his arid conception of duty. And yet his arrival that afternoon had a timeliness which seemed to be an integral part of an elusive pattern.

No abstract extrapolation could ever make order out of it, Simon concluded. And so the only thing still was to find out – to let his own natural impulses take their course, and see where they led him.

'I just hate being shot at,' he said amicably, 'especially by proxy. And I don't think I'd be violating any law by looking for a guy named Rogers if I wanted to. Or would I?'

Haskins stared at him for the briefest part of a minute. His lean, weatherbeaten face was as unemotional as a piece of old leather.

'No, son,' he said at last. 'Just *lookin'* for a guy named Rogers won't be violatin' no laws . . .' He turned abruptly, grasped Jennet by the collar, and propelled him towards the door. 'Git goin', Lafe.' He glanced back at the Saint once more, from the doorway. 'I'll be around,' he said, and went out.

Simon lounged languidly against the bar and tried to put a smoke-ring over the neck of a bottle.

Gallipolis used the peephole to assure himself that Haskins and Jennet had really gone. He turned his face back from the aperture with a discouraged air.

'The hell with it.' He waggled his curly head from side to side and looked at the Saint. 'Are you going too, or have you got any more trouble?'

'You've still got my gun,' Simon reminded him.

The Greek seemed to brood about it. Then he slid back the bar and picked out the Luger from his cache. He handed it to Simon, butt foremost.

'Okay,' he said. 'Now what?'

Simon holstered the gun.

'Why didn't you tell the sheriff what you told me about Rogers?'

'Hell,' said Gallipolis, 'I should help him? I hope you find Rogers. He might have made trouble for me here.'

'What else do you know?'

'Not a thing, friend.' Gallipolis replaced the bar with a movement of gentle finality. 'I guess I better see what's left of Frank. You wouldn't want to take a job dealing stud for me?' Before Simon could think of a fitting way of declining the compliment, he answered his own question with a mournful 'No,' and disappeared down the hall.

The Saint straightened himself with an infinitesimally preoccupied shrug.

'I guess we might as well blow, too, Hoppy,' he said. 'But it all looks too damned easy.'

'Dat's what I t'ought,' agreed Mr Uniatz complacently.

For once it was Simon Templar who did the delayed take. He had reached the foot of the gangplank, busy with other thoughts, when it dawned abashingly on him that his low esteem for Hoppy's mental alertness might after all have been unjust. He half stopped.

'How did you work it out?'

Mr Uniatz removed the bottle neck from his lips with a noise like a dying drain.

'It's easy, boss.' Mr Uniatz expanded with pleasure at being accepted, if only temporarily, into the usually closed councils of the Saint's gigantic brain. 'All we gotta do is find de pool.'

A faint frown began to mar the Saint's heartening attention.

'What pool?'

'De pool you talk to March about on de boat,' Hoppy explained darkly. 'I got it all figured out. De Greek says it comes from a spring, but dat's a stall. It comes from dis foreign pool we're lookin' for. Dat's de racket. I got it all figgered out,' said Mr Uniatz, clinching his point with rhetorical simplicity.

3

Simon Templar had enjoyed a long drink which did not peel the last remaining membranes from his throat; he had told his inconclusive story to Peter and Patricia; he had showered refreshingly; and he had changed at leisure into dress trousers, soft shirt, and cummerband. He was perfecting the set of a maroon bow tie when Desdemona knocked on his door and proclaimed disapprovingly: 'Dey's a lady to see you.'

'Who is it?' he asked, from habit, but his circulation changed tempo like a schoolboy's.

'Same one who was here dis mawnin'.'

He heard the negress flat-footing disdainfully away as he slipped into a fresh white mess jacket.

Karen Leith was in the patio, and her loveliness almost stopped him. She was wearing some unelaborately costly trifle of white, gathered close about breast and waist and billowing into extravagant fullness below. The tinted patio lights touched the folds with some of the sunset colours of her hair. Otherwise it was all white, except for a thin green chiffon handkerchief tucked into a narrow gold belt at her waist.

'So you made it,' said the Saint.

'You asked me.'

Her lips were so fresh and cool, smiling at him, that it was an effort not to repeat his performance of the morning, even though there could be no excuse for it now.

'I couldn't believe I was so irresistible,' he said.

'I thought it over all day and decided to come . . . Besides, it made Randy so mad.'

'Doesn't that matter?'

'He hasn't bought me – yet.'

'But you told him.'

'Why not? I'm free, white, and – twenty-five. I had to tell him, anyway. I asked Haskins not to tell, but I realised I couldn't trust him. Suppose he'd gone ambling off in his quiet crafty way and told Randy, just to see what he could stir up. It'd 've looked quite bad if I hadn't said it first.'

They were still holding hands and Simon became conscious of it rather foolishly. Even though she hadn't tried to draw away. There was either too little reason for it, or too much. He released her fingers and went to the portable bar which he had thoughtfully ordered out before he went to dress.

'Are you sure that was all?' he asked as he brewed cocktails with a practised hand.

'Of course, I did wonder how you made out on your trip this afternoon.'

'As you see, I came back alive.'

'Did you find the barge and the mysterious Mr Rogers?'

'The barge, but not Mr Rogers. He wasn't there. I'm going to meet him tonight.' Simon handed her a glass. 'But it's nice of you to be interested. It's a pity, though, because I shall have to take you home early.'

'What for?' she objected. 'I'm a long time out of the vicarage. I could even enjoy going to a place like the Palmleaf Fan.'

The Saint was a man whose nerves of steel and impregnable imperturbability are by this time as familiar as the contour of their own bottoms to all patrons of circulating libraries and movie theatres, not to mention the purchasers of popular magazines and newspapers. It cannot therefore be plausibly stated that he staggered on his feet. But it must also be revealed that he came as close to it as he was ever likely to come. So it can only be recorded that he picked up his own drink and subsided circumspectly into the nearest chair.

'Let me get this straight,' he said. 'I forced a fugitive from a chain gang, under threats of hideous torture, to guide me to a gambling barge that looked like a prop from a Grand Guignol show. I crawled for miles on my stomach like a serpent, ruining an excellent pair of pants and getting myself stuck in all kinds of intimate places with an assortment of needle points which no good housewife would leave on a potted palm. I had a contest in hypnotism with a singularly evil-looking cotton-mouth moccasin on the bank of a very stagnant canal. I exposed a crooked stud dealer, and was offered his job by a curly-haired Greek with a machine-gun. Some thoughtful soul even took the trouble to send the sheriff after me again, and I had to distract his attention by giving him our friend Jennet as a scapegoat. And do you know where that got me?'

'I think so.' She could even look demure. 'You found out that Rogers worked at the Palmleaf Fan.'

Simon swallowed a mouthful of blended alcohols with a voracity that would have done credit to Mr Uniatz.

'When did you find it out?'

'Oh, several days ago.'

'Of course, you couldn't have told me right away, instead of letting me wriggle all over Florida like a boy scout trying for an eagle badge. I mean, we could have spent the afternoon playing backgammon or visiting an alligator farm, or something else harmless and diverting.'

She was sitting on the arm of his chair now, and her slim fingers rested on his shoulder.

'My dear,' she said. 'I hated to let you do it. But I wasn't sure what else there was. And would you have missed it?'

'You were just doing it for my own good?'

'I didn't know there was nothing else in it than tracking Rogers down. You had to find out. If you were going to follow a trail, you had to follow it exactly as it was laid out. I might have switched you into a short cut that led nowhere.'

The Saint sat up.

'Karen,' he said quietly, 'how much more do you know?'

She sipped her drink.

'This is nice,' she said. 'What is it?'

'Something I made up. I call it a Wedding Night.'

'That sounds more like a perfume.'

He took hold of her wrist with a grip that was more crushing than he realised.

'Why not answer the question?'

She lifted her glass again and then looked at him levelly.

'Haven't I got just as much right to ask you the same question?'

'That's fair enough. I'll answer it. You know just about everything I know. You heard it on the *March Hare* last night. I shot the works – and half of them were guessworks. You also know what I found out today. I haven't kept anything back. But I'm just as much in the dark as I ever was – with the only difference that I'm not wondering any more whether I'm just dreaming that there's dirty work going on, like an old maid looking under the bed for lecherous burglars. The fact that Jennet took a shot at me this morning proves that someone is interested in my nuisance value, whether the shot was only meant for a warning or not. And since your boy friend Randy and his captain are the only people I'd flaunted my nuisance value at so far, they must be in it up to the neck. A baby could put all that together. But that's all.'

'And one other thing,' she said. 'You have a reputation.'

'That's true.' He admitted it without vanity or self-satisfaction as a cold fact. 'Moreover, I'm still doing my best to live up to it . . . Now it's your turn. You told me this morning I could ask you this tonight, and I'm asking.'

'Your glass is empty,' she said.

His grip had relaxed while he talked, and he let her release herself without tightening it again. She made no attempt to massage her wrist, although the red print of his fingers on her satin skin made him realise how he had forgotten his strength. She had a strength of her own which he sensed as a core of steel no less finely tempered than his, underneath the outward beauty of satin and softness and gossamer, and he wondered why it should be so blandly assumed that women with Tanagra bodies and magazine-cover faces could only be either vapid or vicious inside.

He went back to the portable bar and stirred the shaker and refilled his glass, and said: 'If you want to welsh on that, perhaps you've got a reason.'

'You're asking me what I know,' she replied. 'I don't suppose you'd believe me if I told you I don't know much more than you've said already.'

'What you actually said I could ask is what your place is in this party.'

She let him light her a cigarette, and her amazing eyes were like amethysts under his ruthless scrutiny.

'I run around with Randolph March,' she said.

'For what you hope to get out of it?'

'For what I hope to get out of it,' she said, without wincing.

'Then why are you going out with me?'

'Because I want to.'

'Do you expect to get anything valuable out of me?'

'Probably nothing but a few more kicks in the teeth.'

He felt cheap, but he had to harden his heart, even though he was hurting himself as much as he could hope to hurt her.

'Does it make any difference to you if March is mixed up in some dirty work?' he inquired relentlessly.

'A lot of difference.'

'If you could get the goods on him, you could make something out of it.'

'That's right. I could.'

'Meanwhile, you'll string along with him. And I'm sure he expects you to bring back all the information you can squeeze out of me. Your job is to keep him in touch with what I think and find out and what I'm going to do.'

'Exactly that.'

'What would you say if I told you I'd figured all that out long ago, and decided I didn't care? That I knew you'd been put to watch me, but I didn't think you could do me any harm, and so I didn't give a damn? That I knew you might be dangerous, but I didn't mind, because I liked danger and it was fun to be with you. Suppose I told you I was taking a chance with my eyes open, and I didn't give a hoot in hell for any harm you could do. Because I believed you'd break down before you saw me put on the spot. And the hell with it, anyway. Then what?'

'God damn you,' she said in a low voice, 'I'd love you.'

He was shaken. He hadn't meant to goad her so far, or have so much said.

He wanted to take a step towards her, but he knew he must not. And she said: 'But I'd call you a fool. And I'd love you for that, too. But it couldn't make any difference.'

He glanced at his cigarette, and flipped dead ashes on to the terrace. He finished his drink, with leisured appreciation. And he knew that those things made no difference either. In a ridiculous, reckless way he was happy, happier than he had been since the beginning of the adventure. With no good reason, and at the same time with all the reasons in the world.

When he was sure enough of himself he put out his hand.

'Then let's have another cocktail at the Roney Plaza,' he said, 'and decide where we'll go to dinner. And see how it turns out.'

She stood up.

Her quiet acceptance seemed even grateful, but there was far more behind it than he could put together at once. It was so hard to penetrate that dazzling and intoxicating outer perfection. She was all white mist and moonbeams, cold flame of hair and cool redness of soft lips; and swords behind them.

But she took his hand.

'Let's have tonight,' she said.

She could have said it in twenty ways. And perhaps she said it in all of them at once, or none. But the only certain thing was that for one brief moment, for the second time that day, her mouth had been yielding against his. And this time he had not moved at all.

4

At eleven-thirty she was still with him. When he had looked at his watch and suggested that it was time they left the restaurant, she had said: 'I can't stop you taking me home, but you can't stop me calling a taxi and going straight to the Palmleaf Fan.'

So they were driving northwards, and on their right the sea lapped a pebbly strip of beach only about eight feet below them. The houses had thinned out and become scarce, and on the left a tangled barrier of shrubbery grew high out of grassy dunes. Only an occasional car dimmed its lights in meeting and flashed by. The road narrowed, and held down their speed with short scenic-railway undulations.

Simon drove with a cigarette clipped lightly between two fingers, and a deep lazy devilment altered the alignment of one eyebrow to an extent that only a micrometer could have measured. But there was a siren song in the wind that his blood answered, and when he put the cigarette to his lips his blue eyes danced with lights that were not all reflected from the glowing end.

He was insane; but he always had been. There could be nothing much screwier than going out to what looked more and more like an elaborately organised rendezvous with destiny in the company of a girl who had freely declared herself a wanderer from the enemy camp. And yet he didn't care. He had told her the literal truth, within its limits, exactly as he believed she had told him. The evening had been worth it, and they had bargained for that. They had had four hours for which he would have fought an army. Adventures could be good or bad, trivial or ponderous; but there had been four hours that would live longer than memory. Even though nothing more of the least importance had been said. They had known each other; and behind the screens of sophisticated patter and unforgettable cross-purposes their own selves had walked together, clear-eyed, like children in a walled garden.

And all that was over now, except for remembrance.

'We're nearly there,' she said.

And all he had to be sure of now was that the automatic rode easily in his shoulder holster, without marring the set of a jacket which had been cut to allow for such extra impedimenta, and that his knife was loose in its sheath under his sleeve, and that the atavistic physiognomy of Hoppy Uniatz, whom he had stopped to collect on the way without any protest from her, still nodded somnolently in the back seat.

Ahead and to the left, the sand dunes flattened into a shallow gully with a wooden arch at its entrance. Over the arch a single dim bulb flickered in an erratic way that sent crazy shadows writhing across the road. As the Saint slowed down, he saw that the effect was caused by the uncannily lifelike effigy of a negro boy which reclined on top of the arch with a palmleaf fan in one dangling hand. The fan, in front of the light, moved restlessly in the breeze and created the flickering shadows.

'This is the place,' she said. 'It's about half a mile in.'

'Looks like a cheerful spot for an ambush,' he remarked, and turned the car into the shell road.

Flame fanned past his ear, and a report like the crack of doom left the drum bruised and singing. Fragments of something showered from above, and the largest of them fell solidly into his lap. He glanced at it as he instinctively trod home the accelerator, and for an instant a ghostly chill walked like a spider up his back. He had to force himself to pick up the black horror; and then suddenly he went weak with helpless laughter.

'What is it?' Karen whispered.

'It's nothing, darling,' he said. 'Nothing but the hand of a plaster negro – detached by Hoppy's ever-ready Betsy.'

Mr Uniatz leaned over the back of the front seat and stared at the hand remorsefully as Simon tossed it out.

'Chees, boss,' he said awkwardly, 'I am half asleep when I see him, an' I t'ink he is goin' to jump on us.' He tried to cover his mortification with a jaunty emphasis on the silver lining. 'One t'ing,' he said, 'if he's plastered he won't know who done it.'

Karen brushed off her dress.

'He's just a big overgrown kid, isn't he?' she said in a tactful undertone. 'When are you thinking of sending him to school?'

'We tried once,' said the Saint, 'but he killed his teacher in the third grade, and the teacher in the fourth grade thought he'd had enough education.'

It was fortunate that there was half a mile from the entrance arch to the premises, he reflected, so that it was unlikely that anyone at the Palmleaf Fan would have been alarmed by the shot.

The road swung right in a horseshoe. His headlights ran along a thatched wall ten feet high, broken only by a single door, and picked up the sheen of a line of parked cars. There was not a vast number of them, and he imagined that the crowd would not get really thick until the other night spots were tiredly closing and the diehard drinkers flocked out to this hidden oasis for a last two or three or six nightcaps. Simon parked himself in the line, and as he switched off the engine he heard music filtering out from behind the impressive stockade.

'Well, keed,' he said, as Mr Uniatz gouged himself out of the back, 'here we go again.'

She sat beside him for a moment without moving.

'If anything goes wrong,' she said, 'I couldn't help it. You won't believe me, but I wanted to tell you.'

He could see the pale symmetry of her face in the dimness,

the full lips slightly parted and her eyes bright and yet stilled, and the scent of her hair was in his nostrils; but beyond those things there was nothing that he could reach, and he knew that that was not delusion. Then her fingers brushed his hand on the wheel briefly, and she opened the door.

He got out on his side, and settled his jacket with a wry and reckless grin. So what the hell? . . . And as they crossed to the entrance she said in a matter-of-fact way that clinched the tacit acceptance of their return to grim rules that had been half forgotten: 'It's easier to get in here if you're known. Let me fix it.'

'It's a pipe, boss,' declared Mr Uniatz intrusively. 'When de lookout opens de window, I reach t'ru an' squeeze his t'roat till he opens de door.'

'Let's give her a chance to get us in peacefully first,' Simon suggested diplomatically.

It was all strictly practical and businesslike again.

A hidden floodlight beat down on them, and a slit opened in the door – perhaps someone else had thought of Hoppy's method of presenting his credentials, for the slit was too narrow for even a baby's hand to pass through. But there was no need for violence. Eyes scanned them, and saw Karen, and the door opened. It reminded Simon a shade nostalgically of the glad and giddy days of the great American jest that was once known as Prohibition.

The door closed behind them as they entered, operated by a stiffly tuxedoed cut-throat of a type Simon had seen a thousand times before.

'Good evening, Miss Leith.'

The blue-chinned watchdog approved the Saint, and veiled his startlement at Hoppy's appearance with a mechanical smile and an equally mechanical bow.

A flagged pathway led to the entrance of the building itself, which was a rambling Spanish-type bungalow. The second door opened as they reached it, doubtless warned by a buzzer from the gate.

They went into a vestibule full of bamboo and Chinese lanterns. Another blue-chinned tuxedo said: 'A table tonight, Miss Leith? Or are you going back?'

'A table,' she said.

As they followed him, the Saint took her arm and asked: 'Where is "back"?'

'They have gambling rooms with anything you want. If you've got a few thousand dollars you're tired of keeping, they'll be delighted to help you out.'

'I tried that once today,' said the Saint reminiscently.

They went through into a large, dimly-lighted dining-room. The tables were grouped around three sides of a central dance floor; and on the fourth side, facing them, an orchestra played on a dais. Back against one side wall was a long bar. Grotesquely carved coco-nut masks with lights behind them glowered sullenly from the walls. At either end of the bar a stuffed alligator mounted on its hind legs proffered a tray of matches. Electric bulbs scattered over the raftered ceiling struggled to throw light downwards through close rows of pendent palmetto fans, and only succeeded in enhancing the atmospheric gloom. The collective decorative scheme was a bizarre monstrosity faithfully carried out with justifiable contempt for the healthy taste of probable patrons, but with highly functional regard for the twin problems of reducing the visible need for superfluous cleaning and concealing the presence of cockroaches in the chop-suey; and Simon recognised that it was entirely in tune with the demand that it had been designed for.

A silky head waiter, proportionately less blue-jowled as his position demanded, ushered them towards a table on the floor; but the Saint stopped him.

'If nobody minds,' he said, 'I'd rather have a booth at the back.'

The major-domo changed his course with an air of shrivelling reproach. He might have been more argumentative, but it seemed as if Karen's presence restrained him. As they sat down he said: 'Will Mr March be joining you?' – and he said it as if to imply that Mr March would have had other ideas about good seating.

Karen dazzled him with her smile and said: 'I don't think so.'

She ordered Benedictine; and the Saint asked for a bottle of Peter Dawson, more with an eye to Mr Uniatz's inexhaustible capacity than his own more modest requirements.

The orchestra struck up another number, and multicoloured spotlights turned on at each corner of the room threw moving rainbows on the floor. Karen glanced at him almost with invitation.

'All right,' he said resignedly.

They danced. He hadn't wanted to, and he had to keep his mind away from what they were doing. She had a lightness and grace and rhythm that would have made it seem easy to float away into unending voids of rapturous isolation; her yielding slenderness was too close to him for what he had to remember. He tried to forget her, and concentrate on a study of the human contents of the room.

And he realised that there were some things about the clientele of the Palmleaf Fan which were more than somewhat queer.

He wasn't thinking of the more obvious queernesses, either; although it dawned on him in passing that some of the groups of highly made-up girls who sat at inferior tables with an air of hoping to be invited to better ones were a trifle sinewy in the arms and neck, while on the other hand some of the delicate-featured young men who sat apart from them were too well-developed in the chest for the breadth of their shoulders. Those eccentricities were standard in the honky-tonks of Miami. The more unusual queerness was in some of the cash customers.

There was, of course, a good proportion of unmistakable sightseers, not-so-tired business men, visiting firemen, shallow-brained socialites, flashy mobsters, and self-consciously hilarious collegians – the ordinary cross-section of any Miami night spot. But among them there was a more than ordinary leavening of personalities who unobtrusively failed to fit in – who danced without abandon, and drank with more intensity of purpose than enthusiasm, and talked too earnestly when they talked at all, and viewed the scene when they were not talking with a detachment that was neither bored nor disapproving nor cynical nor envious, but something quite inscrutably different. Many of them were young, but without youthfulness – the men hard and clean-cut but dull-looking, a few girls who were blonde but dowdy and sometimes bovine. The older men tended to be stout and stolid, with none of the *élan* of truant executives. There was one phrase that summed up the common characteristic of this unorthodox element, he knew, but it dodged annoyingly through the back of his mind, and he was still trying to corner it when the music stopped.

They went back to the table, and he sat down in the secure position he had chosen with his back to the wall. Their order had been delivered, and Hoppy Uniatz was plaintively contemplating eight ounces of Scotch whisky which he had unprecedently poured into a glass.

'Boss,' complained Mr Uniatz, 'dis is a clip jernt.'

'Very likely,' Simon assented. 'What have they done to you?'

Hoppy flourished his glass.

'De liquor,' he said. 'It's no good.'

Simon poured some into his own glass, sniffed it, and sipped. Then he filled it up with water and ice and tried again.

'It seems all right to me,' he said.

'Aw, sure, it's de McCoy. Only I just don't like it no more.'

The Saint inspected him with a certain anxiety.

'What's the matter? Aren't you feeling well?'

'Hell, no, boss. I feel fine. Only I don't like it no more. It ain't got no kick after dat Florida pool water. I ast de waiter if he's got any, an' he gives me dat stuff.' Hoppy pointed disgustedly at the carafe. 'It just tastes like what ya wash in. I told him we ain't gonna pay for no fish-bath, an' he says he won't charge for it. I scared de pants off him. But dey try it on, just de same. Dat's what I mean, boss, it's a clip jernt,' said Mr Uniatz, proving his contention.

The Saint sighed.

'What you'll have to do,' he said consolingly, 'is go back to Comrade Gallipolis and ask him for some more.'

He lighted a cigarette and returned to his faintly puzzled analysis of the room.

Karen Leith seemed to sense his vaguely irritated concentration without being surprised by it. She turned a cigarette between her own finger and thumb, and said: 'What are you making of it?'

'It bothers me,' he replied, frowning. 'I've been in other joints with some of these fancy trimmings – I mean the boys and girls. I think I know just what sort of floor show they're going to put on. But I can't quite place some of the customers. They aren't very spontaneous about their fun. I've seen exactly the same thing before, somewhere.' He was merely thinking aloud. 'They look more as if they'd come out here because the doctor had told them to have a good time, by God, if it killed them. There's a phrase on the tip of my tongue that just hits it, if I could only get it out?—'

'A sort of *Kraft durch Freude?*' she prompted him.

He snapped his fingers.

'Damn it, of course! It's Strength through Joy – or the

other way round. Like in Berlin. With that awful Teutonic seriousness. "All citizens will have a good time on Thursday night. By order." The night life of this town must have got to a pretty grisly state . . .'

His voice trailed off, and his gaze settled across the room with an intentness that temporarily wiped every other thought out of his mind.

The head waiter was obsequiously ushering Randolph March and his captain to a table on the other side of the floor.

5

How Simon Templar saw sundry Girls, and Sheriff Haskins spoke of Democracy

1

The orchestra uncorked a fanfare, and the room lighting seemed to become even dingier by contrast as a spotlight splashed across to illuminate a slim-waisted creature who had taken possession of the microphone on the dais. His blond hair was beautifully waved, and he had a smudge under one eye that looked like mascara.

'Ladies and gentlemen,' he said with an ingratiating lisp, 'we are now going to begin our continuous entertainment, which will go on between dances to give you a breathing spell – if you can still breathe. And to start the ball rolling, here is that beautiful baby Toots Travis.'

He stepped back, leading the applause with frightful enthusiasm, and Toots minced forward from a curtained arch on the right of the orchestra. She really was pretty, with a Dutch-doll bob and a face to go with it and a figure with rather noticeable curves. She looked about sixteen, and might not have been much more. The orchestra blared into a popular number, and she began to saunter around the floor, waving a palmleaf fan and singing the refrain in a voice which could have been more musical. Much more.

March semaphored boldly across the floor to Karen, and she responded more restrainedly with one hand. He gave no sign of having noticed the Saint's existence. The captain nodded perfunctorily in their direction, and paid no further attention. Simon could hardly see any other course for him. When in a public place one encounters two persons who twenty-four hours ago were kicking one four feet into the air and beating one over the head with an empty bottle as one came down, one can hardly be expected to greet them with effusive geniality. One could, of course, call for the police and make charges; but there had been plenty of time already to do that, and the idea had obviously been discarded. Or one could come over and offer to start again where one left off, but there were social problems to conflict with that, not to mention the discouraging record of past experience.

Toots continued to stroll about after the refrain ended. It began to appear that the needlework in her dress was not of the most enduring kind. Subtly, and it seemed of their own volition, the seams were coming undone. Either because she was unaware of this, or because as a good trouper she bravely refused to interrupt the show, Toots went on circulating over the floor, revealing larger and larger expanses of white skin through the spreading gaps with every pirouette. Mr Uniatz goggled at the performance with breathless admiration.

Simon leaned a little towards Karen.

'Incidentally,' he said, without moving his lips, 'what is that captain's name?'

'Friede,' she told him.

'One of those inappropriate names, I think,' murmured the Saint.

He was recalling his first curious impressions about the captain. It had seemed on the *March Hare* that Friede was far more in command of the situation than March. There had been an aura of cold deadliness about him that the average observer might have overlooked, but that stood out in garish colours to anyone as familiar with dangerous men as the Saint. Throughout the episode of the previous night, Friede had never stepped out of line, had never attempted to dominate, had given March every respect and deference. And yet, when Simon looked back on it analytically, Friede had done everything that mattered. All the constructive and dangerous suggestions had come from him, although he had never obtruded himself for a moment. He had simply put words and ideas into March's mouth, but so cleverly that March's echo had taken the authority of an original command. It had been so brilliantly done that Simon had to think back again over the actual literal phrasing of the dialogue, wondering if he was trying to put bones into a wild hallucination. Yet if that irking recollection was right, what other strange factors might there be inside that rather square-shaped cranium, which now that the captain appeared without his cap was revealed as bald as an ostrich egg?

By this time, Toots's disintegrating seams had left nothing but four wide streamers of black lace hanging from her shoulder-straps. With a last revolution of her curvilinear body which spread them like the blades of a propeller, she reached the curtained doorway. The lights dimmed. There was a round of applause, to which Hoppy Uniatz lent his co-operation by thumping his flat hand on the table until it shuddered under the punishment.

The music and the spotlight struck up again together. Apparently intoxicated by her success, but at the same time handicapped by the shredding of her gown, Toots compromised by coming back without it. She had nothing now but the palmleaf fan, which being only about twelve inches in diameter was not nearly large enough to cover all the vital scenery. Her valiant attempts to alternate concealments and exposures held the audience properly spellbound.

'Stay where you are,' Simon ordered sternly, as Hoppy's chair began to slide away from the table. 'Haven't you ever been out before?'

'Chees, boss,' said Mr Uniatz bashfully, 'I never see nut'n like dis. In New York dey always got *sump'n* on.'

Simon had to acknowledge that the comparison was justified, but he still kept Mr Uniatz in his seat. He was trying to anticipate what the arrival of March and Friede portended. By saying nothing to Haskins about the Saint's felonious activities of the night before they had positively established themselves as asking no favours from the Law, but it was impossible to believe that they had decided to forget the whole thing. Their arrival at the Palmleaf Fan, after Simon had been led there by such a devious trail, had to be more than mere coincidence. And a kind of contented relaxation slid through the Saint's muscles as he realised that by the same portents their personal presence guaranteed that whatever was in the wind was not going to be a waste of anybody's time . . .

The peregrinations of Toots returned to the curtained doorway as the music drew to a conclusion. She stood weaving the fan with slower provocation through the last bars, scanning the audience as though making a choice. The applause grew wild. Mr Uniatz put two fingers in his mouth and emitted a whistle that pierced the room like a stiletto. The strident sound seemed to settle her selection. With a smile she tossed the fan away in his direction, blew him a kiss, stood posed for an instant in nothing whatsoever, and vanished through the curtain as the spotlight blacked out.

The nimble M.C. tripped back to the microphone.

'And now, ladies and gentlemen, just one more sample of what we are offering you tonight. That lovely personality – Vivian Dare!'

Vivian wore a beautifully-cut dress of blue tulle, and had a considerably better soprano than Toots.

'You're very quiet,' said Karen. 'Is the show so absorbing, or are you shocked?'

Simon grinned.

'You may not believe it, but I've been watching Randy most of the time. He seems to like the place.'

'It's the sort of place he does like. He could have bought it for the money he spends here.'

The Saint nodded. He had already observed the extra attentiveness of waiters around March's table, and deduced that this was by no means a first visit. The attraction seemed to radiate to other quarters as well, for two blondes and a brunette were at that moment happily attaching themselves to the party.

'Did he bring you here much?' Simon asked.

'Often.'

'Do you think he's trying to show you that he doesn't need to bring a girl here?'

She laughed.

'That isn't for my benefit. He always had girls to the table even when I was with him. It's his kind of fun.'

She spoke without rancour, without any personal emotion that he could detect, as if she had been mentioning that March had a stamp collection. But once again Simon was brought up against the enigma of her, wondering about so many things that were unsaid.

And he was still watching March's table for the first warning of where danger would come from. Their complete detachment was beginning to make him tense again. Neither March nor the captain had given a sign of greeting or recognition to anyone in the room except the waiters, and Karen, and the ladies of pleasure who had just joined them; and yet he knew that their arrival must have been a signal for wheels to begin turning. He wondered if that was really the only signal there would be . . .

Vivian had begun to carry her song among the tables, and now she was at their booth, addressing the words intimately to Mr Uniatz, who gaped up at her as if in hopes that the blue tulle would begin to come off her before she moved away.

'You are
The promised kiss of springtime
That makes the lonely winter seem long;
You are
The breathless hush of evening–'

Hoppy's chest expanded like a balloon, and he shifted his weight to the detriment of the chair. It had always been one of the tragedies of his life that so many women were blind to his hidden loveliness of soul.

The singer reached out and stroked his cheek.

'You are the angel glow
That lights the stars;
The dearest things I know
Are what you are . . .'

Simon choked over his drink.

'Some day
My happy arms will hold you–'

It was too much for Mr Uniatz. He tried to wrap one arm around the svelte enticing figure that was bending over him; but Vivian was ready for that. A swift kiss was planted on Hoppy's forehead, and his clutching hand caught nothing but a mass of curly hair, which came off in the form of a wig, revealing a strictly masculine haircut underneath.

'You nasty rough beast!' squeaked Vivian, and snatched the wig back from him and fled towards the door.

Like lightning, before Simon could move, Mr Uniatz let go with the carafe of water. It crossed the room like a damp comet, caromed off the clarinet player, boomed off a drum, and came to a cataclysmic end among the cymbals. Then

Simon had Hoppy's wrist and was holding him down with a grip of iron.

'Cut it out,' he gritted, 'or I'll break your arm.'

'We oughta take dis jernt apart, boss,' said Mr Uniatz redly.

'You damn fool!' snarled the Saint. 'They were just waiting for us to start something.'

And then he realised that the room was rocking with laughter. Everyone seemed to be laughing. March's table was in an uproar, with March himself leading it. Even Captain Friede's tight mouth was flattened broadly across his teeth. The clarinettist was helped out by a grinning waiter, apparently being a person of no consequence. The chortling orchestra leader waved his baton, and a new dance number blared out. Giggling couples were filtering on to the floor. The head waiter appeared at the booth and smiled, only a little more restrainedly.

'Your first time here?' he said, more as a statement than a question.

'My friend isn't drunk,' said the Saint. 'But he's a little hasty.'

The head waiter nodded tolerantly.

'Well, there was no harm done. Shall I bring you some more water?'

'Thank you.'

The Saint felt incredibly and incredulously foolish. And yet it had seemed so obvious. Start something, bring on the bouncers, and anything could happen in the resultant brawl.

But the opportunity had been ignored. It had been taken as a good joke.

He lighted another cigarette and tried to say unconcernedly to Karen: 'It's a good thing they've got a sense of humour here.'

'Something happens here almost every night,' she said casually. 'But nobody gets excited.'

Not that, then . . . And yet she also seemed expectant, in a way that he could not pin down on to any outward sign. There was no nervousness in the handling of her cigarette or the leisured sipping of her liqueur. Perhaps it was because of that very tranquillity that he felt on edge, as if he sensed that she was playing a part to which he was not admitted.

Then where was it coming from? A shot from somewhere during a blackout? Too conventional – and too risky. He still couldn't get out of his head the conviction that March and Friede must still be bothered by the protective letter that he had spoken about. And they were here now, much too prominently present to have any expectation of being named as suspects. A poison in the Scotch, or the new carafe of water? Impossible, for the same reason. Then what? Could he have been altogether wrong in every single calculation, and could he be a helpless particle in a ferment that he knew nothing about and for whose chemical combinations he was utterly unprepared?

Hobgoblin centipedes inched up his back into the roots of his hair.

And then the dance had ended, and the exquisite M.C. was skipping up to the microphone again, as the floor cleared and a miniature piano was trundled in.

'Now, ladies and gentlemen, we bring you another of those unique entertainments which have made the Palmleaf Fan famous: that great and goofy singer, the maestro of murky music, lewd lyrics, and dirty ditties – the one and only Jesse Rogers!'

There was a concerted blast from saxophones, trombones, clarinets, and cornucopias; and the man Simon Templar had been looking for walked on.

2

Hoppy Uniatz, still crushed beneath his recent humiliation, swilled whisky around his glass and put it down. He leaned across the table.

'Boss,' he divulged in a despondent whisper that reached every comer of the room, 'I gotta go.'

'Shut up,' snapped the Saint. 'You can go afterwards. This is the guy we came out here to see.'

Mr Uniatz reviewed the performer with sour disillusion.

'It don't mean a t'ing in dis jernt, boss. I betcha he's just a wren wit' pants on.'

Simon could appreciate the justification for Hoppy's prejudice, but he also realised that Jesse Rogers was definitely not the right subject for it.

Rogers was a normal type if there ever was one, even though it was not a type which entirely harmonised with the atmosphere of the Palmleaf Fan. He had more of an air of filling in there while paying his way through college. He had a round and rather juvenile face made studious by rimless glasses, and his shoulders and complexion both looked as if they were indebted to a much more healthy background.

His repertoire, however, certainly did not. His first song ran a gamut of transparent *double entendre* and monothematic suggestion that would have brought blushes to the cheeks of the blowsiest barmaid, and was accordingly received with tumultuous applause. It was plain that he was a popular performer. As the ovation subsided, there were sporadic shouts of 'Octavius!' Rogers smiled with cherubic salaciousness, and said: 'By request – Octavius, the Octogenarian Octopus.'

The difficulties, vices, and devices of Octavius were unfolded in the same strain. They were biologically improbable, but full of ingenious concepts; and they went on for a long time.

A waiter came by the table, picked up the Peter Dawson bottle, and tilted it over the glasses. It was an unproductive service, for Mr Uniatz had not taken his revised standards of alcoholic quality seriously enough to leave anything unpoured. The waiter leaned over with respectful discretion and said: 'Shall I bring another bottle, sir?'

'I suppose you'd better,' said the Saint with the fatalism of long experience. 'Or do you make special rates by the case?'

The waiter smiled politely and went away. The song went on, with the diversions of Octavius becoming more recherché in every stanza. Currently, they seemed to be concerned with some whimsical prank involving bathing girls in Bali.

Karen said curiously: 'What are you making of him?'

'He knows his onions, for what they're worth,' said the Saint judicially. 'I've been trying to estimate what else he's worth. At first I thought something was haywire again, but now I'm not nearly sure.'

'Does he look tough to you?'

'He does – now. He's tougher than Jennet. It's a funny twist, but you're always surprised when a villain you've built up in your imagination doesn't turn out to look like a professional wrestler, and yet some of these baby-faced guys are more dangerous than any plug-ugly knows how to be.'

He felt no incongruity in discussing Rogers so dispassionately with her. The mere fact that she should be sitting there with him at that time achieved a culmination of unreality beside which all minor paradoxes were insignificant. And yet even that apical absurdity had become so much a part of the fantastic picture that he no longer questioned it.

The saga of Octavius ended at last, and Rogers was shaking his head, smiling, in answer to the disappointed yells for more as the piano was whisked away. The M.C. tripped on again like a pixie and said: 'Jesse Rogers will be back before long, ladies and gentlemen, with some more of those sizzling songs. We can't give you the whole show at once. Let's dance again, and then we'll have another treat for you.' The orchestra took its cue, and the ball kept rolling. It could never be disputed that the Palmleaf Fan worked tirelessly in its dubious cause.

Simon still looked between the gathering dancers, and saw that Rogers had been stopped on his way out through the curtained doorway by a waiter. Something about the back of the waiter's close-cropped head seemed oddly familiar . . . Simon was trying to identify the familiarity when Rogers looked directly at him across the room. In that instant the Saint grasped the fleeting shadow of recognition.

It was the waiter who had just taken his order for another bottle of Scotch.

Nothing to make any difference. The waiter had other duties. But Rogers had looked straight across the room. And in the circumstances . . .

Karen Leith's face was a lovely mask. She might not have seen anything.

'So you've seen him,' she said. 'Now what are you going to do?'

'I was just wondering,' Simon replied slowly. 'We might wait till he comes on again and shoot him from here. But the management might resent that. Besides, I want to know where he gets *his* orders from . . . Do you think you're getting enough inside information to please Randy?'

He was deliberately trying to hurt her again, to strike some spark that would end his groping. But instead of hatred, her eyes brightened with something else that he would much rather not have seen.

'Dear idiot,' she said, and she was smiling. 'Don't ever stop being hard. Don't ever let anyone fool you – not even me.'

He had to smile back at her. Had to.

'No nonsense?' he said emptily.

'Not for anything.'

'Boss,' began Mr Uniatz, diffidently.

The Saint sat back. And he started to laugh. It was a quiet and necessary laughter. It brought the earth back again.

'I remember,' he said. 'You wanted to go.'

'I was just t'inkin', boss, it don't have to make much difference. I can be quick.'

'For Heaven's sake, don't go into all the details,' said the Saint hastily. 'Take all the time you want. We know all about the calls of Nature. We can wait.'

'Chees, boss,' said Mr Uniatz, with almost childishly adoring gratitude. 'T'anks!'

He got up from the table and paddled hurriedly away.

Karen made a slightly strangled sound, and quickly picked up her glass. The Saint looked at her and chuckled.

'I should have warned you about him,' he murmured. 'He doesn't mean any harm. He's just uninhibited.'

'I – I was b-beginning to discover that.' Her lips trembled. 'If he ever has any puppies, will you send me one?'

'I'll remember,' said the Saint; but his voice faded as he said it.

The waiter was back again, transferring a fresh bottle and clean glasses from a tray to the table.

Simon studied him again through lazily trailing wisps of smoke, and became doubly sure of his identification. The lines of the tightly trimmed fair hair, as the man leaned over the table, were quite distinctive. He had a square unexpressive face on which the skin seemed to be stretched so snugly over the bony structure that there was hardly any play left for movement. He said, leaning over: 'Are you Mr Templar, sir?'

Like a wind-ruffled pool on to which oil has been floated, everything in the Saint settled into an immeasurable inward stillness; yet there was no change in him that any eye could have seen.

'That's right,' he said calmly.

'Mr Rogers would very much like to see you, sir, as soon as it's convenient.' The enunciation was stiff and without personality, a formal reproduction which conveyed nothing but the bare words it was phrased in. 'I can show you to his dressing-room whenever you're ready.'

The Saint drew his cigarette to a long even glow. And in that time his mind raced over everything, without stirring one fibre of that deep physical repose.

So this was it . . . It seemed simple enough, now, so simple that he had to deride the energy he had squandered on all his preliminary alertness. Rogers had seen him, recognised him, and beaten him to the draw. He didn't remember ever having seen Rogers before, but that was no reason to think that Rogers didn't know him – he had to be more than a name to at least some of the units in the chain of conspiracy. Lafe Jennet might be back on the road at Olustee by that time, but there were plenty of other ways for Jesse Rogers to have learned that the cat was out and the Saint was on his trail. So Rogers – or the men behind Rogers – had merely taken the dilemma by the horns . . .

'Of course,' said the Saint easily. 'I'll be right along.'

The waiter bowed disinterestedly, and moved a little way off. And the Saint found Karen's eyes fixed on him.

'Will you excuse me?' he said.

'We could have another dance first. And then Hoppy'll be back to keep me company.'

It seemed as if that was all she could think of to say, to delay him, without making a confession or a betrayal that they both knew was impossible. He smiled.

'Why not now?' he said quietly. 'Hoppy'll be back, but I wouldn't have taken him anyway. Rogers and I have a little personal business. I came here to see him, so I might as well do it. I don't know what's in his mind, but I'll find out. It's the only certain principle I ever learned – find out. And if he knows that I work that way, and he's ready for it – I'll find that out too.'

She didn't speak or move for a moment.

Then her hand touched his hand, lightly; and the touch was a kiss, or an embrace, or more than that, or nothing.

'Good luck, Saint.'

'I've always been much too lucky,' he said, and turned away at once, and went after the waiter.

He wanted it to be that way, to go into swift movement and the exalting leap of danger that left no time for profitless introspection and static gentleness: he was tired of thinking. There was no bravado in it. He wanted whatever they had waiting – wanted it with an insolent and desperate desire.

'Lead on, Adolphus,' he said, and the waiter's eyes barely flickered.

'Yes, sir. This way.'

They went around the perimeter of the room, past the front of the orchestra, and through the curtained doorway that served the floor show artistes for an entrance. A passage turned to the left, paralleling the wall for a couple of yards, and then turned straight back at right angles.

Simon stopped at the corner of the L and adjusted a shoelace that was perfectly well tied. March and Friede had both been dancing when he crossed the floor, but if it was part of their plan to follow him closely into the back of the building he could do no harm by confusing the time-table. He spent rather a long time over the shoelace, long enough for them to have blundered into him, but no one followed.

He straightened up at last and went on.

The passage was about eighty feet long, ending in a door which from the iron bars over its pebble glass panel he guessed to be an exit from the building. The wall on the left gave out warmth for a few yards as he passed it, and a muted rattle and clink of metal and china that came through it suggested a kitchen. Aside from that blank space, there were plain doors on both sides. A pretty black-haired girl in a gaudy print brassiere and sarong came out of one door, passed them with hardly a glance, and went on to wait for her announcement. Further down, on the other side, a twittering of high-pitched male voices came through another door. It opened, and something in a strapless sequin gown and a silver wig came out, leered at them, said 'Woo!' and vanished through the door opposite like a leprechaun.

The waiter stopped just beyond that point, and Simon came up alongside him.

'The last door, sir, on the left.'

'Thank you.'

The Saint passed him and strolled on. The steadiness of his movement was a triumph of cold nerve over instinct, but he felt as if there was a bull's-eye stencilled between his shoulder-blades. His ears strained for the click of a cocked gun or the premonitory swish of a blackjack, or even a breath too close behind . . .

Then he was at the last door, and as he turned towards it he was able to glance sideways down the length of the corridor through which he had come. The waiter had turned his back and was walking slowly away. There was no one else visible.

Simon laughed, silently and without humour. Perhaps he really was getting old and jumpy, letting his imagination blind his judgment.

And yet there was nothing fanciful about the bullet that had been sent him by the man he was going to see.

He paused for a moment at the door. Without intention, but simply from force of habit, he knew that his feet had made no sound through the approach. But during that pause he could hear nothing within the room – not the least rustle of human speech or movement. There were only the distant undertones which had become unnoticeable through acceptance – the waiter's retreating steps, the chatter from other dressing-rooms, the dissonances of the kitchen, and the distant drift of music. But in spite of that, or because of it, he lowered the hand which he had raised to knock.

Instead, his fingers closed on the door knob. He took one long breath; and then in one feline ripple of co-ordination he threw the door open and slid diagonally into the room.

Two men with round stolid faces like Tweedledum and Tweedledee stood in one corner with their hands held high. Jesse Rogers reclined on a shabby divan with his hands behind his head, a lighted cigarette drooping from one corner of his mouth. There was no weapon anywhere near him to account for the attitudes of Tweedledum and Tweedledee. The single reason for that was a cumbersome 45 Colt which swung around in the hand of a fourth member of the congregation whose lanky legs stretched forward from a chair tilted back against the dressing-table.

Sheriff Newt Haskins spat accurately at the feet of one of his captives, squinted his keen grey eyes at the Saint, and said: 'Well, ain't this nice? Come right in, son. We were sort of expectin' you.'

3

Simon Templar carefully closed the door.

There was rather a lot to assimilate all at once, and he wanted time. The entire tableau gave him the impression of some sort of mad tea-party from *Alice in Wonderland.* Of course, he had already seen the March Hare, he reflected hysterically. And now there was Tweedledum and Tweedledee. Doubtless Sheriff Haskins would turn out to be the Mad Hatter. Jesse Rogers, from his position, looked like a promising candidate for the Dormouse. Presently they would all start singing and dancing, with Toots and Vivian doing a hot rumba in the middle.

That was the way it felt at first. The Saint could have taken a whole army of hoodlums in his stride, and turned up his nose at a forest of machine-guns, by comparison with the cataclysmic shock of what he actually saw. It left him wondering, for perhaps the first time in his life, whether he had any right to be patronising about the pedestrian intellectual reflexes of Hoppy Uniatz . . .

'Hullo, Sheriff,' he drawled. 'You do get around, don't you?'

The sheer electronic energy that it cost him to maintain that air-conditioned nonchalance would have twisted the needle of any recording instrument known to science off its bearings; but he achieved it. And with a simultaneous equal effort he was forcing himself to try and wring a coherent interpretation out of the scene.

The only entirely unplumbed factors were Tweedledum and Tweedledee.

Aside from their generic facial resemblance, they shared the hollow-stomached muscular emphasis of professional bullies – and something more. It was something strange and out of place even in that plethora of improbabilities, something that was bound up by devious psychological links with the strangeness that had struck him about some of the revellers outside.

In another split second he realised what it was. Even in surrender, their carriage had the ingrained rigidity of soldiers on a parade-ground. They only needed the addition of field boots and Sam Browne belts to complete the picture.

Two guns lay on the dressing-table beside Haskins's left shoulder. The sheriff caught Simon's glance at them, and moved his chair a little to offer a better view. He puckered his lips, weasening his face with furrows, and underlined the weapons with a backward jerk of his left thumb.

'Now that you're heah, son, mebbe you can help us. A feller like you should have a right smart knowledge of fire-arms. What do you make of these shootin' irons?'

The Saint made no attempt to get closer – he knew better than to make an incautious move against a man who seemed to have the situation so comfortably lined up. Newt Haskins might look like a piece of antique furniture if he were set down in the streamlined atmosphere of New York's Centre Street, but Simon was not deceived. Haskins wasn't even nervous. He was utterly relaxed – a natural deadly machine buttressed with the simple knowledge that if he shot six times, six men would die.

'One of them is a Smith and Wesson 357 Magnum,' said the Saint.

'An' the other?'

Simon screwed up his eyes.

'It looks like a Webley Mark VI 455 Service revolver.'

'Service, hey?' The sheriff's free hand caressed his neck. 'What service would that mean?'

'It was the official British Army revolver in the last war,' Simon replied slowly. 'I don't know whether they're still using it.'

Haskins peered sidelong at Tweedledum and Tweedledee. 'Do either o' these lads look to you like they mighta been in the British Army?'

Simon shook his head.

'They look more as if they'd belong on the other side.'

'That's how it seemed to me. But I took those irons away from Hans and Fritz less 'n fifteen minutes ago.' Another stream of tobacco juice hit the floor. 'Now, why would you figure one o' these Krauts would be totin' a gun that looks more like it ought to belong to you?'

'I don't suppose I can prove it,' said the Saint, 'but I never owned one of those guns in my life.'

Haskins pushed back his black hat and scratched his head.

'I can't prove you ever did, either, if it comes to that,' he said. 'But it seems to me you still got plenty of explainin' to do. There's a whole lot o' things goin' on that don't make sense, an' you're in the middle of all of 'em.' He motioned towards a chair with the barrel of his 45. 'Now suppose you just sit down, son, an' tell your daddy what goes on.'

The Saint sat down.

'If you don't mind my mentioning it again,' he remarked, 'you seem to bob up pretty frequently yourself.'

'I git paid for that by the county. But I shuah never worked so much overtime before until you hit the town.' The grey eyes were placid but bright as flints in their creased sockets. 'I been mighty tolerant with you, son, on account of you bein' a guest of the city, so to speak. But you don't want to forget that we ain't like Scotland Yard. They tell me they ask all their questions with powder puffs over there, but out here we get kinda rough an' hasty, sometimes, when our patience is plumb wore out.'

It seemed as if there were only the two of them in the room. Tweedledum and Tweedledee, fixed in their arm-lifted pose with the petrifaction of *rigor mortis,* made no more difference than a pair of statues. But the most perplexing nonentity was Jesse Rogers. He had never moved or spoken, but his half-closed eyes behind the rimless glasses had not shifted once from the Saint's face.

'You can smoke, if you like,' Haskins went on. 'But be almighty shuah it's tobacco you're reachin' for.' He watched the Saint kindle a cigarette and put his lighter away. 'You didn't by any chance come in heah lookin' for a lad named Jesse Rogers, did you?'

'You knew that.'

'Shuah. You told me this afternoon. Now, I heard tell you was a smart boy, son, an' comin' to a feller's dressin'-room to bump him off after the whole countryside knows you been chasin' him all day strikes me as a right foolish way of committin' murder. So I just can't see that you was aimin' to do that.'

Simon stretched out his long legs and blew smoke towards the ceiling.

'That's very kind of you, Sheriff.'

'Way down in my heart,' Haskins declared dryly, 'I'm a soft lovin' sort of man.' His gaze brushed over the Saint's dinner clothes. 'So you hadn't no idea of killin' Jesse. At least, not right now. You dolled yourself all up an' just come out here on a party, like. You wouldn't by any chance have brought along that red-headed girl?'

'As a matter of fact,' said the Saint blandly, 'I did.'

'You've got the ball now, son,' Haskins said. 'Keep goin'.'

Simon's mind raced warily ahead, trying to cover all the conceivable ramifications of possibility. And yet he couldn't find a single one which seemed to take a dangerous direction. That was the fantastic part of it. For once in his life, he could face any inquisition without a shadow on his conscience. And in that fact alone there was something more disconcerting than there would have been in any need for lies. Subterfuge and evasion were things that one expected in such adventures with the regularity of treads on a tractor. But Haskins was interested in nothing that the Saint had to conceal. The Saint's only secrets were the lifebelt twisted on to the wrist of the drowned boy, the planting of the body on the *March Hare*, the interview that had followed, and a brief glimpse of a submerging submarine. And Haskins knew nothing about any of those things – even the opposition had co-operated in concealing some of them. The only things that Haskins was concerned with could be dissected under arc lights without any fear that Simon could anticipate. There was no problem of inventing a convincing lie. There was only the much more devastating problem of making the truth believable.

'I haven't one single thing to hide,' said the Saint, and was obsessed with the hollowness of his own candour even while he said it. 'You know just as much as I do – unless you know any more.'

'Don't stop, son.'

The Saint pulled at his cigarette, marshalling the simple facts. When there was no obvious direction for a lie, what could be safer than the naked truth?

'You know why I'm in Miami. Gilbeck sent for me. I showed you his daughter's letter. I don't know one single thing more than what was in it, about what the trouble was. Now the Gilbecks have disappeared, and naturally I'm afraid there's dirty work in it. Naturally, too, I want to find them. But I didn't know where to begin.'

'You made a good start, anyhow.'

'Somebody else made the start – somebody who knew I was looking for them. Jennet shot at me. We caught him and grilled him – maybe that was overstepping the technicalities a bit, but I told you we'd done it. He told us he'd been coerced by Rogers, whom he didn't know anything about except that he'd met him on that barge of Gallipolis's. So I went out there and that's where you met us again. I told you the story then. But Gallipolis had already told me that Rogers worked here, which he didn't tell you. So I came here.'

'So you an' Gallipolis was holdin' out on me.' The sheriff's voice was gentle and chiding. 'Well . . .'

'Gallipolis is a bit prejudiced against the Law,' said the Saint, with a slight smile. 'Personally, I didn't give it a thought. I like taking care of myself. Besides, I've found that my motives are sometimes misunderstood when I try to interest the Law in my troubles.'

'Mebbe that's so.'

'Look,' Simon insisted, 'how hard did you try to give me the benefit of the doubt when you found that note of mine on the *Mirage*? Not any longer than it took you to get out to Gilbeck's and start calling me names—'

'Just a minute, son.' Haskins elongated his neck a couple of inches. 'Who told you that was where I found that note?'

The Saint sighed out a steady feather of smoke.

'Probably,' he said without batting an eyelid, 'the same mysterious person who tipped you off that the *Mirage* was at Wildcat Key.'

It was not such a wild shot in the dark, after all. The sheriff blinked a little and then found dogged consolation in his chew.

'Son,' he remarked, 'I don't mind tellin' you I've been gettin' a mite tired of bein' called to the phone to receive messages from a voice belongin' to A Friend. First thing it was a drowned sailor on the *March Hare*. Then it was to look for the *Mirage* at Wildcat Key. Then it was to see what you were doin' with Gallipolis on his barge, takin' an escaped convict there. To-night it was Jesse Rogers.'

'You mean he called you?' Simon took another puzzled glance at the recumbent figure on the divan.

'That's right, son,' Haskins replied unexpectedly. 'But A

Friend called him first. A Friend told him the jig was up an' there was a long box waitin' for him tonight. So he called me. That warn't much more 'n an hour ago. So I come out. I tramp across country an' let myself in the back, rememberin' about you an' not wantin' to spoil anythin'. Jesse an' me kind of got together. So when he went on, I hid me in the closet.'

The Saint's brows were beginning to draw imperceptibly together.

'What for?'

'For Hans an' Fritz heah.' Haskins shifted his cud from one side of his mouth to the other and gave the first side a rest. 'It seems like your smartness sort of slipped a cog, son. If I hadn't 'a done that, an' taken those fancy shootin' irons away from 'em when they come in – the way we figgered it, you an' Jesse, or what was left o' you, would be lyin' on the floor waitin' for the coroner.'

Simon looked at the two guns on the dressing-table again, and at Tweedledum and Tweedledee again, and at Jesse Rogers again, and felt as if he was balanced on a pinnacle of crumbling ice above an interplanetary maelstrom of emptiness.

'You've taken the ball again,' he said. 'It's all yours. Now you keep going.'

'It was a mighty clever idea, accordin' to Jesse's tip from A Friend an' the way we worked it out,' Haskins proceeded luxuriously. 'After Jesse had done his act, he got a message that you wanted to see him––'

'Wait,' Simon interrupted. 'I hadn't got as far as that. He beat me to it. I got a message that he wanted to see me.'

Haskins barely twitched one shaggy eyebrow.

'That's what the waiter told him, anyhow. I don't misbelieve you, son. Mebbe the waiter was just doin' his part. It don't make no difference. One way or another, you get here. An' when' you walk in the door, like you did just now, Hans an' Fritz are already holdin' Rogers up. Hans will shoot you with the Magnum, while Fritz shoots Jesse with that British gun. Then they leave the right guns beside each o' you, an' duck out the window. When everybody comes rushin' in, it looks just like you'd killed each other in a gun fight – particularly since about four people know that you've been trailin' Jesse all day with a grudge agin him on account of he hired Lafe Jennet to take a shot at you. Havin' come in on some o' that myself this afternoon, I'd 'a been most liable to figger that was the way of it myself.' The sheriff scratched one leg with the toe of the opposite boot. 'Thinkin' it all over, son, it shuah seems to me that somebody was takin' an awful lot of trouble to see that you an' Jesse was both got rid of together with no questions asked.'

Simon Templar put his cigarette to his lips and filled his lungs with warm soothing vapour and forgot to let it out again. His whole being seemed to stand still in the same cumulative and timeless stasis that affected the expansion of his ribs.

But through those fleeting seconds, his brain absorbed fact and association and deduction as completely and meticulously as his lung tissues ingested the smoke. Every molecule of factual knowledge was seeping into its predestined pore. The pattern was all falling into place. Every piece had its revealed significance, even to the most trivial fragments. He didn't know whether to feel stupid or triumphant. Certainly he had expended an astronomical amount of time and energy and cerebration on the trail of a wild goose, but had it been really wasted? The wild goose – to cross metaphors with a lavishness that only a pedant could criticise in the circumstances – had come home to roost. There were only a few vacant spaces left . . .

'It makes sense, Sheriff.' Even the naturalness of his own voice surprised him. 'I've spent about twelve hours letting myself be nursed into the most beautifully eleborate set-up I ever heard of. But how about Jesse? Did he really tell Jennet to shoot at me?'

Rogers spoke for the first time without any expression.

'I did. I didn't have to tell him to hit you, so I thought I'd pass on the order and see what happened.'

'You see, son,' Haskins explained, 'you got yourself mixed up in some powerful big organisin'. I found out tonight that Jesse was workin' heah as what you'd call an undercover man for the Department of Justice. It didn't surprise me so much, neither. I've knowed for a long time that this place was the local headquarters of Mr Hitler's Nazi-American Bund.'

4

'Of course,' said the Saint with an ecstatic lilt in his voice that was too zephyrous for anyone else there to hear. 'Of course . . .'

And he felt as if a fresh wind from out of doors had blown through his head, leaving it clean and light, with all the dark tangles swept away. Everything else was set in its niche now, to be seen clearly from every angle. The only thing that amazed him was that he had failed to find the connecting link long ago. Those last words of Haskins's had supplied it.

The Bund. And those fearfully earnest merrymakers outside. Karen had practically told him when she put the words '*Kraft durch Freude*' into his mouth – and he'd been too preoccupied to grasp it. And the whole atmosphere of the trap into which he had so nearly fallen. Its grim, far-ranging, tortuous Teutonic thoroughness. One could almost see the imprint of the fine hand of Himmler. But between the master hand of Himmler and its victims, in this as in every other corner of that incredible world-wide web of intrigue and sabotage, a more fantastic secret society than any blood-and-thunder writer of fiction would ever have dared to try and make convincing, there had to be major intermediaries, graduates *summa cum laude* of the Himmler school of technique. And who was the intermediary here, the local lieutenant of this greater gangsterism than the pretty Caesars of civil crime had ever dreamed of? Well, not a lieutenant. A captain. Captain Friede. The man whom Simon had always sensed was the real commander even when March seemed to give the orders. It could be no one else. The finger pointed to him beyond any mortal doubt. Sometimes there could be uncertainties; but sometimes there was a clarity of vision that amounted to inspiration, that logic might justify but could not assail. It had to be Friede. And through him, the other threads linked with March, with

Gilbeck, with the Foreign Investment Pool, with a torpedoed tanker, even with a drowned sailor with a lifebelt bearing the name of a British submarine tangled to his wrist. Everything, everything hooked up . . . There were still a few minor questions, but their solution would be direct and unequivocal. The groping was over, and all that was ahead lay straight as an arrow's flight . . .

'Of course,' said the Saint, after a million years, 'Jesse can't have been quite so much under cover as he thought. Somebody had suspected him, and this was the neatest way to get rid of both of us together.'

'That's what I think.' Rogers sat up at last, and Simon discovered that the old-young eyes behind his glasses could be unexpectedly penetrating. 'I've been watching you all this time, and I know you've been telling the truth. But Haskins didn't ask why they should want to get rid of *you*.'

Simon chain-lighted another cigarette. Because of divers accidents, he had been able to reconstruct far more than either Rogers or Haskins. And that was where his incurable madness came back, that gay and crazy quirk of his very own that had led him into so many hairbreadth perils and so much more fun. They had provided the one vital clue, but they still couldn't have his adventure.

'The only thing I can think of,' he said, 'is that this disappearance of the Gilbecks has something to do with it. They knew my reputation, and they knew I'd be bound to take an active interest in that, and they may have thought I was too dangerous to leave at large. That is, if I was ever important at all. They may have just wanted any scapegoat at all, and heard that I was in town, and thought I'd been good enough if I could be manoeuvred into a sufficiently compromising background. But the disappearance of the Gilbecks does seem to have some connection, since Haskins was first put on to me when A Friend sent him to find my note on the *Mirage*.'

His air of baffled candour could not have been more convincing.

'And you still haven't any idea what connection Gilbeck could have with this?' Rogers asked, watching him.

'Not the slightest,' Simon lied tremorlessly. 'If I had, I could catch up on a lot of sleep.'

Rogers sat for a moment longer, and then stood up. He went to the window and whistled softly. Two deputies loomed up in the dark outside. Rogers turned away, and Haskins said: 'Boys, the two lads in the corner have gotten themselves a queer idea that Miami Beach is the Siegfried Line. I want you to take 'em into town an' tuck 'em away so their patriotic passions can get a chance to cool.' He gathered up the two revolvers by the barrels with his left hand, and held them out. 'You better take these along, too, so you can book 'em for concealed firearms.'

'You'll hear more of this,' rasped Tweedledum, as the sheriff's revolver waved him towards the window. 'We've got our legal rights—'

Haskins screwed up one eye and said: 'Our county Gestapo knows all about 'em, an' I'm afraid they'll give you more breaks than you'd get at home. In the meantime, I'm goin' to send you some writin' paper an' let you write your boss an' tell him to keep his goddam *Weltanschauung* at home!'

When the two men had gone out through the window, Simon said boldly: 'If you knew all this before, why didn't you do something about the place?'

'Sometimes a place like this is useful,' said Rogers. 'If we know where the small fry are meeting, it gives us a chance to keep track of some of the big fish.'

'Then who is the big fish here?'

'That's what I was sent here to find out.' Rogers shrugged. 'It seems as if he spotted me before I could spot him. I hope it doesn't make much difference. Somebody else will pick up where I left off, and in the end we'll know him. Even if their plot had worked, it wouldn't have really mattered.'

'It must be very comforting to have the philosophic outlook,' commented the Saint.

Haskins put his big gun stoically away.

'Son,' he remarked, 'it's always been a policy of the Law in this country to let bad little boys alone when they want to play. We let these bunches o' tin soldiers march an' drill around in our peaceful country, an' wave their swastikas, an' heil Hitler, an' make the goddamdest dirty cracks about democracy, on account of it's the policy of democracy to let everybody shout his own opinions, even when it's his opinion that nobody who don't agree with him ought to be allowed even to whisper what he thinks. We let 'em tear hell out o' the Constitootion on account of the Constitootion says anybody can tear anything out of it he wants to. We let 'em use all the freedom that the founders of this country gave their lives to give us, to try an' take that freedom away. We're so plumb scared of gettin' accused o' bein' the same as they are that we even let 'em train an' arm a private army to put over their ideas, rather 'n give 'em the chance to say we denied 'em the liberty they want to take away from us. That's why we're the greatest country in the world, an' everybody else laughs 'emselves sick lookin' at us.'

There was a moment's silence before Simon could say, evenly enough: 'I hope nobody can ever lick your screwy country . . . But do you need me here any more?'

'By this time,' Rogers said, 'they know that the plot's misfired. You can slip the back way with us.'

'I left Haskins's red-headed flame in the main room,' said the Saint 'And another friend of mine in the gents' relief station. I can't just ditch them. If the gang knows that the plot has misfired, they can guess you and Haskins are here with some deputies. They'll be too scared to make trouble without plenty more planning. You go the way Haskins came, and I'll get out the way I came in. I can take care of myself.'

'Check with me at the local F.B.I. office in the morning?' Rogers said.

There was no need for picayune hair-splitting. Their eyes met in the understanding of men among men – an unspoken bond of strength greeting strength. Death had brushed by them lightly, and left them alive to carry on. Both of them knew it.

'If I can,' said the Saint, and was gone.

He went quickly back down the long corridor. He had his own plan of campaign, clear now that its objectives were no longer eddying reflections in a distorting mirror, to iron out; and he knew that time was more vital now than it had ever been . . . The vacuous twittering went on in the men's dressing-room. The pretty black-haired girl, who had apparently completed her act with the usual disasters to the costume, met him at the turn of the passage with what was left of it in her hand and nothing else to obscure the artistic tailoring of her birthday suit. Once again, they passed each other with hardly a glance. He would have passed the Queen of Sheba with the same disinterest. He wanted to see Karen Leith . . .

And she was not there.

Neither was Hoppy Uniatz.

It was more than a temporary absence, a prolonged nose-powdering or hand-washing expedition. The table where they had been was cleared and freshly laid, ready to receive new tenants. There was not a personal relic left on it to let anyone anticipate a return.

Simon's glance swept over the room and discovered other changes. Quite a fair number of new customers had arrived while he was away, but the place was not much more crowded. He hit on the reason in a moment. It was because space had been made by the departure of other patrons. The Strength through Joy boys and girls were no longer to be seen. And incidentally, he was unable to catch sight of the waiter who had taken him back stage, either. It was perhaps not very surprising. The whole of one certain element in the place had been neatly and unfussily evacuated, and nothing but the regular honky-tonk front was left.

The most conspicuous disappearance was that of March and Friede. Their ringside table had already been taken over by another party, and Simon noticed that their girl companions were once more on offer in the wallflower line.

The Saint located the head waiter. He crossed the room very coolly and recklessly, and his eyes were everywhere, like shifting pools of blue ice. He backed the head waiter against the wall and held him there by the simple process of standing tall and square-shouldered in front of him.

'Where are the people who were with me?' he asked.

'I don't know, monsieur.'

The man looked helpless and tried to edge sideways out of the trap. The Saint stopped that by treading hard on his toe.

'Drop the Brooklyn French, Antonio,' he advised bleakly. 'And don't make any mistakes. It'd take me just thirty seconds to do things to your face that a plastic surgeon 'll take six months to put right. And if I see any of your bouncers coming this way I'll start shooting. Now do we talk or do we wreck the joint?'

'Oh,' said the head waiter, recovering his memory, 'you mean the big gentleman and the red-haired lady?'

'That's better,' said the Saint. 'Let's start with what happened to the big gentleman.'

'He left.'

'When?'

'But that was when you were still at the table, sir. He got up and went right out. The doorman didn't stop him because you were still here to take care of the check.'

Simon began to have a weird and awful understanding, but he bottled it down within himself.

He said: 'All right. Now what about the lady?'

'She went as soon as you left the table, sir.'

'Alone?'

The man's mouth compressed.

'Did she by any chance leave with Mr March?' Simon suggested.

The man swallowed. There were guests close by, and waiters hovering within earshot, but the Saint didn't give a damn. Not for anything that might start. He kicked the head waiter thoughtfully on the shin.

'Yes, sir. She went over and spoke to him, and they left almost at once.'

'Including Captain Friede?'

'Yes, sir.'

The Saint nodded.

'You're a good boy, Alphonse,' he said mildly. 'And just because you told me the truth, I'll pay my check.'

'There is no check, sir,' said the head waiter. 'Mr March took care of it.'

Simon went out of the Palmleaf Fan with his hands at his sides, balanced like the triggers that his fingers itched to be on, walking a little stiffly with the cold anger that was in him. Nobody tried to interfere with him; and he didn't know, or care much, whether it was because they had had no instructions or because he looked too plainly hopeful that someone would make a move. But he walked past the two door guards with the contempt of reckless defiance, and was disappointed that it was so easy. That last patronising gesture of March's was something that he would have liked to wipe out before he left.

But as the Cadillac streaked down the oceanside road he realised that it could hardly have been any other way. March and Friede must have been informed within a few seconds of the misfiring of their plot. There was still nothing that could have officially linked them with it, so they might well have stayed and brazened it out; but that would have been purely negative. Their quick departure had not so much the air of a getaway as of a rapid reorganisation.

And again he had to remember Karen. It had seemed once that she was the most likely person to have warned Rogers. But she had had ample chance to warn Simon himself direct, and had not. And immediately he left, she had gone back to March. She was one of the remaining riddles to which he still had no clue. Unless her part was so simple and sordid that he did not want to see it . . .

He tried to shrug her out of his mind.

Everything now seemed to hang on time. It was certain that Friede and March would feel forced to move fast. He wanted to move faster. There was no longer any motive for caution, and wildness could be given full rein once more. All he needed was the supporting troops who had been waiting for his call.

The car swung into the horseshoe drive and stopped in front of the Gilbeck home. And Simon sat still behind the wheel for the time it took him to light a cigarette.

Peter and Patricia would never have gone to bed until they heard from him. And they wouldn't have gone out, because he had told them to stand by. But except for a single light burning in the servants' quarters the house was in blackness.

He went into the hall and through it to the patio. The lights were out there also, and his ears could pick up no sound but the rustle of palm fronds and the ceaseless muted roaring of the surf.

He turned from the patio into the kitchen.

'Where are Miss Holm and Mr Quentin?' he rapped, and

Desdemona looked up from a love pulp and marked her place with a black thumb.

'Dey's in de jailhouse,' she said placidly.

The Saint's eyes froze into chips of steel.

'What jail?'

'Lawdy, man, how should I know? De she'iff man come an' took 'em away, not fifteen minutes ago, I 'spect dey's lookin' for you, too,' said the negress, with the morbid satisfaction of watching her direst forebodings fulfilled.

Simon went back to the hall and picked up the telephone. There was a chance that Newt Haskins might have gone through into the public quarters of the Palmleaf Fan, prowling around to see what he could see and trying to quietly annoy the management. And as a matter of fact, he had.

'I should have known better than to let you kid me,' said the Saint scorchingly. 'But why couldn't you tell me that all the time I was talking to you your deputies were picking up my friends? And what are the charges, and what are you trying to do?'

There was a longish silence.

Haskins said: 'There ain't no charges, son, an' I didn't send any deputies to pick up any friends o' yours.'

'What about the Miami police?'

'Unless your friends have been robbin' a house, they'd hardly make a move without talkin' to me. It looks like you're barkin' up the wrong tree, son.'

'Maybe I'm not, after all,' said the Saint softly, and cradled the instrument before Haskins could make any more reply.

In a matter of seconds he was back in the car, scattering gravel and sand from the driveway as he ripped out of it. It all seemed so plain now that he wondered how any doubt could have detained him for a moment. And the idea that had been part formed in his mind on the way down from the Palmleaf Fan was now a consuming objective which blotted out everything else on his horizon. To face the last cards, and fight out a showdown on Landmark Island or the *March Hare* . . .

The Cadillac screamed on to the County Causeway with supreme disregard for the risk of speed cops. And just beyond the turn-off to Star Island it stopped, oblivious to the exasperated honking of horns behind.

There was no chance to mistake the trim grey shape feeling its way along the steamship channel towards the Government Cut and the open sea. The *March Hare* had already sailed. One couldn't reach it in a car. One couldn't swim after it. One might overtake it with a speedboat but there would still be no way to get on board. And on board, beyond a question, were Patricia Holm and Peter Quentin. He couldn't see them; but he could see Karen Leith. She stood leaning on the after rail beside Randolph March, watching the traffic on the Causeway and laughing with him.

6

How Hoppy Uniatz rode on his Brain Wave, and Gallipolis introduced Another Vehicle

1

What in the absence of a better phrase we must loosely refer to as the thinking processes of Hoppy Uniatz were blissfully uncluttered by teleological complications such as any worry about consequences. His mind, if we must use the word, was a one-way street through which infrequent ideas rolled with the remorseless grandeur of cold molasses towards an unalterable destination. Once it was started, any idea that got caught in this treacly rolling stream was stuck there until it had been through everything that the works had to offer, like a fly in a drop of glue on a Ford production belt.

What Simon Templar sometimes remembered too late, as he had done in this instance, was that the traffic in Mr Uniatz's constricted mental thoroughfares moved at such a different rate from that of everybody else that one was apt to overlook the fact that it really did keep moving. In which error one did Mr Uniatz a grave injustice. It was true that an all-foreseeing Providence, designing his skill principally to resist the impact of blackjacks and beer bottles, had been left with little space to spare for grey matter; but nevertheless some room had been found for a substance in which a planted thought could take root and grow with the ageless inevitability of a forming stalagmite. The only trouble with this adagio germination was that the planting of the seed was liable to have been forgotten by the time the resultant blossom coyly showed its head.

It had been like that in this case; and to Hoppy Uniatz it was all so straightforward that he would have been dumbfounded to learn that the Saint had lost touch with the scenario even for a moment.

Hoppy had only a minor difficulty over transportation. He guessed that the Saint might not like to be left without a car, and so he passed up the Cadillac and selected instead a flaming red Lincoln which caught his eye further down the line. There were no keys in it, but that was an elementary problem, which was quickly solved by tearing the wires loose from the ignition lock and making some experimental connections. A beam of pleasure that would have made a baby scream for its mother spread over his homely face as the engine fired, and in a glow of happy innocence he swung the Lincoln out in a spurt of sand and headed off like Parsifal on the spoor of his Grail.

He had few doubts of his ability to finally find his way to the barge – having been there once, that was another relatively minor problem to a man who in his day had safely shepherded trucks of beer and other such valuable cargo over back roads to other equally well-hidden harbours. He turned unerringly on 63rd Street, sped south on Pinetree Drive, and took Dade Boulevard to the Venetian Way. And before he reached the Tamiami Trail he was warmed with another heart-swelling realisation which he had worked out while he drove. This trip need not be regarded as a purely selfish expedition for the gratification of his own thirst. Hoppy remembered that that afternoon he had produced, out of his own head, a Theory which the Saint had perhaps been too busy to appreciate. Now, while the Saint was disporting himself with the red-haired wren, he, Uniatz, would be tirelessly following up his Clue . . .

The roads looked a little different by night. Hoppy made two false turn-offs, and wasted fifteen minutes getting out of a patch of soft sand, before he found the place where Simon had parked the car that afternoon. When he reached the flat open country beyond the trees he still wasn't sure of his direction. He struck off in what he hoped was the way, letting the growing parchedness of his throat guide him in much the same manner that a camel's instinct leads it to an oasis. Even with this intuitive pilotage, his wide striped flannels were bedraggled from clutching palmettos when the barge at last showed black against the sky.

As Hoppy put his weight on the gangplank a streak of light fanned across the deck, and Gallipolis stepped out of the door. His flashlight streamed over Hoppy and clicked off.

'By the beard of Xerxes!' said Gallipolis. 'Hullo, bad news. What brings you?'

'Uniatz is de name.' Hoppy plodded on up and went inside. The heat of the closed and oil-lighted bar struck at him in a wave. 'I come out to get some more of dat Florida water, see? I gotta toist.'

Gallipolis stopped at the end of the bar. Over his invariable white-toothed grin, his fawn-like eyes stared at Mr Uniatz suspiciously.

'What's the matter – all the joints in town closed up?'

'Dey ain't woit wastin' time in,' Mr Uniatz told him feelingly. 'A lot of fairies wit' goils' clothes on . . . Dey ain't got none of dis stuff dat I want, neider. De water you say comes outa de springs.'

'Oh.'

Gallipolis secured a bottle and glass and slid them along the bar. Hoppy ignored the glass and picked up the bottle. A long draught of the corrosive nectar, to be savoured with the inenarrable contentment which the divine fruit of such a pilgrimage deserved, washed gratifyingly around Mr Uniatz's atrophied taste buds, flowed past his tonsils like Elysian vitriol, and swilled into his stomach with the comforting tang of boiling acid. He liked it. He felt as if angels had picked him up and breathed into him. His memory of the first taste that afternoon had not deceived him. In fact, it had barely done justice to the beverage.

The Greek watched his performance with a certain awe.

'Bud,' he said, 'if I hadn't seen you hose yourself out with that shine before, and if your story about hauling all the way out here to get some more of it wasn't so lousy, I'd think this was a stall.'

Hoppy either did not grasp or did not choose to take up the aspersion on his motives. He waved the bottle at the empty room, breathing deeply while he felt his potion soaking in.

'Sorta quiet in dis jernt tonight, ain't it, pal?' he remarked with comradely interest.

'After you and the sheriff were here I had to tell the gang to stay home for a bit.' The Greek's eyes were softly watchful. 'What's the Saint doing now?'

'He's still out wit' a skoit. I gotta go back after a bit, but he says I can take my time.'

Mr Uniatz picked up the bottle again and made another experiment. The result was conclusive. There had been no mistake. This was the stuff. At long last, after so many arid years of search and endeavour, Mr Uniatz knew that he had discovered a fluid which was sufficiently potent to penetrate the calloused linings of his intestines and imbue his being with a very faint but fundamentally satisfying glow. It was the goods.

He put down the bottle only because, not having been half full when it was handed to him, it was now quite empty, and reverently exhaled a quantity of pent-up air tainted with dynamic fumes. One spatulate finger stabbed at the bottle as it would touch a holy relic.

'Dey's a fortune in it, pal,' he informed Gallipolis in a whisper which vibrated the houseboat like the lowing of a Miura bull.

'If there is,' said the Greek, 'I'd like to know how.'

'Because it don't cost nut'n,' Hoppy said witheringly.

'What do you mean, it doesn't cost anything?'

'Because it comes outa de Pool.'

Gallipolis lowered one eyelid and studied Hoppy out of the other eye.

'I wonder who's ribbing who now?' he said. 'That stuff just comes from a still, bud. It used to be a good racket, but now the Revenuers go about in airplanes and spot them from the sky.'

'Well, where is dis still?' Hoppy persisted challengingly. 'I know a lotta lugs who'd pay big dough for de distribution.'

The Greek reached down and brought up another bottle. His smile veiled the undecided alertness of his gentle eyes.

'Tell me the gag, friend,' he invited. 'There's something screwy when the Saint wants to start selling shine.'

Mr Uniatz laved his throat again. He was face to face with a situation, but the various steps by which he had reached it were not entirely clear. He was, however, acutely conscious of the secondary motive for his visit which he had worked out on the way. The essential rightness of his idea appealed to him more than ever at this stage. He needed some pertinent information to put bones into his Theory. The problem was how to get it. All Greeks were dumb and unresponsive, in Hoppy's racial perspective, and this one appeared to be a typical specimen. Mr Uniatz felt some of the identical delirious frustration which, had he only known it, was one of his own principal contributions to Simon Tempar's intellectual overhead.

Confronted with the need for greater extremes of initiative, Hoppy decided that the only thing was to put more cards on the table.

'Listen, youse. De boss don't wanna sell dis stuff. He wants to bust up de Pool.'

'What pool?' asked Gallipolis, and opened his weary eye.

'De Foreign Pool,' said Mr Uniatz, suffering. 'De Pool where March gets it from.'

The Greek walked over to where the hanging lamp was smoking in the centre of the room and turned it low.

'What March?' he asked as he returned to the bar.

'Randolph March,' groaned Mr Uniatz. 'De guy what has de Pool where—'

'You mean the medicine millionaire?'

Mr Uniatz cocked his ears, but decided to give nothing away. He had heard nothing about medicines before, but it might be a lead.

'Maybe,' he said sapiently. 'Anyhow, dis March has de Pool, an' nobody knows where it's at, an' dat's what we wanna know. Now all you gotta do is tell me where dis stuff comes from.'

'You're making me a little dizzy, big boy,' said Gallipolis with a smile. 'Are you trying to tell me that March is selling this stuff?'

'Soitenly,' said Hoppy. 'It don't cost him nut'n, so it pays for all his dames. So if we get de Pool, maybe de boss won't mind cuttin' you in.'

The Greek dug out another bottle and poured himself a drink.

'I feel a little tired, mister. Suppose we sit down.' He led the way to one of the tables and kicked out the opposite chair. When Hoppy was seated across from him, Gallipolis drank and shuddered. 'I've been peddling this stuff for a good many years,' he said, 'but this is the first time I've heard that March was making it.'

'De Saint is always de foist to hear anyt'ing,' Hoppy assured him proudly.

The Greek's eyes might have been starting to glaze with pardonable vagueness, but he kept on with his heroic effort.

'You think March is making shine at the Pool.'

'So he *has* got a Pool.' Hoppy caught him triumphantly.

Gallipolis wiped a hand back over his curly hair.

'I suppose you could call it that,' he answered exhaustedly. 'He calls it a hunting lodge. But he did have a coupla dredgers and a gang of men working all summer to cut out a channel and a yacht basin so he could take his boat in. I guess that's the Pool you mean.'

Mr Uniatz tilted his bottle again, and gave his œsophagus another sluicing of caustic lotion. His hand did not tremble, because such manifestations of excitement were not possible to a man whose nervous system was assembled out of a few casually connected ganglions of scrap iron and old rope; but the internal incandescence of his accomplishment came as close to causing some such synaptic earthquake as anything else ever had. The swell of vindication in his chest made him look a little bit like an inflated bullfrog.

'Dat's gotta be it,' he said earnestly. 'Dey dig it out so dey can get more water outa de spring. Dey haul it out in de yacht an' pretend it's medicine. Now me an' de boss go down an' take over dis racket. You know where to find dis Pool?'

Gallipolis tilted his chair on the rear legs and rocked it back and forth.

'Sure, mister, I know where it is.' Being a comparative stranger, he could be forgiven for not following all the involutions of Hoppy's thought, and it seemed harmless to humour him. 'An old moonshiner that I buy stuff from told me. He used to have a still near there, but he got chased out when they started working.'

Mr Uniatz leaned forward grimly.

'Coujja take us to it?'

The Greek's eyes narrowed.

'You say there's something in it for me?'

'Can ya take us dere?'

'Well,' said Gallipolis slowly, 'maybe I could. Or I could find a guy who could take you. But how much would there be in it for me?'

'Plenty,' said the Saint.

He stood in the open doorway, debonair and immaculate, smiling, with a cigarette between his lips and a glint in his eyes like summer lightning in a blue sky. He knew that he had come to the last lap of his chase, by the grace of God and the thirst of Hoppy Uniatz.

2

'Old home week,' said Gallipolis. His voice was as mild as a summer breeze on the olive-clad slopes of Macedonia. 'Get yourself a glass and sit down, Mr Saint, I suppose you're also dry.'

'I'll pass up the liquid fine.' Simon sat down and feed Mr Uniatz with a sardonic eye. 'It's a good job 1 figured out that I'd find you here, Hoppy.'

Something in his tone that sounded like a reproof even to Hoppy's pachydermatous sensitivity, made Mr Uniatz sit up with a pained look of reproach on his battered countenance.

'Lookit, boss,' he objected aggrievedly. 'Ya tell me to come here, dontcha, when we are in de clip jernt? So after we hear Rogers I say can I go now, anja say to take all de time I want—'

'I know,' said the Saint patiently. 'That's the way I worked it out, in the end. It took me quite a long time, though . . . Never mind. You've done a swell night's work.'

'Dat's what I t'ink, boss,' said Mr Uniatz, cheering. 'I woiked out everything on my own. Gallipolis is okay. We cut him in, an' he takes us to de Pool.'

The Saint settled back and smiled. He had a feeling of dumb gratitude that made him conscious of the inadequacy of words. It was a coincidence that made him giddy to contemplate, of course; and yet it was not the first time that the glutinous rivers of Mr Uniatz's lucubration had wound their way to results that swifter brains sought in vain. But the recurrence of the miracle took nothing away from the Saint's pristine homage to its perfection. He had boarded the barge, silently as he always moved, just in time to hear Gallipolis make the speech which had tumbled with the clear brilliance of a diamond through the obscurity of a dead end which had brought him within inches of cold despair; and he had not even had time to adjust his eyes to the light that had destroyed the dark.

His strong fingers drummed on the table edge.

'This afternoon you offered me a job, Gallipolis. I'd like to change it around tonight and offer you one.'

'For plenty?' The white teeth flashed.

'For plenty.'

'I may be running a stud juke, but I have a conscience.' Gallipolis filled his glass again. 'If I have to step on it too badly, the price comes high.'

'I want to know one thing first,' said the Saint. 'Were you just stringing Hoppy along when you told him about this hunting anchorage or whatever it's called that March has got?'

'No, sir.'

Simon drew the glowing end of his cigarette an eighth of an inch nearer his mouth, and exhaled smoke like the timed drift of sand spilling through an hour-glass.

It was so beautiful, so perfect, so complete . . . And yet, twenty-four hours ago, it had seemed impossible that among the million coves of the Florida coastline he could ever find the base of the mysterious submarine which had first given him a hint of the magnitude of what he might be up against. Twenty-four minutes ago, it had seemed even more impossible that he could discover the destination of the *March Hare* in time for the knowledge to offer any hope . . . And now, with a word, both questions were answered at once. And once again the answer was so simple that he should have seen it at once – if he had only known enough . . . But no one who was not looking for what he was looking for would have thought anything of it. A man like March could have a hunting lodge in the Everglades without causing any comment; and if he wanted to dredge out a channel and an anchorage big enough to accommodate a vessel the size of the *March*

Hare – well, that was the sort of eccentric luxury a millionaire could afford to indulge. Haskins might have known about it all the time, and never seen any reason to mention it. And now the Saint couldn't go back to Haskins . . .

Again the Saint brightened the tip of his cigarette.

'In that case,' he said, 'you could do your little job of guide work.'

'Uh-huh.' Gallipolis drained his glass. 'You could hire bloodhounds cheaper. How many people do I have to kill?'

'That all depends,' said the Saint benignly.

'I thought there was a gimmick in it,' said the Greek. 'Let's quit beating around the bush. You've got something on Randolph March, and I don't mean that boloney about him making shine. He'd be pretty big game, Mr Saint, I wonder if he' mightn't be too big for the likes of you and me.'

Simon's eyes wandered estimatively over the room.

'You aren't doing much business, are you?' he said.

'I can thank you for some of that. When the sheriff starts calling at a place like this, you ease up and like it. The good-will doesn't last when they start loading your customers into a wagon and carting them off to the bastille.'

'If you had a grand,' said the Saint abstractedly, 'you could open up somewhere else and have quite a nice joint.'

'Yes,' said Gallipolis. 'If I left that much money, every sponge diver in Tarpon Springs would be pickled in red wine for three days after I die.' He rubbed slender fingers through his hair and looked at his palm. 'If there really is that much dough in the world, mister, I can take you out to the middle of the Everglades and find you snowballs in a peat fire.'

Simon took a roll out of his pocket and peeled off a bill.

'What does this look like?'

'Read it to me,' said the Greek. 'My eyes are bad, and I can't get by the first O.'

'It's a century. Just for an advance. To earn the other nine, you take me to this place of March's. And I want to get there the quickest way there is.'

'The quickest way is overland through the swamps,' said Gallipolis tersely.

He got up from the table and moved towards the back of the bar.

The Saint said, deprecatingly: 'It's true I'm carrying a lot of money, but Hoppy and I are carrying other things too. They go bang when they see machine-guns.'

'You're damn near as suspicious as I am,' Gallipolis said petulantly. 'I'm looking for a map. I thought we might study it a while.'

He pulled out a folded sheet from behind the counter, while Hoppy's gun hand tentatively relaxed from its hair-trigger hovering.

Gallipolis spread out the map on the counter and said: 'Turn up the lamp and come here.'

Simon complied, and bent over the sheet beside him. The Greek pointed to a spot on the lower west coast of the state.

'March's lodge is somewhere in here on Lostman's River, near Cannon Bay. The nearest town is Ochopee, and that's about seventy miles from here on the Tamiami Trail.'

The Saint gazed down at the vast green wilderness on the map marked 'Everglades National Park.' Only the thin red line of the Tamiami Trail broke its featureless expanse of two thousand square miles or more. In all the rest of that area from the coastal creeks inland there was nothing else shown – nothing but the close-packed little spidery bird-tracks that cartographers use to indicate a swamp. It was as if exploration had glanced at the outlines and then decided to go and look somewhere else. Only a finger's length from Miami on the large-scale map, they offered less informative detail than a map of the moon.

And that was where he had to go – quickly.

It had to be him; he knew that. He couldn't run back crying for Haskins or Rogers. It was outside Haskins's county, anyhow, and he could put decimal points in front of the probability of getting a strange sheriff interested. Rogers would not be much easier. Rogers would probably have to get authorisation from Washington, or an Act of Congress, or something. And what was the jurisdiction, anyway? What charges could he bring and substantiate? Any authorities would want at least some good evidence before going into violent action against a man like March. And there was not one shred of proof to give them – nothing but the Saint's own suspicions and deductions and a little personal knowledge for which there was no other backing than his word. It would take hours to convince any hard-headed official that he wasn't raving, even if he could ever do it at all; it might take days to get the machinery moving. The State Department would brood cautiously over the international issues . . . And he had to be quick.

Quick, because of Patricia and Peter. Who were also the last and most important reason why he had to hesitate to call for official help. They were hostages for the Saint's good behaviour – he didn't need to receive any message from the ungodly to tell him that. The counter-attack had been made with the breath-taking speed of blitzkrieg generalship. The pincers movement against himself had been balked, and without a pause one of the flanking columns had swung off and trapped Peter and Patricia. Yet even if Simon could enlist the forces of the Law and send them into the fight, Captain Friede would only have to drop the hostages overboard somewhere with a few lengths of anchor chain tied round them, and blandly protest his complete puzzlement about all the fuss. And the Saint had no doubt that that was exactly what he would do . . .

'Ochopee.' The Saint's voice was quiet and steely cold. 'What is there there?'

'Tomato farms,' said Gallipolis, 'and nothing much more except a lot of water in the rainy season. But I know an Indian there. If there's any guy living who can take you through the Glades to where you want to go, he's it.'

Simon laid a paper of matches along the scale of miles and began to measure distances.

Gallipolis stopped him.

'You're on the wrong track. We pick up the Indian at Ochopee, but you couldn't get down from there. You'll have to come back thirty miles to where you see this elbow marked 27 in the Tamiami Trail. March's place can only be about ten miles from there. Of course, it might be nearer twenty-five or thirty the way you'd have to go. If we started early tomorrow morning, we might be able to get in there by the following day.'

The Saint figured quickly. It was a hundred miles to Ochopee and back to the bend of the elbow where they would enter the swamp. If that left March's harbour only about ten miles away—

'We aren't going on bicycles,' he said. 'We can drive to Ochopee in an hour and a half. We should be able to pick up your Indian and get back to the elbow in another hour easily. That ought to get us to Lostman's River early in the morning.'

The Greek cupped one hand and supported his chin with one arm on the bar.

'Mister,' he said dreamily, 'you're talking about something you just don't know. You're talking about covering ten miles of Everglades. That's oak and willow hammocks, and cypress and thorns and mud and quicksand and creek and diamond-back rattlesnakes and moccasins – and at night I'll throw in a panther or two. This ain't walking around Miami. That web-footed Indian might get you there alive if I can talk him into it, but even he'd have to do it by day.'

Simon made rapid calculations on the course of the *March Hare.* The yacht could probably tick off twenty knots, and might do more with pushing. It was two hundred and fifty miles if she went around Key West to Cannon Bay on the Gulf, which would take her twelve hours or more. But if the submarine operated out of Lostman's River too, the chances were that the astute Captain Friede knew other channels through the Keys which might save as much as a hundred miles.

The Saint folded the hundred-dollar bill and flicked it towards Gallipolis, and said: 'Let's just pretend that Randolph March and I are having a private war. I want to pull a surprise attack, and I haven't got time to mess around. Do we start right now, or do we play charades while the price goes down a hundred dollars an hour?'

'What do you think?' asked Gallipolis.

'I think,' said the Saint, 'that we start now.'

Gallipolis picked up the bill and tucked it away. He tilted back his head, pinched his lower lip, and studied Simon's flawless Savile Row tailoring.

'My Indian's named Charlie Halwuk, and the last time I saw him he told me he was a hundred and two years old, which may be stretching it a bit – it's a Seminole trick. What I'm trying to tell you is this. If he sees you in that rig-up, instead of starting out on any heap big hunting party, he'll want to take you down to an Indian village and marry you to a squaw.'

Simon looked down at his night club costume.

'Have you got anything else?'

'I've got some things a guy left here on account and never came back. He was about your size. Come along with me.'

The Greek strode off down the hallway of the house-boat, past the darkened poker room, and turned into a state-room on the left. He lighted a match and touched the wick of an oil lamp. A locker disgorged high leather boots, heavy woollen socks, khaki pants and shirt. Gallipolis tossed them on a bunk.

'They look like hell, but I had 'em washed. Suppose you try 'em on. They'll be more comfortable where you're going, anyhow.'

The Saint changed, while Gallipolis went back to the bar. The fit was not at all bad. Perhaps the boots were a trifle large, but that was better than having them too small. Simon strapped on his shoulder holster again, and found a shabby hunting coat to put on over the gun.

There was a newspaper among the outer litter on the bunk, and Simon picked it up and found that it was dated that evening. He had to turn to the second page to find a follow-up story on the tanker sinking. The reason for that was plain enough, for nothing new had developed. He realised that there was no reason why anything ever should, and he began to wonder if by a fortunate fluke the explosion had been just a little too sudden for the ungodly; and he was tempted to be glad that he had never said anything about the submarine. The plot should have called for at least one survivor to spike the theory that the disaster was due to spontaneous combustion, which seemed to be the accepted explanation pending the verdict of a Commission of Inquiry. After his own capture of the planted lifebelt, the loss with all hands must have been one of those unforeseen accidents to which the best conspiracies were subject.

The only additional information was that the tanker was sailing under the American flag, but had loaded with oil at Tampico and cleared for Lisbon – it was presumed that she had been working up the coast for the shortest possible dash across the ocean. It was a minor point, but it helped to round out the picture and dispose of another lurking obscurity. There had to be at least a good superficial reason for a British submarine to have done the sinking; and beyond Lisbon was Spain, at the back of France, with Franco responding to the strings pulled in Rome, where Mussolini's wagon careered behind the maniac star of Berlin. It could all be plausible . . . And the Saint wondered whether it was right that he should ruthlessly call it good fortune that no man had come out alive from that latest sacrifice to the ravening ambition of the hysterical megalomaniac who was putting out the lights of Europe as a screaming guttersnipe would break windows . . .

He went back to the bar room and found Gallipolis regarding Hoppy with a despairing frown.

'That cricket outfit is going to wow the Indians,' he told Simon apprehensively. 'But I gave you the only things I've got that'd come near fitting him. Maybe he can swap it for a blanket. Anyhow it'll help keep the rattlesnakes away.'

'We're goin' out huntin', ain't we?' argued Mr Uniatz. 'I buy dese sport clothes in Times Square, so dey can't be nut'n wrong wit' dem.'

Gallipolis gave it up and pushed back the bar.

'When I'm walking wide-eyed into trouble, I like my chopper,' he explained. He took his Tommy-gun out of the floor cavity, picked up a can of cartridges, and weighted down another pocket with a heavy automatic. A powerful flashlight followed. Simon was keyed for treachery like a taut violin string, but there was no sign of it. Gallipolis turned down the lamp until it flickered out, shone the flashlight against the door, and said: 'Come on.'

They followed the path across the palmetto land, with the Greek leading the way. There were small fleecy clouds playing tag with the moon, but the stars gave a steady glimmer of illumination that relieved the fluctuating dark. A frog barked in the canal, and the night was full of the gabble and screech of insects.

Simon stopped for a moment to examine Mr Uniatz's Lincoln again under the flashlight.

'This is what you came in, I suppose,' he said.

'Dat's it, boss,' assented Mr Uniatz unblushingly. 'I borrow it from de dip jernt, on account of I t'ink I am goin' back.'

'We'd better move it out – it's probably on the air by now. I'll stop about a mile up the road, and you can park it and get in with us.'

He started the Cadillac and let it go, and braked again after they had been on the highway about eighty seconds and the last of Miami had fallen behind. While the lights of the following car went out, and he waited for Hoppy to join them, he took another look at the Greek.

'I don't want you to misunderstand anything, comrade,' he murmured, 'but there's one other side to that grand I promised you. If I can buy you, I expect anybody else can. But you ought to remember one thing before you go into the auction market. Hoppy and I are both a little quick on the trigger sometimes. If we thought you were going to try to be clever and turn that perforator of yours the wrong way, your mother might have to do her job all over again.'

Gallipolis gave him the full brilliance of his limpid black eyes.

'I never met a big shot like you before, mister,' he said curiously. 'Does anybody know just what your angle is?'

'Believe it or not, I've done most of my killings for the sake of peace,' said the Saint cryptically.

The Cadillac swept on again until the speedometer touched seventy, eighty, eighty-five, and crept towards ninety. Bugs battered shatteringly against the windshield and disintegrated in elongated smears. Simon's face was a mask of cold graven bronze with azure eyes. Then the world about them disappeared entirely, and they were roaring through mist westward on the Tamiami Trail.

3

A single light showed like a puffball through the fog and rocketed up to meet them.

'This is Ochopee,' said the Greek, and touched Simon's arm.

The Cadillac slowed down. The light turned out to be a single bulb over a pump in front of a darkened filling station. It was the only sign of life in the shrouded town.

'Boss,' said Mr Uniatz from the back seat, in a voice of glum foreboding, 'dey pulled in de sidewalks. If dey's a bar open now it's because somebody forgot to lock up.'

Gallipolis said: 'Charlie Halwuk lives on a dredge about half a mile on the other side of town.'

'What sort of dredge?' Simom asked.

'There's a lot of 'em around here. They used 'em to build the road, and then left 'em. Now they're nothing but skeletons with most of the planking gone. Keep straight ahead.'

Simon drove on. Above the whisper of the engine the night emphasised its silence with the clatter of crickets and a throaty chorus of bullfrogs. It sounded like a thunderclap when the Greek said: 'Turn here.' Simon pulled over, and saw the headlights glisten on two lines of milky water.

'There's sand underneath it,' said Gallipolis. 'Go on.'

They followed the ruts for a tenth of a mile or more, and then Simon stopped again. A great float boat, with grinning ribs at the stern topped with a crazy superstructure, showed starkly in the double glare of the headlights. The Saint switched on the spotlight and played it from side to side.

Gallipolis called: 'Charlie!' musically, and said: 'Blow your horn.'

The howl of the klaxon rasped through the cheeping stillness, and when Simon took his hand from the button the bullfrogs had stopped their oratorio. Close beside them on the left, the air was suddenly beaten to tatters with a deafening whirr like the wings of a thousand invisible angels. White shapes floated upwards, loomed briefly in the headlight beams, and were gone.

'Birds,' said Gallipolis mechanically. 'We frightened them away.'

In the back, Mr Uniatz said pessimistically: 'I bet de jernt has been padlocked.'

The Greek reached down beside him, turned around, and magnanimously presented Hoppy with a fresh quart of shine.

'I'm charging this stuff to you at a buck a bottle,' he told Simon. 'It's a good thing I brought some along.'

Simon sat still. A man had come slowly erect on the deck of the abandoned barge and was standing like a wood carving in the blaze of the spotlight. Over dirty white ducks, a long-sleeved jacket glowed with the colours of the rainbow. A red neckerchief was knotted about the man's throat. The face of well-seasoned ancient mahogany was topped with long straight black lustreless hair.

It was the sight of the face that kept Simon so still. A black moustache covered wide, thick lips. The slightly negroid nose was straight and aquiline. Wrinkles made deep by the sorrows of a thousand years branched upwards from a firm strong chin. Large flat eyes lay close to his head.

The Indian stared straight into the spotlight, and his paunched eyes burned unblinkingly like the eyes of some jungle animal looking unmoved into the noonday sun. He moved as smoothly as rippling water, and with less sound. One second Simon was watching him on the dredge; in the next, he was beside the car.

Gallipolis said: 'We were looking for you, Charlie. If you want to make twenty-five bucks, this gentleman with me has a job to do.'

'Got drink?' asked Charlie Halwuk, and stretched out his wrinkled hand.

Simon said over his shoulder: 'It won't hurt you to share your bottle, Hoppy.'

Mr Uniatz surrendered it grudgingly. Charlie Halwuk took it and tilted it up.

The Greek said confidentially: 'It's strictly a Federal offence, but we'll all have to drink with him. A Seminole has an idea that any party starting out to do anything just ain't worth a damn if they're dry.'

'Okay,' said the Saint, and wondered if he had at last stumbled upon the dark secret of Hoppy's ancestry.

Charlie gave the bottle to Gallipolis and wiped his mouth with the back of his hand. The Greek took two swallows and passed it on. Simon touched it perfunctorily to his lips, and slid it back into Hoppy's clutching paw. Mr Uniatz emptied it, tossed it out of the window, and breathed with deep satisfaction. Simon expected smoke to come out of his mouth, and was disappointed.

Charlie Halwuk had also watched the demolition with respect. He pointed a finger at Hoppy's blazer.

'Plenty good drinker, big boy,' he stated admiringly. 'Plenty pretty clothes. Him damn good man.'

'Chees,' said Mr Uniatz unbelievingly. 'Dat's me!'

Gallipolis pointed to Simon.

'This is the Saint, Charlie. He's a good man, too. They say he's one of the world's greatest hunters with a gun.'

The Indian's round wrinkled eyes shifted impassively to take in their new target

'You know Lostman's River?' Gallipolis went on.

Charlie nodded.

'The Saint wants to go down there where all that digging went on last summer.'

'Take boat?' asked Charlie Halwuk.

'No,' said Gallipolis. 'He wants to go through the Everglades, and start tonight.'

The Seminole stared unmovingly.

'Take canoe?' he asked.

Gallipolis nodded.

'Plenty miles. Plenty tough,' said Charlie Halwuk. 'No can do.'

'I'll make it fifty dollars if you can take us there,' Simon put in.

'Plenty rain,' said Charlie. 'Plenty bad. You great hunter. Rain too much for you.'

'Damn the rain!' Simon leaned across Gallipolis. In the light from the dashboard his blue eyes glinted with tiny flecks of steel, but his voice was quiet and persuasive. 'You're a great hunter and a great guide, Charlie Halwuk. I've heard about you from many people. They all say there's nothing you can't do. Now, I have to get to this place on Lostman's River, and get there right away. If you won't take me I'll have to try it by myself. But I'm going to get there somehow. I'll give you a hundred dollars.'

'Plenty big talk,' said Charlie Halwuk. 'You get marsh buggy, maybe me go too.'

Gallipolis slapped a hand down on his thigh.

'By God, he's got it!'

'What the devil is a marsh buggy?' Simon asked.

'They use it prospecting for oil around this part of the country,' the Greek explained. 'It's a combination boat and automobile that'll run over any sort of ground and float across streams and rivers. It's a hell of a looking thing with wheels ten feet high and cleated tyres that only carry four pounds of air.'

It sounded like a fearsome vehicle, but its advantages sounded considerable. Simon felt a microscopic flicker of excitement as he wondered if their prospects were brightening.

'Where can we get one of these amphibious machines?' he

asked; and the Greek lifted his shoulders to shrug them and then stopped them in the middle of the movement.

'There's a prospecting company at Ochopee that owns four, but you'll probably be the first guy who ever tried to rent one by the day.'

'Could you drive it?'

'Hell, no. I'm not so keen on riding in one either, but for the price you're paying I'll try anything.'

'I'll get you a marsh buggy, Charlie,' said the Saint, and opened the back door. 'Get in. We're starting right away.'

'Wait,' said the Indian. 'Get gun.'

Simon watched him climb up the side of the dredge, admiring his fluid agility. The Seminole might claim to be a hundred and two, but his limbs worked with the suppleness of a twenty-year-old acrobat. He was back again in a moment with a light double-barrelled shotgun.

'I t'ought dey used bows'n arrers,' said Mr Uniatz, open-mouthed.

'That's only when they're acting in movies,' Simon explained to him. 'This one hasn't been to Hollywood, so he still uses a gun.'

'And good, too,' added Gallipolis, as Charlie climbed into the car.

They sped back to Ochopee. Gallipolis guided the Saint to a tremendous corrugated-iron garage that looked more like an airplane hangar about a hundred yards down a rutty turning off the main street. A small frame house adjoined the garage. Gallipolis gestured at it with his thumb.

'The manager lives in there. Maybe you can do business with him, but he's a crusty guy.'

The Saint got out and banged on the bungalow door. Somewhere back of the house a dog barked viciously. Simon knocked again.

From a window opening on to the porch a man's voice

said heatedly: 'Get the hell away from here, you damn drunk, or I'll run you off at the end of a gun.'

'Are you the manager of the prospecting company?' Simon inquired placatingly.

'Yeah,' snarled the voice. 'And we do our business in the daytime.'

'I'm sorry,' said the Saint, with the most engaging courtesy he could command. 'I know this is the hell of an hour to wake you up, but my business won't wait. I want to rent one of your marsh buggies and get it right now.'

'Don't be funny,' came the grinding reply. 'This isn't a garage running "See the Everglades" tours. We don't rent marsh buggies. Now run away and play.'

Muscles began to tighten in the Saint's jaw.

'Listen,' he said with an effort of self-control. 'I'll leave you a brand-new Cadillac as security. I don't know what your machine is worth, but if it'll do what I've been told it will I'll pay you a hundred dollars a day for it, cash in advance.'

The man inside laughed raucously.

'I told you we weren't in the rental business, and a hundred bucks a day is peanuts to the owner of this she-bang.'

'Where is he?' Simon persisted. 'Maybe he'll listen to reason.'

'Maybe he will,' agreed the man sarcastically. 'Why don't you go and talk to him? You can find him at Miami on his yacht, the *March Hare*. Now get the hell out of here and let me sleep before I put some bird-shot into you!'

Simon started to walk back a little shakenly towards the car. But the shock lasted for exactly three steps. And then it began to be transmuted into something totally different, something so exquisite and precious that the blood in his veins seemed to turn into liquid music.

'I told you he was a bastard,' said Gallipolis philosophically. 'What do we do now?'

Simon slid in behind the wheel. His eyes were sparkling.

'We take a March buggy anyhow.' He turned to Hoppy. 'You get out and stay here by the porch. I'm going to move on down and start a little work on the garage door. I don't know how many men there are in that bungalow, but I don't expect there are more than two. They'll come out in a hurry when they hear me breaking the lock. You take care of them.'

'Do I give 'em de woiks?' asked Mr Uniatz hopefully.

'No,' said the Saint. 'No shooting. We don't want to wake up the rest of the town. Don't be any rougher than you have to.'

'Okay, boss.'

Mr Uniatz vanished into the shadowy mist; and Simon started the car and turned it through an arc that ended close to the garage with the headlights flooding the corrugated-iron door. Simon got out and examined the fastenings.

And the rich beauty of the situation continued to percolate through his system with the spreading recalescence of a flagon of mulled ale. He had no belief that this oil prospecting outfit had any connection with March's more nefarious activities – otherwise the manager would certainly have been a much smoother customer – but the coincidence of its ownership lent a riper zest to what had to be done anyway. Even with everything else that was on his mind, the Saint's irrepressible sense of humour savoured the situation with an epicurean and unhallowed glee. To set out on that desperate sortie in a marsh buggy that belonged to Randolph March had a poetic perfection about it that no connoisseur of the sublimely ridiculous could resist . . .

Nor did there seem to be any great obstacle in the way. The door was secured with a padlock that could have moored a battleship; but the hasp and staple through which it had to function, as in most cases of that kind, were not of the same stuff. Simon went back to the Cadillac and found the jack handle. He slipped one end of it under the lock and levered skilfully. With a mild crash, one half of the rig tore completely out of its attachments.

In the bungalow, an apoplectic voice yowled: 'What the hell do you think you're doing?'

A light came on, and the irate manager burst from his dwelling, pounded across the porch, and charged valiantly towards the depredator who was destroying his garage.

He was a brave man, and he had a shotgun, and moreover he considered himself quite athletic. It therefore filled him with some confusion to find his avenging rush checked by a single arm that appeared from nowhere and encircled his body, clamping the shotgun against his own chest. The manager struggled frenziedly, but the arm seemed to have the impersonal solidity of a tree that had suddenly grown round him. His fluent cursing made up for his physical restriction for a couple of brief moments, until a large portion of the road seemed to heave up in the most unfriendly manner to smack him on the head and turn the whole of his brain into a single shooting star that floated off like a dying rocket into a dark void . . .

Mr Uniatz ambled up with the man over his shoulder as Simon finished sliding back the doors.

'Boss, dis must be de only one.'

'Tie him up and gag him,' said the Saint.

With the aid of the headlights which now shone into the garage he was inspecting the nearest of the fabulous machines that were stabled there.

It looked like an automobile engineer's nightmare, but there was no doubt that it also looked highly utilitarian. For coach-work, a boatlike body, blunt at both ends, hung between the four gigantic wheels. There was no luxurious upholstery, but it had an encouraging air of being ready to go places. The huge balloon tyres would serve the dual purpose of flattening out to lay their own road through mud and sand and buoying up the contraption when it was in the water, while in its aquatic manœuvres the deep flanges on the rear tyres would continue to propel it after a fashion by turning them into a pair of extempore paddle wheels. He recognised the steering controls as being of the tractor type, and hoped that he had not forgotten a lesson in their manipulation which he had once been given by a friendly farmer.

He found a yardstick on the wall and measured the gasoline in the tank. It was nearly full, but he located an extra five-gallon can and put it in the back. He found a switch that kindled the two powerful high-slung headlights. He squeezed into the driving-seat, and the starter unhesitatingly twisted the engine into a clattering roar of life. He took hold of the two clutch levers, put his feet on the two brake pedals, and gingerly worked the thing out of the garage.

He stopped it again in the road, and drove the Cadillac into the space that it left vacant. Hoppy by that time had made a compact bundle of the unconscious manager, which under Simon's direction he jammed into the back of the car. They closed the garage doors and returned to the marsh buggy, in which Gallipolis and Charlie Halwuk were already installing themselves.

The Indian appeared to be quite unconcerned by the short spell of violence which he had witnessed.

'Too much plenty can happen,' he said stoically, as Simon and Hoppy got in. 'Better take food.'

The Saint turned, settling beside him.

'I thought we'd be there by morning.'

'Maybe morning,' said Charlie Halwuk noncommittally. 'Maybe night. Plenty damn big country. Plenty too much trouble maybe. Maybe two-three day.'

'Maybe plenty damn glad I bring some shine,' contributed Gallipolis.

Simon lighted a cigarette. The check frayed at the tightly drawn fibres of his nerves, but he could hardly dispute its sober sanity.

'Where can we get food at this time of night?' he queried steadily.

'There's a general store a short way down the road,' said Gallipolis. 'Of course, they don't keep open all night, but I don't suppose that will bother you.'

'We'll open it.'

The marsh buggy started off again, and warped itself into the main street like some grotesque clumsy insect picking its course with great fiery eyes.

Simon stopped a short distance from the store that Gallipolis indicated, and switched out the lights. He moved through the mist like a wraith to the back of the building, and went to work on a flimsy window more stealthily than he had worked on the garage door. It took him less than two minutes to master it; and for the next ten minutes he was tracking down canned goods, an opener, a coffee pot, and a frying pan, and passing them out for Hoppy Uniatz to porter back to the buggy. He pinned two ten-dollar bills to the broken window with an ice pick, selected two bottles of Scotch and a bottle of brandy to complete the provisioning, and prudently took those to the buggy himself.

They rolled westwards, scattering wisps of fog.

Driving the buggy was not so easy as driving a car. The lever-and-pedal system necessitated by the obvious impossibility of applying conventional steering to wheels of that size was tricky to handle. To make a left-hand turn, for instance, you fed more power to the right-hand wheels, and disconnected and braked the left-hand ones, the sharpness of the turn being governed by the relative violence of both manipulations, up to the point where the buggy would practically whip round on its own axis. Keeping a straight course at any speed was much harder to do. The Saint was able to nurse it up to about thirty miles an hour, and found the pace more hair-raising than any driving he could ever remember having done.

A warm breeze laden with dampness beat across his face and ruffled his hair. In addition to the mechanical difficulties of control, he had to follow the road by clairvoyance rather than sight, for both sides were swallowed up in the mist. It seemed endless hours, endless leagues more than the estimated thirty miles on the map, before Charlie Halwuk touched his shoulder with an arresting hand and said: 'Turn off road here.'

Simon eased off the throttle and swung to the right. There was a fleeting moment of instinctive panic when the buggy nosed over the graded banking and felt as if it was rolling off the edge of the world. Then the headlights picked up a narrow unrailed bridge of logs which led across the broad ditch.

'This was your idea,' Simon told Charlie and Gallipolis impartially, and set his teeth as he sent their crazy chariot bucketing down.

The lights dipped woozilv and rose slowly again towards the sky. When they levelled again, the way was barred with a solid curtain of sickly green that glittered with an unearthly luminiscence. It took him some moments to realise that he was facing a motionless barrier of sawgrass with heavy stalks alight with clinging beads of dew.

'Plenty grass,' said Charlie Halwuk. 'But bottom got some sand right here. Drive on.'

For an interminable hour the Saint clung to the levers with sweating hands as the marsh buggy ploughed on through. The parted grass gave off smoky clouds of midges and mosquitoes. They filled the air with a vicious droning hum that was audible above the rattle of the engine, beat against the headlights like a living storm, and massed into savage onslaught against every inch of exposed human flesh. The intermittent glugs of Hoppy's bottle alternated with stinging slaps of his palm. Gallipolis fanned himself and cursed interestingly in his mother tongue. Simon, with both hands occupied, finally stopped and tied his handkerchief round the lower part of his face for a modicum of protection, and took off his coat and draped it over his head like a bonnet in an attempt to save his neck and ears. Only the Seminole, at home in the lands of his ancestors, seemed completely untroubled. He sat almost somnolently beside the Saint, directing their passage with occasional grunts and touches on Simon's arm.

The sawgrass ended as suddenly as though some celestial gardener had taken a stroke with a stupendous scythe. Ahead was a clear wide space of flat metallic blackness. The mist hung above it in lowering clouds, letting the headlights sweep out to light a forest of death.

White with age, hoary with moss, and stark as the blasted timberlands of Hades might have been, the great gnarled cypresses loomed on the far side of the clearing, their upper branches lost in the low ceiling of fog.

'Plenty slow,' said Charlie Halwuk. 'Go on.'

Simon went into bottom gear, and the great wheels settled down. It seemed as if the ground beneath them melted away, turning into a sheet of slaty liquid, foul and oleaginous, that threatened to rise and engulf them and suck them down. They sank into it relentlessly until it swirled sluggishly above the hubs of the wheels.

'Chees!' said Hoppy, and was quiet after that.

Simon could have reached beside him and touched the enveloping wetness with his hand. Slashing like an antediluvian swimmer, the marsh buggy went on.

Wings flashed startlingly ahead, beating branches; and the night was wild with hoarse cries as a hidden colony of egrets took to flight and crashed blindly heavenward before the approach of the terrifying intruder in their preserves. The amphibian wallowed on into the blanched grey forest, and the world of reality was gone.

A rudder at the stern of the hybrid craft, geared in with the dual clutch mechanism, took hold and lent its help to the steering, and the Saint had already developed a fair amount of assurance in the handling of his charge; but now there were new problems in the threading of a path through the trees. His piloting was an outstanding blend of inspiration and desperation. He judged each opening to a nicety, driving through gaps where there were only inches to spare; and yet as if they were caught in some gargantuan bagatelle table each opening, instead of bringing them to a clear passage, only brought them face to face with another tree.

Twice he turned hopelessly to the phlegmatic Indian, to have his unspoken question met by Charlie Halwuk's flat 'Drive on.'

Shining eyes came redly towards them, moved together into a single stop light, and vanished as a twenty-foot alligator sank below the surface like a waterlogged tree.

The wheels began to churn on a different note, and Simon realised that they were not making any progress.

'We're stuck,' he said, as though he were afraid some unseen listener might hear.

'Log,' said Charlie Halwuk. 'Plenty back. Then go on.'

The Saint reversed. The ten-foot flanged wheels at last took hold and dragged them backwards. He found another opening and coddled the marsh buggy through it, and sighed wearily at the sight of more grass ahead. He pointed without speaking.

The Indian said: 'Plenty more grass now. Then swamp again. Then hammock. You keep a little more left.'

Black mud boiled up under the landboat even as he spoke. The Saint fed more gas. Dripping water, the machine began to climb with a changing cadence, shaking itself like a mechanical bear. Beyond, the grass looked as if it stretched endlessly. Simon felt stifled and had to pull off his masking handkerchief in spite of the mosquitoes, searching for a draught of breathable air.

Life became a game of pressing down sawgrass and wondering how many times Charlie Halwuk would say 'Drive on.' Without warning, they were in a swamp again. They got out of it. Then still more grass; and, suddenly, trees. They plunged into trackless jungle – a nightmare of dodging matted vines, fallen logs, and pliant unbreakable trailers that seeped down from above to claw at their faces with inch-long horns. At no time was there anything like a trail, or anything to point a direction; he sometimes wondered if he was driving round in circles, destined eventually to find himself back where he had been two hours before. But the Seminole never seemed to know any uncertainty, and kept warning him to veer left and right with as much wooden confidence as if he had been watching a compass.

Then at last, as though he were emerging from the

dreamland of a dispersing anæsthetic, Simon began to realise that he could see around him, that the shining green under the headlights was fading, and above and about them the blackness was turning to a dull grey. Then, far above, the matted branches were touched with a thin blush of fire.

'Look,' said the Saint.

Beside him, Charlie Halwuk said: 'Day.'

The marsh buggy pushed on into the blistering dawn.

7

How Simon Templar found a New Recipe for Roast Pork, and Hoppy could No Longer control his Toist

1

Heat came with the morning – a sticky, oppressive heat that stewed itself softeningly into every bone and cartilage. The Saint had known jungles and deserts, but he had never felt himself overwhelmed with such torrid enervation. The mists fled before the sun, leaving the swampland a visible vastness of tangled draperies that seemed to have neither beginning nor end; but over the riotously intertwining foliage the humidity still weighed down like an invisible blanket. His arms ached with the strain of fighting the twin clutch levers, and his whole body felt as if it had been left overnight in a Finnish bath.

'How much further, Charlie?'

Simon found that his voice also had sunk into a lower key. He used his sleeve to wipe perspiration from the clutch handles.

The Indian pointed away from where the climbing sun was slanting into their eyes, and said: 'Over there. Maybe ten miles. Maybe fifteen. Maybe more. Dunno.'

'For Christ's sake,' Simon swore. 'I thought it was only ten miles when we left the road. Now it's maybe more. What am I doing – driving this goddam tank backwards?'

'Plenty hard,' said the Indian impassively. 'No can go straight. Plenty long way round.'

'We should have gone back to Miami and bought an aeroplane,' said the Saint dispiritedly.

'If you wanted to land anywhere in this country,' said Gallipolis, 'you'd have to get out with a parachute.'

It was only too plain, as Simon stared at the landscape ahead, that the Greek was not exaggerating. Simon took time off to light another cigarette, and admitted it. There was nothing else to do but what they were doing.

Charlie Halwuk said: 'Can go back.'

Simon caught the glint in the Seminole's flat black eyes, and twisted his lips back to the reckless smile that so seldom left them.

'I'm hungry and sleepy and the mosquitoes have taken enough blood out of me for a transfusion, and I've tooled this cockeyed charabanc around all night through stuff that I didn't think anything on wheels would go through,' he drawled. 'After that, what's another day more or less? I always wanted to see these Everglades, anyway. Let's have some breakfast, and I'll drive on.'

They built a small fire to boil water to make coffee, since that was the only way to disguise the colour of the swamp water and at the same time reduce its probable bacterial content. They ate corned beef and canned beans cold – or as cold as the outside temperature allowed them to be, which was really lukewarm. And the Saint drove on.

On and on.

It was like winding through a labyrinth with walls which only Charlie Halwuk could see. There was the sun now to give Simon a sense of direction, but that would have been no help to him if he had been alone. The trail that Charlie Halwuk knew would have looked on a map like the track of an intoxicated eel. And always the wilderness opened before them with sullen hostility and timeless patience, as though it were a sentient hungry thing that knew they must weaken in the end and be devoured . . .

The marsh buggy chugged through endless alternations of

jungle and swamp and grass and groves where the ghostly remnants of cypress trees spired upwards to make circular pincushions of mysterious pools. As the heat grew more stifling, jutting ends of logs became the sun-roofs of assorted turtles basking in friendly fashion beside deadly cottonmouths. As the buggy approached, snakes and turtles quietly slipped away, leaving nothing but widening circles in stream or pool; and roseate spoonbills, blacknecked stilts, burrowing owls, and stately herons rose before their intrusion and took refuge in the air. But only once the Seminole caught Simon's arm as a small bird much like a falcon rose before them.

'Look,' he whispered.

The Saint's eyes followed the speeding flash of blue and grey.

'Everglade kite,' said Charlie Halwuk. 'Maybe last time white man ever see. One time plenty. No more. Twenty, thirty maybe, now. Soon come be gone like Indian. White man never see!'

Time crawled on as slowly as they moved.

The marsh buggy took to shallow milky water. Simon wrenched it along the serpentine course for a few hundred yards, and then the denseness of a bayhead barred them with a wiry thorny wall. The soil about them was a deep quaking humus that clung like salve to the broad soft tyres. Following Charlie Halwuk's pointing, the Saint turned south and skirted the impenetrable barrier until he found a knoll of comparatively higher and drier ground. He stopped there for another brief rest and a cigarette.

Mr Uniatz moved his neanderthal bulk, yawned with the daintiness of a breathing switch engine, and said: 'Dis jalopy is makin' me seasick, boss. When do we eat again?'

Simon saw from his watch that it was after one o'clock.

'Very soon, I think,' he said, and started the buggy again.

Almost at once, as if in answer to the movement, a dog

hidden somewhere in the undergrowth yapped loudly. Others joined in, shattering the barren deadness with their snarling bedlam. The noise was so sharp and savage and unexpected that the Saint's hackles rose and Gallipolis fumbled for his gun; but the Indian showed a trace of pleasure.

'*Chikee* there,' he said. 'My people camp. We get plenty *sofkee*. Drive on.'

In a hundred yards the bayhead fell away. Simon pulled up in astonishment.

They had run into a great moss-draped amphitheatre floored with dry loamy ground. A fire burned in the centre, blazing brightly in the hub of ten enormous logs arranged like the spokes of a wheel. High above the fire was a roof of thatched palmetto leaves supported by four uprights driven into the ground. Pots and pans interspersed with dried meat and herbs hung from the rafters. At one corner of the tribal fire-place was a mortar hollowed from the head of a cypress log, where their arrival failed to interrupt an ancient squaw who sat pounding corn with a wooden pestle.

Chikees formed a square around the central kitchen. They were similar to the roofed fire-place, except that they had floors of plaited saplings raised several feet above the ground. Blanketed forms roused from the floors at the stopping of the marsh buggy, while others rose from where they had been sitting on the fire logs; and when Simon stepped down and stretched his aching limbs he found himself surrounded by a curious group of them.

Charlie Halwuk spoke quickly, and the circle of faces lightened. A clatter of welcome, which Simon decided was friendly, broke out in the liquid Seminole tongue.

'They give us *sofkee*,' interpreted Charlie Halwuk, and got down.

Mr Uniatz followed stiffly and Gallipolis without his gun. One of the Seminoles reached out suddenly and felt the material of Hoppy's blazer. He made a comment which brought back several excited echoes. More Indians crowded up, chattering guttural enthusiasm for the screaming colours of the blazer, and formed a guard of honour to escort Hoppy to a log which served as a chair. Charlie Halwuk watched the demonstration with a certain possessive pride.

'Him damn good man,' he said, reverting to a previous impression.

'Boss,' Hoppy said pathetically, 'what goes on?'

'They like you,' said the Saint. 'You seem to have carried away half the Seminole nation with your irresistible charm. For God's sake try to look as if you appreciated it.'

A wizened Indian, whom Charlie Halwuk treated with the deference due to a chief, ceremoniously passed out *sofkee* in coco-nut bowls. It proved to be ground cornmeal mush, undoubtedly wholesome enough, but a dish which any gourmet could have spared from his menu. Fortunately the other items were more appetising. There came turkey stew, sweet potatoes, and cowpeas. There were also oranges. Simon bit into one, and found his mouth suddenly curdled into an acidulous ball.

'Plenty wild, plenty sour,' said Charlie contentedly. 'You eatum long time, then like 'um.'

Simon decided that that was another exotic taste which he could afford not to acquire.

When the meal was finished, the Greek's eyelids were drooping and Mr Uniatz was snoring majestically in the shade, watched by an immobile circle of worshippers. The Saint felt his own eyes growing heavy. Against all his deeper impulses, he forced himself to let the insidious lethargy take its course. To give time to sleep, in the circumstances, seemed like a kind of treason; and yet he knew that it was as vital as eating. If he were to arrive at the destination where he was going with any of his faculties below their peak, he might almost as well not make the trip at all.

He awoke refreshed after an hour of concentrated oblivion, to find Charlie Halwuk squatting beside him.

'Lostman's River three miles,' announced the Indian as if there had been no interruption. He found a stick, and rapidly drew an intricate outline in the soil. 'We here now.' He made a cross and indicated the space between the cross and the indentations of the coastline. 'In here, quicksand. Plenty bad. No can do. We go this way.' A wide spiralling hook. 'Too bad. Twelve miles – maybe more.'

'It's been about that distance ever since I can remember,' said the Saint.

Charlie Halwuk stared reflectively up towards the red ball of the sun.

'Plenty rain. We go on?'

'You spoke about rain last night,' Simon retorted. 'If you could produce some it might freshen us up. Do we pay your people for the meal?'

'You give chief big boy's coat. He make you son.'

The Saint chuckled.

'I've already got one daddy in Miami. See if you can talk Hoppy into it.'

While the Indian went to his task, Simon found some water and rinsed his face. Gallipolis followed his example. Shaking tepid drops out of his curly hair, the Greek studied Simon with a sort of unwilling perplexity.

'I had you all wrong, mister,' he said. 'When I saw you in that monkey suit last night, I didn't really think you could take three hours of this. Now I won't even back Charlie Halwuk to stand up longer than you.'

'Don't put up your money too quickly,' said the Saint. 'We haven't arrived yet.'

But he smiled when he said it, in spite of himself. He was taking a new lease of confidence. He had lived soft by these standards for a long time; but he knew now that he was the same man that he had always been. With the short rest, strength had flowed back into him. A half-forgotten indomitable resilience picked him up again and loosened his thews with freshness. If he failed, he knew now, it would not be because he had failed himself.

He checked the level of the gas tank again and found that their fuel was more than half gone. He poured in their reserve supply with a silent prayer that it would be enough.

Then, as he climbed into the driving seat again he saw an historic sight.

Across the clearing, followed by Charlie Halwuk, and at a more respectful distance by the rest of the Seminole village – braves, squaws, and papooses – came Mr Hoppy Uniatz. Arm in arm with him walked the chief, proudly wearing Mr Uniatz's appalling blazer. In exchange, Mr Uniatz had acquired a ruffle-pleated Seminole shirt with a pattern of vivid rainbow stripes.

The procession reached the marsh buggy and stopped. The chief put both his hands on Hoppy's shoulders and made what sounded like a short oration. The rest of the tribe grunted approvingly. The chief stepped back like a French general who has just bestowed a medal.

Hoppy got into the marsh buggy and said hoarsely: 'Boss, get me outa here.'

The tribe stood like wooden totem poles, silently watching, as Simon engaged the clutches and the huge wheels rolled again.

'I never knew,' said the Saint, in an awed voice, 'that you were a graduate of the Dale Carnegie Institute.'

Mr Uniatz swallowed bashfully.

'Chief say him come back,' interpreted Charlie Halwuk complacently. 'Marry chief's daughter. Damn good.'

The heat beat down until it felt like a tangible weight on Simon's scalp and he felt certain that at any moment the shallow patches of water about them would break into a boil. But it hardly seemed to affect him physically any more. He was getting his second wind, and the discomfort was almost welcome because it left him no energy to feed into his imagination. He didn't want to do too much thinking. There were too many things in the background of his mind that were not good to think about. He wanted to black them out and concentrate on nothing but the grim task of getting to the only place where thinking would do any good.

And then came the rain.

A crackling sound, as sharp as the sound of a brush fire, heralded the foresweep of a blast of humid air. Black stormclouds drove westwards before it and curtained the brazen sun with palls of gunmetal. For seconds the world seemed to stand motionless under the strain of a supernatural compression. Then the clogged skies burst open and let loose the deluge that Charlie Halwuk had prophesied.

This was no gentle shower greening the fields of England, no light drizzle blending with the sea spray on the coasts of Maine. It was flat and hard and tropically brutal, pounding straight down to gouge a million tiny craters out of the swamp water and blot out all vision beyond a few yards with its grey dripping wall.

They drove on. Their clothes were soaked as suddenly as the storm struck, but each sodden body turned into a ball of steam. It stung their faces like a sort of soggy hail, and smashed in thousands of tiny dancing shell-bursts over the engine cowling. But the marsh buggy kept going, as ponderous and impervious as a great groping tortoise. Time had no more significance; it ceased to exist, smothered under the borderless avalanche of leaden wet.

As the afternoon wore on there was an almost imperceptible change.

'Quit soon now,' said Charlie Halwuk.

Twenty minutes later the beating in the hammocks and bayheads was still, as abruptly as it had begun, and bars of light from the setting sun broke through the vanishing clouds.

The marsh buggy completed the fording of another sluggishly rolling stream and Simon stopped to squeeze some of the dripping water out of his hair.

And then he was aware of another strange noise.

It was like nothing he had ever heard before. Superficially, it was nothing but a chorus of ferocious squeals and gruntings. But it had a savagery and a blood-lust in it that was worse than the roar of a tiger or a panther's scream – a shrill bestial fury that sent cold trickles crimping up his spine.

'What on earth is that?' he asked.

'Plenty wild porkers,' said Charlie Halwuk. 'Plenty bad. They catch somebody. Plenty better we go other way.'

Simon had started the marsh buggy moving when the full meaning of the speech dawned on him. He let go the clutch levers.

'You mean *somebody*?' he demanded incredulously. 'A man?'

The Indian pointed down the stream to the right. Simon could see nothing at first; but with a sunken reckless defiance he used opposite brake and clutch to jerk the buggy around and plunge it back towards the stream.

'No can help,' Charlie Halwuk said sharply. 'Porkers tear you up plenty quick. Plenty better you stop.'

'To hell with it,' said the Saint grittily. 'If wild pigs have caught a man there, I'm not going to run away.'

And then he saw it.

Straight ahead was a mass of tangled roots which might have bordered a mangrove island. A single tree stood up above the level of undergrowth, and a flutter of human clothing moved in its branches. At the base of the tree, a clear patch of ground was dappled with darting black evil shadows; and as the buggy ploughed nearer the grunting of slavering tusked mouths swelled in a vicious crescendo.

'Those hogs are meaner than wildcats,' said Gallipolis, rising with his machine-gun. 'Better let me use this on 'em.'

'Wait a minute,' said the Saint, and turned to the Indian. 'How far are we from the lodge now, Charlie?'

'Maybe mile. Maybe little more.'

'Could you hear shooting that far in this country?'

'Hear it more. Shooting no good anyhow. Porkers worse than wild boar.'

Simon's mouth set in a stubborn line. If he had behaved as he perhaps should have behaved on that mission, he would have shut his eyes and gone on. But to leave any innocent human being to that horrible squalling doom was more than the flesh he was built out of could have done. Besides, any human being who was found so close to March's secret hideaway might be a more important rescue than he could guess.

He reversed the buggy and watched the course of the stream for a few seconds. It rippled deep into the roots along the shore of the islet . . .

Before anyone could have forestalled his intention, Simon grabbed a wrench and opened the drain plug under the gasoline tank.

'What the hell!' yelped Gallipolis; and the Saint smiled at him satanically.

'Get tough about it and I'll let it all go,' he said gently, and the Greek sank back as Mr Uniatz crowded the muzzle of a warning Betsy into his sacro-iliac.

Simon dumped about two gallons and then tightened the plug again while the floating oil spread into smudged rainbows as the moving water carried it downstream.

He flicked lighted matches into it until it flashed into flame. Burning brightly, it floated down to the rain-soaked island and seeped its fire in among the knotted roots. The feet of the savage pigs were suddenly enveloped in a sheet of fire, and their ravening grunts turned into ear-splitting shrieks of terror. There was a wild rush into the water, where their lean black bodies churned frantically away from the searing blaze. Most of them reached the opposite shore, and went on without stopping through the rustling underbrush like a frenzied herd of Gadarene swine.

The blazing gas smoked blackly and died out without having been able to set fire to the freshly-sodden mangroves. Simon nosed the marsh buggy into the island, grasped an overhanging bough, and pulled himself up on to relatively dry land in time to catch the slight limp figure that fell more than it climbed down out of the tree in which it had found precarious sanctuary.

The reddening sun that was slipping down under the horizon struck a last flare of even more vivid red from the tousled mane of her hair. Incredibly, it was Karen Leith.

2

'I was just wondering where you'd got to,' murmured the Saint in classical understatement.

In place of the billowy white dress of the night before, she wore a blue slack suit that might once have been trickily cut in a stylish travesty of a labourer's dungarees. Now, muddy and torn and bedraggled, it was something that no self-respecting labourer would have been seen in. And yet he discovered, with a little surprise, that she had a quality which could transcend even those detractions. The wet clinging clothes only revealed new harmonies in her figure, and the grime on her tired face seemed if anything to enhance the fairness of its modelling. It was something that Simon took in at this time without letting it sway the icy detachment that was creeping into him.

Hoppy Uniatz was impressed for a different reason. His eyes had a somewhat crustacean aspect as they goggled at the girl.

'Boss,' he said earnestly as though he were trying to argue the apparition away, 'I leave you wit' dis wren in de clip jernt.'

'That right, Hoppy,' said the Saint.

'You don't bring her out here witcha.'

'No, Hoppy.'

'Den how,' demanded Mr Uniatz logically, 'can she be sittin' up in dat tree?'

Gallipolis mopped his steaming forehead with a wet bandanna and said: 'This whole damn business is getting too much for me.'

'Have any of you got a cigarette?' asked the girl calmly.

Simon took out his case. The contents were on the damp side, but the metal had saved them from total dissolution. He offered it to her, and helped himself. He noticed that her slim hands were soiled and scarred, and yet their unsteadiness was so rigidly controlled that he had to look closely for it.

'Well,' he said after he had given her a light, 'I know that this life of sin is full of mysteries, but for once I think Hoppy has got something.'

Her deep violet eyes studied the Martian contours of the marsh buggy, and then deliberately went over the four men – Hoppy, Gallipolis, Charlie Halwuk, lastly the Saint. Simon realised that none of them could have looked much more civilised than she did, and wondered if she saw the same stony purposefulness in all of them that he saw in her. He had to hand that to her also. In spite of the ordeal that she had just been through, she was keyed with the same delicate inner core of steel that he had sensed in her once before.

'Apparently,' she said, 'we're all literally in the same boat.'

'Marsh buggy,' Simon corrected disinterestedly. 'It runs on land too, believe it or not. It isn't exactly a Rolls Royce, but it's a lot more use in the Everglades.'

'On land?' Her voice had a quick lift. 'You mean this thing can take us out of the swamps?'

'It brought us in.'

'Simon,' she said, 'thank God you brought it. Don't let's waste any more time. I've got to get to the road—'

The Saint sat on the side of the buggy, his forearms on his knees. He eased his lungs of a long plume of smoke. The mantle of his detachment wrapped him in a cold armour of aloofness and gave his blue eyes an impersonal hardness that she had never seen before.

'I think you're taking a lot for granted, darling,' he said in a voice of tempered tungsten. 'The only question at the moment is whether we should take you with us where we're going, or whether we should turn you loose again to keep walking.'

The shadow that passed through her eyes might have been dark and dull with pain; but the eyes themselves never flinched.

'I know,' she said. 'I should have begun at the beginning.'

'Try it now,' he suggested dispassionately.

She drew the end of her cigarette hot and bright.

'All right,' she said in a tone that attempted to match his. 'I suppose you know that Captain Heinrich Friede is one of the chief Nazi secret agents in the United States.'

'I figured that out.' Simon flicked ash into the oozing creek. 'And your dear Randolph March is his principal stooge, or a sort of playboy financier of the Fifth Column. Go on from there.'

'You know that Randolph March has a hidden harbour that he calls a hunting lodge somewhere over there.'

'Hoppy found that out. All by himself. I can still top you. He keeps a German U-boat parked in it, and they go out and torpedo tankers.'

'That's right.'

'You're quite sure it is? You've seen this submarine?'

'I saw it today for the first time. It's there now.'

'And what else?'

'The *March Hare*.'

'Once again we don't fall over backwards. You know that because you were on board. As a matter of fact, I happened to see you.'

'There are two other people on board.'

'I know. Friends of mine. Arrested by phony deputy sheriffs.' The Saint's voice had the silky edge of a razor. 'How were they when you left them?'

'They were still all right. They'll still be all right – according to what you do. They're hostages for you.'

'Then we're still waiting for you to contribute. When do you start paying your way with something we don't know already or hadn't guessed for ourselves?'

She seemed to be holding herself in with terrible patience.

'What else is there that matters?'

'There's still the minor detail of what your stake is in this carnival.' Simon's voice was without emotion, his face a smooth carving in brown marble. 'We seem to keep running into you in a whole lot of funny places – most of them somewhere near Randolph March. You were with him and Friede when I met you. You came to visit me just at the time when one of their stooges twice removed took a shot at me that started a most ingenious trail towards my tombstone. You kept quiet about Rogers until I'd planted the very evidence against myself that I was meant to plant. You came with me to the Palmleaf Fan to be in at the death; and when the death failed to take place, you joined up with Randy and Friede again and beetled off. I skipped a lot of that while it was going on because it was fun, as I told you. But the fun is all over now, Ginger. It's nothing but straight answers – or else.'

Her lips gave a funny little quirk.

'Dear man,' she said, 'who do you think tipped off Rogers?'

He lifted his eyes to hers.

'According to the sheriff,' he replied unyieldingly, 'it was a mysterious kibitzer called A Friend. If that was you, say so.'

'It was.'

'Then why didn't you say anything to me?'

'I told you before dinner, last night – you had to go through it all, in case you got anything else out of it. And then, if I'd told you at the Palmleaf Fan, you know you'd have still gone in to Rogers anyhow, and the plot would have worked. But I knew he belonged to the F.B.I., and I knew he'd be more cautious. I hoped that if I told him it might save you from being killed.'

'That was nice of you,' said the Saint politely. 'So after you'd done that, you went back to March and Friede and helped them to kidnap my friends.'

'I didn't. I wanted to cover myself. I went over and said that I didn't know what went on, but you'd said something just as you left that sounded as if you already knew what the trap was and you'd organised things to take care of it. A couple of minutes later the waiter came and whispered to Friede, and he said I was right. He was raging. He gave a lot of orders in German that I couldn't catch, and we all left. While they were getting the *March Hare* ready to sail, some men brought your friends on board.'

'I saw you enjoying the joke with Randy as you went past the Causeway.'

'I had to stay with them then. The one thing that mattered was to find out where they were going.'

Without shifting his eyes, the Saint blew smoke at the mosquitoes that were starting to rise in thickening clouds into the twilight.

'You still have a last chance to come clean,' he said ruthlessly. 'Who are you working for?'

She seemed to make up her mind after a hopeless struggle.

'The British Secret Service,' she said.

Simon looked at her for a moment longer.

Then he put his face in his hands.

It was a few seconds before he raised it again. And then the expression in his face and eyes had changed as if he had taken off an ugly mask.

It was all clear now – all of it. And he felt as if he had taken the last step out of suffocating darkness into fresh air and the light of day. He didn't even have to ask himself whether she was telling the truth. If the unshadowed straightness of her wonderful eyes had not been enough, the circumstantial evidence would have been. No lie could have fitted every niche and filigree of the pattern so completely. He could only be astounded that that was the one answer he had never guessed.

Impulsively he reached out for her hand.

'Karen,' he said, 'why didn't you tell me?'

'How could I?' But her face and voice were without rancour. 'I wouldn't have been any more use if I'd been suspected. I'd put too much into getting where I was. Even for you, I couldn't endanger any of it. I knew you were supposed to be a sort of romantic Robin Hood, but how could I know how much of that was to be trusted? I couldn't take a chance. Until now – I've got to.'

'Finish it now,' he said quietly.

She put her cigarette back to her lips and drew at it more evenly than she had done since he lighted it. It was as though a die had been cast and a decision made, and now for the first time she could rest a little while and let herself go with the tide.

'It started as a very ordinary assignment,' she said. 'The Foreign Office knew about Randolph March, as they know about most people who might give them trouble one day. They knew he'd spent a lot of time in Germany since 1933, and had a lot of powerful Nazi friends, and a lot of leanings towards their point of view. But he isn't the first rich man who's thought the Nazi system might be a good thing. You know the technique – you scare a rich man into the Fascist camp with the bogy of Communism, because he's worried about his possessions, and you scare the poor man into the Communist camp with the bogy of capitalism; and then the Communists and the Fascists make an alliance and clean up . . . Well, after Czechoslovakia, they found out that March was doing some heavy speculation in Nazi bonds.'

'Through the Foreign Investment Pool?'

She nodded.

'So when the real war started, he was somebody to be watched. It was more or less routine at first – until I found out about Friede. Of course, I had to pretend that I had Nazi sympathies myself, but it was a long time before they'd open up at all. Even then, they never let me get near anything important – most of what I did find out was from listening at keyholes. Until last night . . . But before that, I'd heard the word "submarine" once. I suppose I'd worked out the tanker business more or less the way you did. But if that was the scheme, I had to find the submarine base. That's why I went with them last night, because it seemed almost certain that they'd be going there. I was right. So as soon as I knew all I had to know, I slipped away. That was this morning . . . I saw from the map that the road couldn't be very far away, and I'd have made it by now if those wild pigs hadn't attacked me.'

The Saint thought back over the country they had traversed, and smiled rather grimly.

'I don't suppose they've even bothered to try and catch you,' he said. 'Because they know better. We've been pushing this wall-eyed wheelbarrow through the swamp for about fourteen hours with an Indian guide who has X-ray eyes; and we haven't arrived yet.'

'But I've got to get out!' she said desperately. 'You can take me. I can identify myself to the British Ambassador in Washington. I've only got to get to a telephone. He'll drop a word to the State Department, and in half an hour the Navy and the Coastguard will be here.'

'Looking for a most illegal German submarine base,' said the Saint. 'But not particularly interested in a couple of friends of mine.'

She stared at him almost incredulously.

'Are you still thinking about them?'

'It's a weakness of mine,' he said.

She sat still.

Then she let the stub of her cigarette fall carefully into the stream. She reached out and took his own cigarette case out of his pocket, and helped herself to another. She waited until he gave her a match.

She said: 'For three months I've let myself be pawed by Randolph March and leered at by Heinrich Friede. I've pretended to sympathise with a philosophy that stinks to high heaven. I've let myself gloat over the invasion of peaceful countries and the bombing of helpless women and children and the enslaving of one nation after another. I've made myself laugh at the slaughter of my own people and the plundering of Jews and the torture of concentration camps. I've even let you walk blindly into what might have been your death, while all my heart loved you, because I'm not big enough to decide who is to live and who is to die while the civilisation that made us is trying to save all the lights in the world from going out. And all you can think of is your friends!'

Simon Templar gazed at her with clear eyes of bitter blue. For a long time. While the intensely even tones of her voice seemed to hang in the sultry air and beat back savagely into his brain.

Like an automaton, he lighted the fresh cigarette he had taken, and put his cigarette case away. In the infinite silence, every scintilla of feeling seemed to empty out of his face, leaving nothing but a fine-drawn shell that was as readable as graven stone.

The mask turned towards Hoppy Uniatz.

'Do you think you could drive this thing?'

'Sure, boss,' said Mr Uniatz expansively. 'I loin it on de farm at de reform school.'

The Saint's eyebrows barely moved.

'Of course, you wouldn't have thought of volunteering before.' His accent was amazingly limpid and precise. 'Will you take it back the way Charlie Halwuk tells you?' He turned to the motionless Indian. 'Which way is where we were going, Charlie?'

The Seminole raised a mahogany arm.

'Plenty straight into sun. No can miss now.'

Simon stood up, and caught a bough over his head, and swung himself on to the quivering shore.

'Thanks – Karen,' he said.

Her lips were white.

'What are you doing?' she asked shakily.

His smile was suddenly gay and careless again.

'You've got enough men to look after you, darling. I'm going to see if I can find Patricia and Peter before the Navy gets there. Give my love to the Ambassador.' He waved his hand. 'On your way, Hoppy – and take care of them.'

'Okay, boss,' said Mr Uniatz valiantly.

He hauled back on the clutch levers. The giant wheels made a quarter turn, and stalled. Hoppy started the engine again and raced it up. Too late, the Saint saw what had happened. A log that had drifted down while they were talking had nosed in between the back wheels and embedded itself in the soft bank of the stream. But by the time he saw it, he could do nothing. Never a man to waste time on niggling finesse, Mr Uniatz had slammed the clutches home while the engine roared at full throttle. There was a deafening screech of rending metal, and every moving part came to a shuddering standstill with an unmistakably irrevocable kind of finality.

Mr Uniatz pumped homicidally at the starter and succeeded in producing a slow spark and a soft puff of expiring smoke.

'Let it rest,' said the Saint wearily, and glanced at Karen again. 'I did my best, darling, but I think Fate had other ideas.'

3

'I'll have to go on foot,' said the girl. 'The way I started. If I had a guide—'

'What about it, Charlie?' Simon interrupted.

The Seminole shook his head impassively.

'Indian go. Maybe three-four days. White man no can do. White man die plenty quick.'

Karen Leith covered her eyes, just for a moment.

The Saint touched her shoulder.

'We may be able to steal a boat and get you out through the islands,' he said. 'But we've got to get to the base first. And we've got to step on it.'

Without the bright beams of the march buggy to light the way, an attempt to get through the trackless Everglades at night was hopeless and might well be fatal. And there was not much more time. Florida twilights were short, and darkness would drop like spilled ink as soon as the sun was gone.

Simon stood up.

'Charlie, you lead. We've got to make Lostman's River before dark. Travel fast, but be as quiet as you can.'

The Indian nodded and got out. The ground quivered badly under Simon, but Charlie Halwuk's moccasined feet seemed to possess some native buoyancy that prevented them from sinking.

Karen spoke to him with tormented calm.

'You'd better keep your eyes open, too. There may be a party out looking for me, in spite of what he said.'

'If man come, I hear,' stated Charlie Halwuk.

He parted branches and moved on. The procession formed behind him.

The Indian's course was deceptively casual to watch, but it was like trying to follow the course of a dodging jackrabbit. He ducked under vines, found passage through tight-packed foliage, and used roots and tufts of grass as stepping-stones with the sure-footedness of a mountain goat. Behind Simon and the girl, Gallipolis began a whispering flow of his inexhaustible Greek profanities. Bringing up the rear, Hoppy Uniatz, who in spite of his nickname had never had any practice in the art of agile skipping about on treacherous knolls, uttered occasional louder epithets as he floundered along.

Presently they came to another narrow stream.

'Cross here,' said Charlie Halwuk, and forded out into the knee-deep water.

The others waded after him. They were nearly across to the opposite bank when Simon noticed that the densest of hammocks screened the shore to bar their way. The Indian slipped sideways along it, working upstream. Then he held up his hand, stopped for a moment, and returned to Simon.

'Go down other way,' he said imperturbably. 'Crocodile up there. Make bad to get out.'

'Crocodiles!' The girl's fingers tightened on Simon's arm, and he knew she was thinking of her own crossing of that same brackish water some time before. 'I didn't know there were any in Florida.'

'Plenty here,' said Charlie.

He moved on noiselessly through the water, found a clump of bushes which looked no different to Simon than the rest, and pushed them aside like a gateway on to the shore. The Saint climbed after him into a cavernous cathedral dank with dripping Spanish moss and roofed with a lacework of twisted branches, so dark that it gave the illusion that night had already fallen. They went on.

The journey became a nightmare race against fleeting time, with every obstacle that the most prolific combination of soil and moisture could erect to impede them. Gallipolis kept up his blasphemous monotone; but Mr Uniatz, whose chassis had been designed for weight-lifting rather than cross-country running, was reduced to an asthmatic grunting. And always the Indian ahead was a tireless space-eating will-o'-the-wisp that kept just a few yards in the lead but could never be overtaken, even though the ground grew firmer at last and the thorny scrub began to thin out. Karen stumbled against the Saint, and for a while his arm held her up; but presently she pulled herself free and fought on indomitably at his side again.

And then, at last, Charlie Halwuk stopped and looked back. Simon caught up with him, and found himself gazing through a last thin screen of vines into the pinkish afterglow of the vanished sun. A breeze stirred, wrinkling water that lay in a wide roseate pool. The Indian pointed.

'Lostman's River,' he said.

Simon stared at it while the shadows deepened perceptibly. Karen Leith came up beside him and clung to his arm, but he scarcely noticed her. He was feeling an absurd weakness that foreran a new flood of strength as he let himself bathe in the mad magnificent knowledge that they had made it, in spite of everything. They were there.

This was the secret outpost of the conspiracy, the field headquarters of March and Friede. He took it in.

The *March Hare* was there, riding at anchor in the broad pool, a slash of pastel grey across the river with porthole lights beginning to reflect themselves in the darkening water like orderly ranks of stars. Between it and the shore was moored a whale-backed shape of a deeper and more glossy grey, most of it hardly breaking the surface, but with its periscope and conning tower outlined in sharp silhouette against the sheen of the pool.

To his right, a small dock shaped like a slender capital T pointed from the water into the shore, at a place where a group of corrugated-iron buildings, probably storehouses, clustered around a huge aluminium-painted fuel storage tank. Tied up to the dock was a small open motor-boat, rubbing gently against the piling in the river current. A little further on, another long low building broke the dusk with two yellow lighted windows, but even they were not much more than a hundred yards from where he stood.

On his other side, Hoppy breathed heavily and drained the last drops from the bottle he had brought with him from the abandoned marsh buggy, and dumped it into the undergrowth. Its extinction hardly seemed to reach his attention under the stress of the awe-inspiring realisation that was silting up in the small hollow space inside his head.

'Boss,' Mr Uniatz said reverently, 'is dis de Pool?'

'This is it,' said the Saint.

'Boss–' Mr Uniatz wriggled with the brontosaurian stirring of an almost unconquerable eagerness. 'Can I try it?'

'No,' Simon said ruthlessly. 'You stay here with everybody else. I'm going ahead to reconnoitre. The rest of you keep quiet and don't move until I give you a signal. Gallipolis, let's have your flashlight. When I blink it this way, come after me.'

He pressed Karen's hand for a moment as he released himself from her arm. Then he was gone.

He stayed just within the edge of the jungle, for the river bank had been cleared for some distance around the lodge. Mud sucked at his boots, and more mosquitoes found him to make a buzzing and stinging hell out of every step; but already with his natural instinct for the wilds he was learning the tricks of movement in that new kind of country, and he felt a boyish kind of excitement at the awareness of his increasing skill.

He waded through a narrow winding arm of the river that crossed his path, circumnavigating another evil cottonmouth that curled like an almost indiscernible sentinel in a clump of lilies; and then he was almost directly behind the lodge. The river broadened in front of the building, arching out towards the Gulf in a sheltering bay. There was more dark formidable land on the other side, its coastline dimly broken by other tortuous creeks that carried the drainage of the Everglades out to sea; and he had to admit that the submarine base had been chosen with a master tactician's eye. Without knowing every secret marker of the channel that had been dredged to it, no one could have found it by water in anything larger than a skiff; and even then only a Seminole pilot would be likely to escape getting lost among the myriad islands and shoals that still lay between it and the sea.

Silently as a roaming panther, Simon stepped out of the sheltering jungle and crossed the clearing towards the blacker shadow under the wall of the lodge, where one of the lighted windows was like a square hole in the darkness striped with narrow black lines. As he reached it he saw that they were bars, and his pulses gained a beat in the rate of their steady rhythm. But a curtain inside made it impossible to see through.

He shifted towards the corner which might bring him round to a door.

An owl hooted mournfully in the thickets behind him, where the shrill chorus of innumerable insects made a background din above which one might have been tempted to believe that no slight sound could have been heard. And yet as Simon turned the corner he did hear a different sound – a sharp rustle that jerked his muscles into involuntary tension like the warning trill of a rattlesnake.

Then he saw that it was not a snake, but a man who had stepped out of the shadow of the doorway.

They stared at each other for an instant in the stillness of surprise.

Out there in the open, there was just enough relief from the darkness for Simon to see him. He was a huge crop-headed bull-necked man in dirty ducks, naked to the waist, with a boiler chest matted with thick hair. A revolver hung in a holster at his hip, and one of his great hands grabbed for it while the other reached for the Saint.

He was too slow with both moves.

The Saint leaped at him a fraction of a second sooner. It was no time for drawing-room niceties, and Simon was not in the mood to take chances with a gorilla of that build. As he went in, his left knee led for the groin while his fist simultaneously pistoned into the vital plexus just under the parting of the ribs. It was like punching a pad of solid rubber; but the man buckled with agony, and then Simon had him. He had him on the ground and he had the massive arms pinioned in a leg scissors, and because he dared not risk another gasp he had his hands locked on the brawny neck and his thumbs crushing mercilessly into the man's windpipe. And after a little while something seemed to give way, and the guard was quite still.

Simon got up and rolled him back into the thickest shadow.

He listened for a few seconds, and could hear nothing but the insect and owl concerto. Satisfied that the scuffle had raised no alarm, he tried the door that the man had stepped away from. It was locked, but a search of the guard's pockets produced a key that fitted. Knowing then that he must be very near the end of his original quest, Simon turned the lock and confidently went in.

He found himself in a small, barely-furnished room lighted with a single dim hanging bulb. The room was stifling. A slim brown-haired girl lay on an iron cot with her face buried in the pillow. She started up as the Saint came in, showing him brown eyes made dull with fear and hopelessness, set in the face of a wayward Madonna. A frail grey-haired man sitting in a cheap wooden chair beside the cot raised a haggard, unshaven face and made a protective movement towards her with one thin arm.

'What is it now?' he asked tiredly, and tried ineffectually to stiffen the gaze of his weak eyes.

Simon looked at him with triumph and bitterness and pity blending in his long comprehensive glance.

'Lawrence Gilbeck, I presume,' he said unoriginally. 'I'm Simon Templar. I believe Justine sent for me.'

4

The flare of half-incredulous relief that leaped into the girl's eyes died again slowly into a more hopeless despair.

'So you came,' she said in a low voice. 'And I got you into this – you and Pat. Now you'll die here with us.'

'It's no use,' echoed Gilbeck stupidly. 'Justine told me; but you shouldn't have come. You don't know what you're up against. There isn't anything you can do.'

'That remains to be seen,' said the Saint grimly.

He switched out the light, and presently found his way to the dim glow of the window. Pulling the curtain aside, he aimed his flashlight through the screen in the direction of where he had left the rest of his party, and blinked it three times. The flashes could hardly have been seen from the *March Hare*. He dropped the curtain back and spoke quietly into the dark.

'Follow me out, and try not to make a sound.'

He crossed to the door and opened it. It was full night outside now, and the moon had not yet risen. Simon let them pass him out of the steaming prison and closed the door again and locked it and dropped the key. That would take care of any other surprise visitors for long enough to let him know that an alarm had been raised; and he knew that the guard would never tell his story to any mortal ears.

He led them across to the shadow of the storehouses at the end of the pier, and from there into the edge of the jungle directly opposite, where he knew Charlie Halwuk would lead the others in answer to his summons. He stopped when he thought it would be safe enough to talk. From where he squatted on a dead log, he still had a fan-shaped field of vision that held the lodge at one edge and the storehouses at the other, with most of the clearing and the *March Hare* in the distance in between. With an old soldier's trick, he lighted himself a cigarette without letting any more light escape than a glow-worm would have made.

'Justine,' he said, 'have you seen Pat?'

'No.' Her voice was ragged, perplexed. 'Isn't she with you?'

'They caught her,' said the Saint passionately. 'Along with a friend of mine named Peter Quentin, who means quite a lot to me too . . . They're probably still on the yacht. I rather expected it. Friede would keep them as close to him as he could, for safety.'

There was a subdued crackling in the underbrush, but it was not made by Charlie Halwuk, who had already reached the Saint's side like a shadow. The noise was made by Karen and Hoppy and the Greek as they followed him.

The moon was just starting to tip the horizon then, spreading a faint glimmer ahead of it by which they could all see each other after a fashion. The Saint moved his cigarette like an indicative firefly.

'Miss Leith, Mr Uniatz, Mr Gallipolis, and Mr Halwuk,' he introduced. 'Our travelling League of Nations . . . These are some Gilbeck people I came here to rescue, among other things.'

The two girls studied each other in silence, and then Justine said uncertainly: 'I'm frightened.'

Karen put an arm round her, but she still looked at the Saint.

Lawrence Gilbeck shook his head like a punch-drunk prizefighter, and said: 'I don't want any of you to take any risks for me, but I would like to save her.'

'You're getting soft-hearted in your old age, aren't you?' Simon remarked with carefully-measured vitriol. 'You threw in your wealth on the side of the most high-powered mob of gangsters who have ever pillaged the world. You weren't worried about an odd hundred American seamen who were to be blown to pieces by Friede's submarine. But you are worried about your darling daughter. You got her into this – you played with fire and got yourself burned. What made you get so sentimental?'

'It was the submarine – so help me God!' Gilbeck said with a groan. 'I didn't know anything about it, at first. I went into March's Foreign Investment Pool as an ordinary business proposition. I knew they were buying Nazi bonds, but there's no harm in that. Or there wasn't. America was a neutral country, and there's nothing wrong with buying anything in the market if you think it'll show a profit. I was in it as deep as I could be before I found out the truth about March's scheme.'

'And what is the truth?' Simon asked mercilessly.

Gilbeck ran trembling fingers through his sparse, dishevelled hair. At that moment he looked less like the popular conception of a Wolf of Wall Street than anything that could be imagined.

'The truth is that they were ready to stop at nothing – nothing at all – to try and alienate American sympathy from the Allies.'

'We'd figured that out too,' said the Saint. 'And I'm still waiting for the truth about yourself.'

'I'm guilty,' said the millionaire feverishly. 'Guilty as hell. But I didn't know. I swear I didn't. It just crept up on me. Look.' The words came faster, the desperate outpouring of vain remorse. 'We were going to make money because March convinced me that these Nazi bonds were going to rise. Then the war started. The bonds fell lower. We had our money in 'em. We *had* to want them to go up. Then the only thing was to hope the Germans would win. We *had* to hope that, if we wanted to save our money. So we couldn't be unsympathetic, could we? In fact, if we could do a little to help them– You see? We'd be helping ourselves. So we couldn't be hostile to the Bund, could we? And other things. Little things. Helping to spread propaganda – the stuff about "Well, after all, it's six of one and half a dozen of the other" and "We helped the Allies once and they never paid their war debt" and "Look what the British did in India and South Africa." You know. And the cleverest of all propagandas – to discount any facts that the Allies could advance on their side by saying that they were just propaganda too. And from there it went to some discreet lobbying in Washington. Supporting Isolationist Congressmen. Criticising Roosevelt's foreign policy. Trying to block the repeal of the Arms Embargo and the Johnson Act – anything that would obstruct American help to the Allies. You know.'

'Go on.'

Gilbeck swallowed so that his mouth twitched.

'That's all. That's how it was. Just like that. Step by step. One thing led to another – so gradually and so harmlessly – so logically that I didn't see where I was getting to. Until they thought I was completely sewn up, and didn't care what they told me. God knows how many other men they made slaves of in the same way. But they'd got me. I'd always known that March had been to Germany a lot, and said that the Nazis were very much maligned; but I only thought of that as a private eccentricity. He'd had dinner with Goebbels and gone hunting with Goering and even visited Hitler at Berchtesgaden, and he thought they were all charming people. Anything that was said against them was "all propaganda." Only as this went on it got worse. He said once that he wouldn't mind seeing Hitler running this country – men like us would be much better off, with no more labour troubles and that sort of thing. He even hinted that he wouldn't mind helping to get him here . . . That was when I was going mad – when Justine wrote to you. But I couldn't do anything. I'd let myself slip too far. They could have ruined me – I think I could even have been sent to jail . . . Then March told me about the submarine.'

'We're waiting,' said the Saint inexorably.

'That was too much. Even for me. It wasn't like killing people indirectly, with political manœuvres. You could forget about that, if you tried hard. Talk yourself out of it. But this was direct murder.' Gilbeck twisted his hands together. 'That was when I found a little belated courage. I knew there was only one thing I could do. I had to expose the plot, whatever it cost me – even if I lost everything I had and went to jail for it. It might even have been a relief in the end, if I could take my medicine and not be haunted any more. Only – I still didn't have quite enough courage. I still wanted to make a last attempt to save myself. I thought if I told March and Friede that I'd decided to expose them and take the consequences, I might make them give up their ideas.'

'Yes,' said the Saint.

'That was the day you were expected.' Gilbeck's voice fell lower, but it seemed to gain steadiness with the security of confession. 'Justine hadn't told me then who you were – she just said you were friends of hers. I knew that March was fishing down the Keys. I thought I could go down in the *Mirage* and talk to him and still be back to meet you. I – didn't know what a fool I was.'

'What happened?'

'You know how you found us . . . They – laughed . . .'

'The *Mirage* was found abandoned at Wildcat Key,' said the Saint. 'What happened to the crew?'

Justine Gilbeck suddenly sobbed, and buried her face in Karen's shoulder.

'I see,' said the Saint, in a quiet glacial breath.

'I wished they had killed us too, then,' Gilbeck said. 'But they hadn't quite made up their minds if we could still be useful. They brought us here in a speedboat. They threatened – horrible things. And under that room – where we were – there are a hundred pounds of high explosive, with a radio detonator that Friede said he could fire from five hundred miles away, from the *March Hare* or the submarine, just by sending the right signal. He told us that if anything went wrong he'd do it. But – there was something about a letter you said I'd left. That was afterwards. I didn't know anything about it, but they wouldn't believe me. They promised to torture us . . .'

'I know about that, too. I'll tell you one day.'

The Saint sat still, while a hundred other things turned through his brain. He knew everything now, and all mysteries had been made clear. There was nothing left – except the most important thing of all . . .

He moved over closer to Gilbeck, and the cigarette end in his cupped hands shifted a little to throw a fraction more light on to the millionaire's face.

'Brother,' he said, and his voice was a thing that merely uttered the form of words, with no more warmth or persuasion than a printed page, 'if you were free again, what would you do – now?'

'I swear by everything I know,' Gilbeck answered, 'that I'd do what I meant to do before – only without any compromise. I'd tell everything, and I'd be glad to take my punishment for what I've had a hand in.'

The Saint stared at him for seconds longer; but even at the end he knew that he had found an ultimate sincerity bred of remorse and suffering that no man would shake again.

He moved his hands, and let Gilbeck's anguished face fall back again into the dark.

'All right,' he said. 'I'm going to give you your chance.'

He went back and found Charlie Halwuk in the gloom.

'Charlie,' he said, 'how far is the nearest town up the coast?'

The Indian studied.

'Chokoloskee. Maybe fifteen, maybe twenty miles by Cannon's Bay.'

'Is there a telephone there?'

'No telephone. Plenty fishing.'

'Where is the nearest phone?'

'Everglades. Three, four miles more.'

'There's a small motor-boat here at the dock. Could you take it to Everglades in the dark?'

'Sure. Me fish plenty. Know all ways from Chokoloskee round Florida Bay.'

Simon turned.

'The dock is straight ahead,' he said, so that they could all hear. 'Get going – and be quiet about it.'

The file started off, led by the Indian, while Simon paused to hiss out his cigarette in a pool of mud. As Lawrence Gilbeck passed him, he saw that the millionaire walked in a pitiful imitation of a man reborn; yet he knew that the real rebirth was in the spirit.

He overtook them on the pier, dropped into the pilot cock-pit, and ventured an instantaneous glint of his flashlight on the fuel gauge. Miraculously perhaps, it showed clear full.

Charlie Halwuk slipped in beside him and said: 'How many go?'

'Not me,' said the Saint. 'I'm staying. How many others?'

'Take two. More, we go out by sea. Take plenty water. Long time.'

Simon climbed back on to the dock.

'Karen and Justine,' he said. 'Get in.'

Justine Gilbeck got in, lowered by Hoppy's mighty arm; but Karen Leith was still at the Saint's side.

'I heard,' she said. 'I'm not going. Send Gilbeck.'

'You have to go,' said the Saint frozenly.

Gilbeck was close enough to hear. He touched Simon with a trembling hand.

'Please leave me,' he said. 'Send the girls.'

'The others are going to have to stay here, and whatever

they do won't be easy,' Karen said unfalteringly, but she was speaking only to the Saint. 'If there's going to be trouble, you only want people who can be useful. I know how to handle guns. What good would he be?'

'And the British Secret Service?' Simon asked.

'I only have to get my message out. None of the others can take it – not even you. You have reputations against you. Gilbeck's name is on his side. He can even talk direct to the State Department, which none of us can do. And they'd have to listen to him.'

The Saint had no quick answer, because he knew there was no answer to the truth. And because he could say nothing quickly, he was silent while the girl turned away from him to Gilbeck.

'You can do my job for me,' she said. 'I've been working on March for the British Secret Service. Before you do anything else, call the British Ambassador or the Naval Attaché, in Washington. My name is Karen Leith. And you must give them the word "*Polonaise*." Will you remember that?'

'Yes. Karen Leith. *Polonaise*. But—'

'Then just tell them everything you've told us. And say that we're still here. That's all. Now hurry!'

With a sudden certainty of resolution, the Saint picked Gilbeck's light body up before he could protest again, and dumped him lightly and silently as a feather into the boat. He thrust the revolver he had taken from the strangled guard into the millionaire's skinny hands.

'Take this, in case of accidents. And stop arguing. If you want this second chance, you've got to do what you're told.' He turned to Charlie Halwuk, going on in the same crisply urgent undertone. 'There's a couple of long oars in the back. Don't start the engine until you're well away.'

The Seminole nodded sagely.

'Me paddle plenty far.'

'Think you can get away if you're followed?'

'Tide plenty high. White man never catch me.'

'Good.' Simon straightened up, releasing the painter from the cleat where it was hitched. 'Then get going.'

'Just a minute,' said Gallipolis.

There was a queer emphasis in the way he said it, an abnormal timbre in his musical voice that gave the conventional phrase something it should never have had. There was a satiny menace in it that sent clammy tentacles of hideous intuition frisking up Simon Templar's spinal cord as he turned.

The Greek stood ten feet away, starlight touching his white teeth as he smiled his flashing smile, and glinting dully against the barrel of his ready Tommy gun.

'Stay right where you are,' he said in his melancholy tone, 'because I'm handy with this. If the folks in that boat think they can make a getaway I'll show them. The second they start to push away from this dock I'll drop them in a pile.'

Simon's tall form was still and rigid, while a bitterness such as he had never known ate through him like consuming acid, and he frozenly reckoned his chances of covering those ten feet of intervening space before the crashing stream of lead would melt him inevitably into tattered pulp.

'Forget it, mister,' Gallipolis went on, as though he had read the thought. 'You wouldn't get half way. I'm going to take a hand in this auction, before you send off that putput. All you bid was one grand, and it sounds as if Randolph March would pay me more than that for you.'

The Saint remained motionless, with a strange cold pulse beating in his forehead.

Behind Gallipolis, on the edge of the dock, a small flat animal was crawling. As he watched it, it had been joined by its mate, and it came to him incredulously that these small animals were in reality hamlike human hands, and that what he had taken for a long black nose was the barrel of a gun.

Eliminating all doubt, the nose suddenly belched orange and purple fire, with a crashing roar that drowned all the impact of a heavy slug. But all at once Gallipolis had no face any more. It had dissolved into a formless smear as the flattened bullet spread through it from behind in an enlarging splash of brains and splintered bones. The Greek lurched as if he had been hit by a truck, and then dropped forward on to his face and hid the horror in the dock planking.

The horrific but at least integral face of Mr Uniatz rose dripping over the side of the pier into full view.

'Dat son of a bitch,' said Mr Uniatz, in a voice hoarse with righteous fury. 'He's takin' us for a ride all de time. I got such a toist, boss, I can't wait no longer. So I drink a pint of dat slop before I find out it ain't what he has in de bottles. Dis ain't de pool we are lookin' for at all!'

8

How Simon Templar fought the Last Round, and Heinrich Friede went his Way

1

'If we get out of here,' said the Saint, 'I'll give you a lake of it. If we get out.'

But he spoke so quickly that the line didn't waste an instant. He knew quite simply what that single shot meant, on their side and the other. But there was no use in arguing about it. It had saved everything and blown everything to hell, with one catastrophic explosion. And that was that.

'Get back behind those storehouses – everybody,' he snapped. 'Charlie, get moving.'

He stooped, and in one flowing movement shoved the motor-boat away, snatched up the sub-machine-gun that had tumbled out of the Greek's lifeless hands, and raced after Karen and Hoppy towards the clump of small buildings at the end of the pier. He crouched there with them in partial shelter, and jerked his automatic out of its holster to give it to Karen Leith.

'You said you could use it,' he reminded her. 'Now show me. The fat's in the fire, but I think we can create a diversion while the boat gets clear.'

From out in the anchorage came sounds of disorganised movement and some confused shouting. To the right of them, a door of the lodge was flung open, flinging a long strip of pallid illumination across the open shore; and Simon remembered the second lighted window which he had not waited to investigate after he had located Gilbeck and Justine. But only one man came plunging out, and then stopped uncertainly while he tried to orient himself to the disturbance.

He stayed in the beam of light from the doorway just one instant too long. Happy's Betsy snorted in its ear-splitting bass, and the man's arms and legs seemed to whirl wide of his body like the limbs of a spun marionette before he fell to the ground. He kicked twice after he was down, and then he was quite still.

Mr Uniatz lowered the gun which he had been holding poised for a finishing shot.

'Chees, boss,' he said disgustedly. 'I ain't been gettin' enough practice. I t'ought I was gonna hafta waste anudder sinker on him.'

Simon thought he saw a dim alteration in the silhouette of the submarine's conning tower, as if something might be emerging from it. In any case, an extra shot would not be wasted if it kept the general attention centred in their direction and away from the water. He plugged a bullet somewhere in the right direction, and heard it ricochet whining into the night.

Nobody else had come out of the lodge and it seemed a fair chance that there had been no one else in it.

'Spread out that way,' he directed Hoppy. 'They don't know what sort of a raid they're up against yet, and we may as well give them something to think about.'

Mr Uniatz still lingered for a moment, nursing his cosmic grievance.

'I don't get it, boss,' he complained. 'If dis ain't de Pool, what de hell are dey beefin' about?'

'Maybe they were fond of Gallipolis,' Simon told him. 'You never can tell. We'll talk about it some other time. Slide!'

'Okay.'

Mr Uniatz edged away. His idea of stealth was rather like

that of a prowling bison, but it was adequate for the circumstances. And at least it needed no more detailed instructions. The Hoppy Uniatz who struggled in leviathan agony with the coils and contortions of the Intellect, and the Hoppy Uniatz of the life of direct action and efficient homicide, were two men so different that it was hard to associate their responses with the same individual. But it was in such situations as this that Mr Uniatz came into his precarious kingdom.

Simon tried to follow him with his eyes and ears, lost him for a while, and then felt a weird tingle as something like a deliriously gaudy snake reached into the wedge of light from the lodge doorway and drew back quickly with the gun that the dead man lying there had dropped clutched in his maw. It was a half instant before he realised that the jazzy colouration was due to the sleeve of the Seminole chief's shirt which Hoppy still proudly wore. Thus having augmented his armament, Mr Uniatz let off another shot which drew an answering shriek from somewhere out in the bay.

The babble of incoherent voices that came over the water was dying away as a new, crisper and harsher voice began to dominate them with a rattle of commands.

'Friede,' said the Saint inclemently, and felt the girl's left hand in the crook of his elbow.

'I only wish we could spot him,' she said.

Somehow there was nothing that jarred him in the cold-blooded way she said it.

Abruptly, a searchlight on the upper deck of the *March Hare* sizzled into life, thrusting a white spear over the tree-tops below the lodge. It swung high and wild for a moment, and then dipped towards the waterfront and began to sweep towards them, cutting a blinding arc out of the bay.

Simon raised the machine-gun, settling his fingers on the grips; but before he had chosen his aim the gun that he had given Karen spat twice, shatteringly, across his right eardrum. At the second shot, the white blade of light shrank suddenly back into a small red eye that faded and went out. A faint tinkle stole over the pool, belatedly, to confirm the visual evidence.

'At this range, darling,' said the Saint respectfully, 'I'll admit you've shown me.'

'I used to be pretty good,' she said.

Friede's voice began barking fresh orders, but it was too far for the guttural German to be distinguishable. However, dim figures could be seen moving on the *March Hare's* lighted decks, and Simon lifted the Tommy gun again.

'It won't do any harm to keep them busy,' he remarked, and hosed a short burst along the length of the yacht.

As the clatter of the Tommy gun died away, and its echoes went dwindling across the startled Everglades, one or two hoarse yells floated back to suggest that the expenditure of precious ammunition might have shown another small profit. There were also four or five answering shots, aimed at the fiery flickering of the machine-gun's muzzle. They were born out of tiny sparks that blossomed on the yacht's deck, and spanged to extinction among the corrugated-iron shelters to left and right. The darkness gave them a curious impersonality, making them seem as unfrightening as the first heavy drops of a thunder shower or a June bug banging against a lighted window.

Then all the lights on the *March Hare* went out as somebody pulled a master switch.

'I was afraid they'd think of that,' Simon said conversationally.

He strained his eyes to penetrate the obscurity of the bay. The moon had risen higher, thinning the darkness of the sky; there was enough light for him to see the pale beauty of Karen Leith's face beside him, watching with the same intentness as his own. But over the water, against the sombre unevenness of the opposite river bank, the illumination was deceptive and full of shadows that seemed to take form from imagination and then disappear. Yet he could see nothing that looked like the motor-boat in which he had sent off Charlie Halwuk and Justine and Lawrence Gilbeck. He had not kept track of the time, but it seemed as if they should have had almost enough leeway, with the current helping them, to steal far enough down river to be safe. Certainly he had heard none of the outcry or shooting that should have announced their discovery.

Karen was thinking the same thoughts.

She said: 'Do you really think they can make it?'

'Once they get clear,' said the Saint, 'it's in the bag. I've done some travelling with that dried-up Seminole, and I can't think of any place I wouldn't back him to make in this country.'

It seemed quite natural that there was nothing to say about themselves. They were there. Without a guide, the jungle at their backs held them as securely as a prison wall.

'I wish you could have done something about your friends,' she said.

'They may get a chance to do something about themselves in the excitement,' he said, and they both knew that they were just talking. 'They're wonderful people for getting themselves out of trouble.'

He was still listening. In a few more seconds, if nothing had gone wrong, it would be time to hear the motor-boat engine starting its racket somewhere in the distance to the south-west. But it had not come yet. The jungle seemed to have fallen unearthly still, for the owl had departed to more peaceful glades, and not more than half the shocked insects had tentatively begun to resume their choir practice since the last burst of firing had stunned them to an abnormal silence.

Then there was a muffled grating of wood, and a splash

far fainter than a leaping fish would have made; and Simon suddenly was aware that a vague shape that had been drifting shorewards on the murkily moonlit water was neither the product of an overstrained retina nor the floating stump of a tree. At the same instant Hoppy fired twice, and the crack of Karen's gun jumped in on the heels of those explosions. Simon took a fraction longer to bring up the Tommy gun, but the thundering stammer of death that poured from it made up in quantity for its tardiness. The response came in shouts and screams, and a single thin piercing wail that seemed as if it would never stop before it was smothered in a choking gurgle. The boat ceased to drift cross-stream and swung lazily round with the current, and something human plunged away from it with a loud splash and floundered wildly back towards the submarine. Karen's gun spoke once more, and the splashing stopped as if it had been cut off with a knife.

The Saint's teeth showed in the dark mask of his face.

'I wonder how the bastards like our blitzkrieg,' he drawled.

'I like it, anyway,' she said, and the cool tension of excitement was in her voice, with no kind of fear. 'Now I know what it must feel like to fight Hitler's invaders. You're only scared until the first shot is fired. And then you hate their guts so much that it doesn't matter what they can do, if you can only get some of them before they get you.'

' "They shall not pass",' he said crookedly. 'I only wish we could make it stick. But there'll be more landing parties, and we haven't many more shots between us.'

'I'm only glad,' she said, 'that we could be together like this – just once.'

Their hands held in an understanding that more words could only have made trivial.

Hoppy Uniatz fired three times more at spaced intervals but without any audible repercussion.

Then a new sound penetrated the Saint's ears – a faint

pervasive hum that almost blended with the contiuous buzzing of mosquitoes. He had barely time to recognise it as the carrier hum of a loudspeaker before Heinrich Friede's magnified voice blared clearly across from the yacht.

'If Mr Templar is there, will he please fire one shot?'

Simon hesitated a moment. Then—

'What the hell?' he said grimly to Karen. 'They must know it's my outfit. The police or the Coastguard wouldn't have opened fire without some sort of parley . . . But stand by to duck.'

He fired one shot, trying to aim it at the voice, and then flung the girl aside and dropped flat beside her behind the flimsy cover of the nearest storehouse. But the hail of machine-gun fire which he had half expected to cut loose in reply did not come.

'Thank you,' said the voice. 'Now I think you have done enough damage. Another party has already landed higher up the river, and you will certainly be captured in a short time, but I should prefer not to lose any more men. Therefore unless you surrender at once, we shall start working on Miss Holm and Mr Quentin, quite slowly and scientifically, so that their cries can be broadcast to you. If you wish to avoid this, you can signify your surrender by firing two shots close together.'

Then Patricia's Holm's voice came clearly through, without a faltering syllable, so that he could almost see the brave set of her chin and the undaunted steadiness of her eyes.

'Hullo, Simon, boy . . . Don't listen to the big ape. He's only saying that because he knows he can't catch you.'

'Tell him to go to hell,' Peter put in.

But a single sharp cry overtook the last word, and was instantly stifled.

'I shall give you ten seconds to decide, Mr Templar,' said Captain Friede.

Simon bowed his head over the sub-machine-gun, and his hands were clenched on the grips as if he could have torn the weapon apart like a stick of putty.

Karen Leith gazed at his face of frozen granite.

Then she pointed her gun to the stars and pulled the trigger twice, quickly.

As if in answer, far to the west, a motor-boat engine awoke to spluttering life.

2

The square bulk of Mr Uniatz lumbered uncertainly out of murk.

'Boss,' he said blankly, 'was dat you? Dijja mean we say uncle to dem Heinies?'

'No, Hoppy,' said the girl. 'I did it.'

The Saint looked at her strangely.

'At least,' he said, 'I shouldn't have expected you to help me break down.'

Her hand slipped over his, and her lovely face held the ghost of a smile of great understanding.

She said: 'My dear, they *could* have taken us. In the end. You know it as well as I do. Why should anyone suffer for nothing? Probably we shall still all be killed, but it may be quick. And we've done all that we hoped to do. Our messengers got away. Listen.'

He listened, steeping his spirit in the methodical chugging of the motor-boat far off in the dark, before it was drowned out by the more steady thrum of a speed tender putting out from the *March Hare* – knowing that she had only spoken the truth, and glad of it, but still trying to reconcile himself to the paradox of defeat in victory. And he wondered if that might only be because his own personal pride had not yet been subdued, so that his insignificant individual fate must still obtrude on a cataclysmic background in which millions of individuals no less important to themselves would yet be consumed like ants in a furnace.

And through that, after seconds that might have run into centuries, he came back to a sanity as immeasurable and enduring as the stars.

Everything else went on. But there was a difference. A difference beyond which nothing could be changed. And yet the only way he could show it was in the recapture of the old careless mockery which had always gone ahead of him like a banner. Because other rebels and outlaws like him would still come after him and the great game would still go on, as long as the spark of freedom was born into the souls of men.

'Of course,' he said. 'And they still haven't killed us yet. They could have their hands full even after they've got us.'

The speedboat was creaming in towards the dock.

'Ya mean, boss,' said Mr Uniatz dumbly, 'I can't do no more practice on dese mugs?'

'Not just now, Hoppy. We've got to get Patricia and Peter back with us first. After that we may be able to do something.'

And if he thought that the change was very slight, the doubt could never have been heard in his voice.

He threw the Tommy gun on the ground away from him, and with a similar gesture the girl tossed her automatic after it. More slowly, perplexed but still reluctantly obedient, Hoppy Uniatz followed suit. They stood in a silent group, watching the tender slacken in towards the pier landing.

Simon took out his cigarette case and offered it to Karen, as easily as if they had been standing in the foyer of a New York night club waiting for a table, while men leaped out of the speedboat, ran down the pier, and fanned out at the double into a wide semi-circle with the efficient precision of trained storm troops – which, he reflected ironically, was what they probably were. But without giving them a glance he struck a match and held it for Karen. Their eyes met over the flame in complete understanding.

'We did have fun, anyway,' he remarked.

'We did.' Her voice was as steady as his; and he never wanted to forget the unchanged loveliness of her proud pale face, and the cool violet of her eyes, and the tousled flame of her hair. 'And thanks for everything – Saint.'

He touched the match to his own cigarette and flipped it away; but light still dwelt on them. It came from the converging beams of three flashlights in the ring that was closing in on them.

Simon looked round the circle. Some of the men were in German naval uniforms, others in ordinary seaman's dungarees, but they all had the square dry-featured brutalised faces which Nazi ethnology had set up as the ideal of Nordic superiority. They were armed with revolvers and carbines.

Another man ran around the outside of the group, beyond range of the lights, and said, '*Verzeihen Sie, Herr Kapitän. Die Gefangene sind verschwunden.*'

'*Danke.*'

The second voice was Friede's. He strode through into the light. His heavy-jawed face was hard and arrogant, the flat-top mouth clamped in an implacable line that turned down slightly at the corners. His stony eyes swept quickly and unfeelingly over his three captives, ending with the Saint.

'Mr Templar, this is not all your party.'

'You may have noticed a guy on the dock with his head blown open,' said the Saint helpfully. 'He was liquidated quite early in the proceedings. In fact, we did that ourselves. He didn't seem to be able to make up his mind which side to be on, so we put him into permanent neutrality.'

'I mean the Gilbecks. Where are they?'

'How are your ears?'

The captain did not move his head. But through the stillness everyone could hear the monotonous putter of the motor-boat engine far out in the sweltering night.

Friede's pebbly stare pored over the Saint from under lowering lids for long crawling seconds.

Then he turned and rasped fresh orders at his men.

Carbines prodded the Saint, driving him with Karen and Hoppy towards the barred lodge room from which he had released Lawrence Gilbeck and Justine. Somebody went in ahead and turned on the light again as they were herded in.

Outside, there was an exclamation and some throaty muttering as the dead body of the guard was discovered, cut short by another of the captain's wolfish commands. The storm troopers who had followed into the prison room cleared the doorway for Friede to march through. He stood back, but the lane stayed open.

After a very brief pause of intense silence, Patricia and Peter were hustled through, to be pushed over with Simon and Karen and Hoppy into the back centre of the room.

Peter said casually: 'Hullo, Chief. It's a funny thing. I've never been able to make out where you collect such an ugly-looking bunch of boils to play with.'

Patricia Holm went straight to the Saint. He kissed her quickly, and his left arm still lay along her shoulders as he turned back to smile genially at Captain Friede.

'Well, Heinrich, dear carbuncle,' he murmured, 'this makes a very cosy little get-together. Now what shall we do to amuse ourselves? If we only had some old treaties we could cut paper dolls. Or there's nearly enough of us to form a glee club and sing the pig trough or Horse Vessel song.'

But one more man still had to arrive to make the get-together truly complete, and he came last through the doorway as two of the seamen moved back to close it.

Randolph March's weakly handsome face was a little drawn with strain, and his fair hair was pushed just a lock or two out of its usual clean smooth grooming. In the same way, his soft white collar was just a little crumpled at the neck. The symptoms were insignificant in themselves, and yet taken together with the equally unexaggerated wildness of his eyes they made a definite picture of a man whose nerves were falling infinitesimally short of the standard of discipline that circumstances were demanding of them.

'The Gilbecks,' he said to Friede; and his voice was

roughened to just the same slight but revealing extent. 'If they got away in the motor-boat—'

'I know,' said the captain.

'Why don't you send someone after them?'

'Who?'

'Well, you've got plenty of men, haven't you? There are two speedboats—'

'And no pilots. No one here could find his way very far outside of our own channel. You know what these creeks are like. We chose this place for that reason.'

'Then they're bound to get stuck themselves, and we can catch them.'

'I'm afraid,' said the captain, 'it may not be so easy. Our friend Templar and his party got here. They must have been guided. Unless Miss Leith . . .'

Both the men looked at Karen; and as if the full force of things that had been temporarily eclipsed by more immediate alarums rushed back on him as he studied her, Randolph March took a half step towards her with his mouth growing tight and ugly.

'You treacherous little bitch!'

'One moment.' The captain's intervention had no hint of chivalry – it was plainly and practically dictated by nothing but cold-rolled efficiency. Recriminations were a waste of time; therefore he had no time for them. 'Let Miss Leith tell us.'

Karen gazed at him with calm contempt.

'It's always so nice to deal with gentlemen,' she said satirically. 'You wouldn't be rude, would you– You'd just fetch some hot irons and get on with it . . . Well, as far as this goes I can save you the trouble. I didn't bring them here. We met accidentally, on the way. And they had a very good guide of their own.'

'Who was it?'

'An Indian.'

Simon Templar flicked ashes peacefully on the floor.

'Let me help,' he suggested affably. 'After all, there should be no more secrets between any of us. To be exact, he was a bird from the Seminole Escort Bureau, by the name of Charlie Halwuk. A great hunter, I'm told, and certainly a wonderful pathfinder. After the way he brought us here, I'd back him against any homing pigeons you can trot out. So we sent him off with the Gilbecks. He seemed quite sure he could leave anybody who chased him high and dry on a sandbank for the mosquitoes and crocodiles to finish; but of course I don't want to stop you trying.'

Friede stared at him for a second longer, and then turned back to Karen. The mask that he had worn in the first meeting on the *March Hare* had been dropped like an old coat. No one could have had any doubt now as to who was in command. Randolph March, gnawing his moustache by the doorway, had become a relative nonentity pillared by his captain's emotionless authority.

'Miss Leith, why were you trying to run away from here?'

'I got bored with the company.'

'Perhaps,' said Friede, 'you were not taking yourself seriously enough in the observation you made just now.'

The girl regarded him with unwavering eyes and her red lips curled.

'I just don't want you to think you frighten me,' she said. 'As it happens, that's another thing I'll be glad to tell you. I was on my way out to tell the world about this submarine base of yours, and how it hooks up with Randy's Foreign Investment Pool.'

'You are an inquisitive journalist, an ally of Templar, a blackmailing adventuress, or an agent of the Department of Justice?'

'Guess once more.'

'You are some kind of Government agent.'

'That's right,' she said calmly. 'And I mean the British Government.'

There was a great silence in the room.

Captain Friede's face did not change. It was like a mould of hard-baked clay, without feeling or flexibility, behind which cogs and connections turned with the insentient functionality of an adding machine. Only in the drooping of the heavy lids over his obsidian eyes was there a sign of the reflex of personal viciousness.

Then he swung back to March.

'Go back to the yacht and get on the radio telephone to Miami,' he ordered, and his tone had lost the last pretence of deference. 'Call Nachlohr and tell him to get the emergency squad together. The motor-boat will take at least three hours to get to Everglades – there is no other place they could head for. The emergency squad can drive across in about two hours, once they are collected. Tell Nachlohr to take all necessary measures. Gilbeck must not reach a telephone, at any cost.'

The Saint stopped breathing.

It was the weak point in everything he had built on, the vital flaw in the one hope for which he had sacrificed all of them there.

Perhaps his brain had never worked so fast. The pressure of it made his head reel; and yet somehow he knew, almost without being able to believe it, that he held the faintest betrayal of dismay out of his face. In fact, he even forced another shade of carefree impudence into his taunting smile.

'It's a lovely idea, Randy,' he said encouragingly, 'and it'll certainly make everything much more exciting. Jesse Rogers and I were just talking along those lines in the Palmleaf Fan last night – you remember that conference you arranged for us. On account of your suspicions about him were perfectly right; only they should have gone further. He really is an agent of the F.B.I., and it seems he'd found out even more about your local Bund than you suspected. In fact, he had a complete membership list, and the boys who weren't pinched last night are just being closely watched to see who else will get in touch with them. The guy listening on the wire will get a big kick out of it when you talk to Nachlohr – that is, if Comrade Nachlohr is still in a place where he can receive telephone calls.'

The Saint took another pull at his cigarette, and his smile became even more demoralising as he drew reckless strength from the reactions that their faces were less quick to conceal than his.

'And there's one other thing you may have forgotten,' he went on in the same blithe and bantering voice. 'You remember the letter I told you about that Gilbeck had written? Well, when I finally found out where this base was, I brought it up to date with some postscripts of my own before we started off on this trip, and mailed it off to Washington in case of accidents. I'll admit I hoped to be able to rescue all the hostages before the big guns went off. But in a few hours they'll be going off, just the same . . . So what with one thing and another, Heinrich, old *Drekwurst*, it looks as if you're going to have to make a lot of good excuses to your Fuhrer.'

3

It worked.

It had to. The bluff was flawlessly played, as few living men but Simon Templar could have played it; but that only gave it a little extra certainty. The barest essential minimum of confidence would have served almost as well. For its real magnificence was in the basic conception.

It was unanswerable. Friede and March might suspect that an indefinite amount of it was bluff – although Simon had said it in a way that would have left only the most optimistic opposition any grounds for pinning much faith to that idea. They might have some evanescent motes of doubt. But doubt was the only thing that fundamentally had to be achieved. Doubt would work just as effectively both ways. For the stakes were too high to let Friede and March take the gamble. They couldn't even dare to waste precious time on an inspirational chance which if it failed would leave them worse off than before.

Simon read all these things in their faces, and knew the lift of a forlorn triumph which made every sacrifice worth while.

Friede stared at him with those vengefully hooded eyes.

'You sent that information to Washington?'

'By air mail,' Simon confirmed, and only wished he had had enough foresight to make it true. 'They've probably got it by now, and I expect the Navy and the Coastguard and the Marines will be on their way before morning.'

Randolph March loosened his collar.

'They don't have to find anything,' he said. 'We can – can kill all these people and sink them in the swamp. Nobody could find them. Then we all say that Gilbeck must have gone off his head, and everybody knows the Saint's reputation – if we send the submarine out to sea—'

'You sickly fool!' Friede turned on him with impersonal

savagery. 'What about the Indian? And how do you think you can discredit Gilbeck as easily as that? What about the stores and other things here that a naval expert would recognise?'

'We could sink them in the river—'

'Without leaving any traces – in the time we've got? And wouldn't the investigators think of that? It would only take one diver to find them.'

'Then what can we do?'

Friede stood with the immobility of a carving in Saxon stone, yet in his stillness he epitomised all the qualities that had been developed and glorified in the system which he represented – the crude driving force and brutality of the Vandals who had left their tribal name to posterity as a synonym for the destroying barbarian, fatefufly combined with an infinitude of patient and painstaking and pitiless cunning that the Mongol invaders had left Eastern Europe for a legacy that was to filter westwards and lend its aid to the creation of a greater shambles than Genghiz Khan ever aspired to. There was no mistaking the power and competence of the man: the only mystery was the strange contagious warp which had taken those abilities and bent them irrevocably to the service of death and desolation.

'We have to leave here,' he said at last; and his voice was bluntly commonplace and precise, considering nothing but the immediate tactical problem. 'Another base can be found for the submarine, probably; but in any case it must not be captured at all costs . . . I'm afraid you will have to lose the *March Hare.*'

'Must I?' March sounded like a pouting child.

'The choice is yours. But you cannot stay here. On the other hand, if you try to escape in the *March Hare*, the Coastguard seaplanes will find it without much trouble. The submarine has at least a good chance of escape. I think you would do much better to come with us. There will be other work for you, and you can be sure that the Fatherland will not forget you.'

The guard of seamen stood stiffly around the room like soldiers on parade, like robots, without initiative or feeling of their own. It gave Simon an eerie sensation to watch them. They would live or die, kill or be killed, as they were commanded, and all the time think only along one narrow track of blind mechanical obedience. They were a deadlier army than Karel Capek ever dreamed of in his fantasy of the revolt of the robots. And the Saint had a frightening prescience of the holocaust that must lay waste the earth before free and sentient men could triumph over those swarming legions from whom everything human had been stolen but their bodies and their ability to carry out commands. They were the new zombies, the living dead who existed only to interpret the ambitions of a neurotic autocrat more sinister than Nero . . .

Friede snapped an order at one of them to fetch some rope, and the man saluted and hurried to the door. Before he could get out he had to halt, salute again, and make way for a young man who arrived at the entrance at the same moment.

The young man wore only a white undershirt and a pair of soiled cotton trousers, but his cap was worked with an officer's gold thread. He had very blond hair and a callous high-cheek-boned face, and his blue eyes had the inner unseeing brightness of a fanatic. He held a revolver in one hand. He looked at Friede and raised his other hand and said: '*Heil Hitler.*'

'*Heil Hitler,*' responded Friede almost perfunctorily, and went on in clipped methodical German. '*Leutenant*, it has become necessary to remove the submarine immediately. You will prepare to sail at once. Take on all the fuel you can carry, also all the spare food supplies from the *March Hare*. You will also take as much as possible of the reserve ammunition and torpedoes from the stores on shore here. You will be ready in not more than two hours. I shall be going with you myself and I shall give you your destination later. That is all.'

'*Jawohl, Herr Kapitän.*'

The lieutenant raised his hand again, turned on his heel, and went out. His young hard voice began rattling its own orders outside.

A moment later the seaman returned with a full coil of rope. Friede jerked his head curtly at the five prisoners.

'Search them and tie them up. Use another rope to tie them to the beds. And be sure that both jobs are well done.'

Randolph March lighted a cigarette with hands that were not quite perfectly steady. Then he put the hands in his pockets and gazed about the room, trying not to pay too much attention to what was going on, and taking especial care not to directly meet the eyes of any of the captives. It was a different approach from that of Friede, who followed every move with implacable if unmoving vigilance. But in his own way March was trying to ape the captain's cold-blooded self-possession, although the faint shine of moisture on his forehead and the almost imperceptible whitish lines around his mouth worked against him.

'What are you going to do with them?' he asked.

'Leave them here,' replied Friede, without taking his eyes from what the seaman was doing, and in a tone that somehow seemed to leave the trend of the sentence unfinished.

March puffed his cigarette jerkily.

'Why don't we take the girls?'

'What for?'

'Er – hostages. We might still be followed. But even the Navy might hesitate to attack us if they knew we'd got them on board.'

'It might also help to relieve your own boredom,' said the captain cynically.

March swallowed.

Friede switched a glance to him for just long enough to sum him up like a butcher inspecting a sample of steer beef on the hoof, and said: 'It might be possible if you were prepared to share your relief with the rest of the crew. But even then it might give just as much trouble as relief. Apart from jealousies, seamen are superstitious. A wise commander humours them. This isn't a time to risk troubles that we can eliminate.'

He might have been devoting excessively laborious precautions to planning a picnic.

March paced his corner of the room in short zigzags to which he tried to give the same air of casualness.

'The Foreign Investment Pool will be blown up,' he said.

'Yes.'

'That means – that means almost everything I had.'

'Unfortunately.'

'Then – then I'm not going to have very much left.'

'My friend,' said the captain, with terrifying simplicity, 'have you stopped to consider how you would be able to reach any of your resources after Gilbeck's confession has reinforced Templar's report to Washington?'

Randolph March came to a halt in his pacing. It was as if the full meaning of the place where he had arrived was dawning on him at that time. His face was suddenly old and ugly, and his eyes emptied as though they were taking in a vista of the years that were left to him.

Simon saw him without pity, even with an arctic and eternal satisfaction. For what March had been and for what he had done there could be no excuse that could stand up to judgment, for what he suffered on account of it there could be no sympathy that was not maudlin; and in a world where civilisation was fighting for its very life there was no room for such inanities. It was that kind of vacuous sentimentality which had allowed the powers of the jungle to grow strong – that perverse broad-mindedness which insisted on acknowledging every argument for the other side while discounting all the irrefutable evidence on its own side, which strained every nerve to make excuses for a murderer while it pigeonholed the sufferings of the victims who did not need any excuse. It was against such injustices masquerading under the name of Justice that the Saint had always waged his relentless battle; and now at this time he was glad that Randolph March had to suffer even a fraction of what had been suffered by the men and women and children who had been crushed under the juggernaut to which he had freely given his aid.

And besides that, the Saint had something else to think about.

It was no more than a faint flickering star far down on a dark horizon; but it was by such flickers that he had cheated death many times before, and once again that one star had not gone out.

For once again, so ridiculously that it seemed like part of an interminable routine, and yet just as logically as it had ever happened in any case before, he still had his knife. The search that had been made would not have left any of them any hidden weapons of the expected kind; and yet once again it had failed to discover the slim sheath strapped to his left forearm. And it was still possible, in spite of the knots that had been ruthlessly tightened in the stiff new rope, that the long fingertips of his right hand might be able to reach the hilt of that keen blade. Perhaps . . .

Simon held on to that attenuated hope. And at the same time yet another thing was obtruding itself on his consciousness.

It was a peculiar acrid smell that was starting to creep into the room. It had a sharpness that was quite distinctive, that fretted his nostrils in a perplexed effort of recognition as the atmosphere grew heavier with it.

'It isn't quite so much fun as you thought it was going to be, is it, Randy, old boy?' he was saying. 'It's worrying about all sorts of things like that that gave Heinrich his bald dome. You'd better take some March Hare Tonic along with you if you want to save your own crop.'

March glanced at him almost vacantly, and took another deep hot pull at his cigarette.

And all at once Simon knew the meaning of that curious pungent odour in the air. One sentence out of Peter Quentin's first report on Randolph March drummed through his head in a monotonous rhythm. His eyes stayed fixed on the burning cigarette with a kind of weird fascination.

'But – that can't be right.' March turned back to Friede, and it seemed that his voice was harsher and higher pitched. 'I can't lose everything. Everything! What am I going to live on? Where can I go?'

'You can be sure that the Party will take care of you,' Friede said dispassionately. 'I can't tell you yet where we shall be going. I shall communicate with Berlin after the submarine is at sea. But you would be wise not to make too much of your own personal losses. Please remember that Templar's interference has cost the Reich a much greater setback in organisation and preparation than the loss of your private fortune. In this service, as you should know, the individual is of no importance. I hope you agree with me.'

'I hope you do, too, Randy,' said the Saint; and now his mockery had a finer edge, a crystallising direction that was founded on that acrid-smelling cigarette. 'It's a bit different, isn't it? You had a lot of fun being a plutocrat of the Fifth Column, while you could enjoy your mansions and yachts and aeroplanes, and plan your sabotage and propaganda over nice cold bottles of champagne with a glamour girl at each elbow. Now I hope you're going to enjoy doing a lot more hard work on beer and *ersatz* cheese, while a lot of big shots like Heinrich crack the whip. It will be a very refining experience for you, I think.'

March gulped, a little dazedly, as the Saint's insinuatingly derisive voice drove each of its points home with the leisured aim of a skilled surgeon operating a probe, and the drawn lines around his mouth whitened and twitched a little more.

Captain Friede saw and heard the cause and effect also. His eyes had narrowed on March while Simon spoke, and it was significant that he had not tried to make the Saint stop talking. He had gone back into a reptilian stillness from which he roused again with the same reptilian speed.

Simon saw the flare of his small nostrils that was the only warning. And then the captain had taken three quick steps across to March, snatched the cigarette from his mouth and thrown it on the floor, and stamped his heel on it.

'*Dummkopf!*' he snarled. 'This is no time for that!'

But he had moved too late. March had already sucked enough marijuana into his lungs to make a maneater out of a mouse. His eyes sparkled with a wide hollow brilliance.

'Damn you—'

His voice cracked, but not his muscular co-ordination. Like lightning he whirled and snatched a carbine from the slack hands of the nearest unsuspecting guard. He fanned the barrel across the captain's chest.

'It's not going to happen like that, do you see?' The words ran together in shrill desperation. 'I won't let it! I'm going to fool all of you. I'm going to keep you here. I'll turn you over to the Navy myself. When they get here I'll say you tried to fool me, but I was too smart for you. I captured you all myself. They won't take anything away from me. I'll be a hero—'

Simon's heart sank again.

It was like watching a slow-motion nightmare, in which horror advanced with infinite sluggishness and yet was preceded by a paralysis which prohibited doing anything about it. March was crazy, of course – his threat could only have been uttered by a man at a hop-headed height of hysteria that could eliminate cold facts by forgetting them. But that same madness, combined with the strange dislocation of the senses of time and space that was a unique property of the drug, also destroyed itself.

March might have thought that he could cover anyone in the room in a split second; but he was wrong. Friede only nodded, slightly and unhurriedly, to another guard who was half-way behind March. A revolver shocked the room twice with its expanding thunder . . .

Simon's frosted blue eyes settled again on Captain Friede as the Nazi looked up from a body that finished jerking a mere instant after it sprawled over the floor.

'I hate to admit it, Heinrich,' he said, 'but I couldn't have thought of a more poetic end for him myself.'

'He was not the first fool we have had with us,' Friede said with complete coolness. 'And he will not be the last. But as long as we can find pawns like him, we shall not be afraid of many puny efforts like yours.'

'It must be wonderful to feel so certain about everything,' said the Saint, with a coldness that had no fundamental difference, even though it had far less reason.

The captain walked calmly around the room, testing the bonds of Hoppy Uniatz, Karen Leith, Peter Quentin, Patricia Holm, and lastly – with especial care – the Saint.

Then he hit the Saint six times across the face, with icy calculation.

'That,' he said, 'is for some of your humorous remarks. I only wish it was practical for us to take you to Germany, where the discipline of a concentration camp would do much more for your education. But as it is, you will be removed from the need for discipline . . . I hope Gilbeck did not omit to tell you that there are a hundred pounds of high explosive under the flooring of this room with a detonating device which I can fire by radio from the submarine. As soon as we are sufficiently far away, I shall permit myself the luxury of pressing the button . . . I leave you and your friends to look forward to that moment.'

4

It was dark in the room before their eyes could adapt themselves to see by the drift of moonlight that filtered through the small window. Friede had switched off the light when he went out, with a deliberation which told as plainly as words that he did it for a last finishing touch of sadism, to eke the ultimate ounce of mental torment out of their wait for death by stealing the small comfort of companionship that light might have given them. March's body had been left ignored where it had fallen. The storm troopers had been withdrawn, all of them to help hasten the readying of the submarine, except one man who had been posted outside the door. They could hear him pacing up and down like a sentry.

They had not been gagged; and Simon did not believe that that was any oversight. It belonged with the same psychology as the putting out of the light. Light could have aided courage; voices alone, speaking in darkness, might be more likely to give way, and in so doing snowball the self-made agony of nerves wrung out under intolerable strain.

That was how Friede would have seen it.

But Patricia Holm broke the silence first, in a voice that held only practical anxiety.

'Simon, boy, are you all right?'

'As fit as a flea, darling,' he said. 'I don't think Heinrich tried to do too much serious damage, because if he'd really knocked me out I might have missed a lot of these two hours of interesting thinking that he was so pleased about giving us.'

And even while he spoke he was working, the muscles of his arms and shoulders cording in the titanic effort to stretch a few millimetres of slack out of the ropes on his wrists, so that his finger tips might grip the hilt of his knife and ease it out of its sheath . . .

In the darkness there were sounds of other efforts, and the quick subdued catching and releasing of laboured breath.

'I just wish,' Peter Quentin said strainingly, 'you'd had the sense to mind your own fool business and let us mind ours. If we want to come to a place like this to get away from you, isn't that enough to tell you we don't want you? Anyone might think you were a detective snooping for evidence for a divorce.'

'It was the deputy sheriffs that worried me,' said the Saint. 'If I'd known that you and Pat were just looking for some jungle love I'd have gone back to the Palmleaf Fan. I was just afraid they might have picked you up because they'd found out she was under sixteen.'

'Make it under nine,' said Patricia. 'You should have left us here just for being taken in by an old chestnut like that.'

'It was just as good a chestnut as it always has been,' said the Saint. 'In fact, it was better than usual in this case. The sheriff had already paid us a call earlier in the day, and you had every reason to believe that I might have raised some more hell at the Palmleaf Fan. Which as a matter of fact was what did happen, to some extent.'

'Tell us,' said Patricia.

The Saint told them, while he writhed and fought and rested and fought again. It was worth telling, to pass the time, and it kept all their minds away from other things. But in spite of what he was doing, his voice never lost its concise and self-contained inflection. He might have been telling a story that there was all the time in the world to discuss.

By the time he had finished they knew everything that he knew himself. The picture was complete. And there was silence again . . .

'A sweet set-up,' Peter commented at length. 'I just wish I could have had your pal Heinrich to myself for a few minutes.'

It seemed like the only thing to say. But Hoppy Uniatz had other ideas.

'Boss,' he said heavily, 'I still don't get it.'

'Get what?' Simon asked, very kindly.

'About de Pool.'

'Hoppy, I tried to tell you—'

'I know, boss. Dis here ain't de Pool, at all. But you hear what March says before dey give him de woiks? He says after we come here de Pool is all blown up. We ain't never blown up nut'n. So dey must be some udder hijackers tryin' to muscle in on dis shine. I don't get it,' said Mr Uniatz, reiterating his major premise.

'It's just a general craze for blowing things up,' Simon explained. 'It'll die out after a while, like miniature golf and the Handies.'

There was another lull. There should have been so much to say at a time like that, and yet at that time there seemed to be so little that was worth saying.

Outside, above the slow pacing of the sentry, the heavier tramping back and forth of laden men went on, with the sounds of creaking tackle and clunking wood, of muttering voices and the intermittent sharp spur of commands.

Karen Leith said reflectively: 'I don't know how the rest of you are getting on, but I'm supposed to have been trained in all the tricks of getting out of ropes, and I'm afraid these knots are too good for me.'

'For me too,' said Peter.

Even the Saint seemed to have stopped struggling.

Patricia said in a sudden eerie whisper: '*What's moving around in here?*'

'Shut up,' said the Saint's low voice. 'Just keep on talking as you have been.'

And the sound came from a different part of the room from where he had last spoken. In the dim moonlight their straining eyes watched a shadow move – a shadow that crept here and there on the floor. But it was not Randolph March come to life again, as the first ghostly brush of horror in their flesh had suggested, for his shape could still be seen lying where it had fallen.

They were tongue-tied for a while, trying to frame sentences that would sound natural.

At last Peter said, with purpose: 'If only Hoppy and I were loose, we could jump the guy at the door and get his gun and kill some more of the swine before they got us.'

'But they would get you, Peter.' Again the Saint's voice came from another place. 'There are plenty of them, and one gun-load wouldn't go very far.'

'*If* we were loose,' said Patricia, taking her tone from Peter, 'we could sneak off and hide in the jungle. They couldn't afford to spend much time hunting for us.'

'But they'd still get away,' said the Saint.

'Maybe dey wouldn't have room for all de liquor,' said Mr Uniatz, developing his own fairytale. 'Maybe dey gotta leave a whole case, so we can find it.'

'If I could get out,' Karen said, 'I'd do anything to try and stop the submarine.'

'With what?' Peter demanded.

'I wish I knew.'

There was a tiny snapping sound, a very thin long-drawn squeak, then a slurred rustle.

Peter made a restive movement.

'I know it's all quite stupid,' he remarked, 'but I wish you'd give us some of your ideas, skipper. Just to pass the time. What would you do if you could do anything?'

There was no answer.

The silence dragged through long tingling seconds.

Patricia said softly, and not quite steadily: 'Simon . . .'

The Saint did not answer. Or was it an answer when two spaced finger-taps beat almost inaudibly on the floor?

There was nothing else. They had lost track of the moving

shadow, although there might have been a new angular patch of blackness in one dark corner near where the shadow had last moved. But the square of luminance from the window had spread itself on the floor in a way that built up deceptive outlines. In the straining of their eyes, all shadows seemed to run together and dissolve like ephemeral fluids. Each of them at some time tried to count other shapes that could be dimly distinguished and identified. One two, three – and the counter . . . and begin again.

But it was quiet. The ears could create sound in protest, as the eyes could create form and movement. The magnified sifflation of a breath, the screak of a cot-spring, the pulse of their own bloodstream – anything could be built into what the mind wanted to make of it. It even seemed to Karen once that something moved underneath her, like a snake slithering under the floor, so that her skin tightened with instinctive fear.

Presently Peter spoke.

'At a time like this,' he said loudly, 'the Saint would begin to tell one of his interminable stories about a bow-legged bedbug named Aristophagus, who would find himself in a number of complicated and quite unprintable dilemmas. Not having Simon's virginal mind, I can't really deputise for him. So let's play some other silly game. We all try to give the name of a song with our names in it. Like if your name was Mary, you'd say *Mary, Mary, Quite Contrary*. Or Hoppy could say *Hopping This Finds You As It Leaves Me, In Love.*'

There was another inevitable lull.

'*Pat Up Your Troubles In Your Old Kit Bag*,' said Patricia.

'You started it, Peter,' Karen observed. 'Where are you?'

'*Peter Me Of Love*,' said Mr Quentin engagingly.

'*Karen Me Back to Ole Virginny*,' she answered.

'This is getting worse and worse,' said Patricia. 'When do we get down to *Holm Sweet Holm?*'

It was something fantastic to remember, and yet coldly dreadful to go through. Somehow, with feverish desperation, they kept their voices going. They worked through every name that they all knew, and gravitated from there into emptier and wilder devices.

And the time crawled by.

The square patch of moonlight moved across the floor, and slid gruesomely over part of the inanimate face of Randolph March. The sentry shuffled endlessly back and forth outside. The speed tender had made three or four droning trips across the bay. The laboured tramping to and fro of the men shifting stores had dwindled; the underplay of their voices had died to rare guttural murmurs, and the barking of commands had become more infrequent. New sounds had also entered the audible background – clankings of metal distorted by the echoes of water, voices muffled by distance and mingled with vague scrapings and splashings. For a while there had been a deep humming noise that had stopped again.

They had no way to keep track of the minutes that had passed. But each one of them knew how their little span of life had been going by. And not one of them had yet uttered any speculation about the one voice that none of them had heard for so long.

Karen Leith said at last, almost in a sigh: 'They must be nearly ready to sail by now.'

'We did what we could,' said Patricia Holm.

'Chees,' said Hoppy Uniatz, 'dese mugs ain't never been raised right. I see plenty a suckers take de heat, but dey always get a smoke an' a pull from de bottle foist. I never see nobody get de woiks wit' a toist in him like I got.'

With all of them crowded in there, the sweltering heat had filled up the room so that it was like a physical compression, which cramped breathing and weighed into the brain, with a relentless pressure that tempted thought into the hazy liberty of delirium. Another snake might have rustled under the floor beneath Peter Quentin. There might have been a repetition of the scuffling sound that he had heard before, the thin creak, and the snap, and a muffled thudding that was not quite the same. The shadows that had been still might have begun moving again. He would not have been sure.

He said, roughly: 'I hate to remind you, but we weren't talking about your grisly past. We were in the middle of a hot spelling game, and it's up to you, Hoppy. It goes R-I-F-L. And I think we've got you for another life.'

'O,' said the Saint.

Nobody stirred. It was a stillness in which pins could have dropped on velvet with an ear-stunning clatter.

'I'll challenge you,' Peter, said at last. 'There's no such word.'

'Riflolver,' said the Saint.

There was a quick march of steps outside, and the door was opened. The single light went on.

Heinrich Friede stood in the entrance, with the sentry just behind him. His lips were flattened over his teeth in a smile of sneering vindictiveness that embraced them all, so that the creases that ran down from his nose cut deeper into his face.

'We are about to leave,' he said. 'I hope you have enjoyed the anticipation of your own departure. You will not have much longer to wait – perhaps half an hour. I shall press the button as soon as we have reached open water.'

Peter and Patricia and Karen and Hoppy looked at him once, but after that they looked more at the Saint. It might have seemed like a tribute to personality or a gesture of loyalty; but the truth was many times more mundane. They were simply letting their eyes confirm the incomprehensible evidence that their ears had offered a few seconds before.

For the Saint was there, sitting at the end of one cot,

exactly as they had seen him last, with his hands behind him and the bruises of Friede's violence swelling in his face and his shabby clothes sandy and dishevelled. Only perhaps the reckless disdain of his blue eyes burned brighter and more invincible.

'I hope you have a nice voyage, Heinrich,' he said.

'It is a waste of time to tell you,' Friede said, 'but I should like one particular thought to cheer your last moments. You, in your unimportant dissolution, are only a symbol of what you represent. Just as you have tried to fight us and have been out-generalled and destroyed, so everyone on earth who tries to fight us will be destroyed. The little damage you have done will be repaired; your own futility cannot be repaired. Console yourselves with that. The rest of your tribe will soon follow you into your extinction, except those whom we keep for slaves as you once kept other inferior races. So you see, all you have achieved and all you die for is nothing.'

The Saint's eyes were unmoving pools of sapphire.

'It is a waste of time to tell you,' he mocked. 'But I wish you could know one thing before you die. All that you and your kind will destroy the world for is no more in history than a forest fire. You'll bring your great gifts of blackness and desolation; but one day the trees will be green again and nobody will remember you.'

'I leave you to your fantasy,' said the captain.

And he was gone, with another click of the switch and a slam of the door.

They heard him striding away, his footfalls dying on the ground outside, walking again hollowly on the planking of the pier, then ceasing altogether. They heard the last crack of command, and a soft plash of water. The seconds ticked away.

'Simon,' said Patricia.

'Quiet,' said the Saint tensely.

They had only their hearing to build a picture with, and

the sounds that reached them seemed to come through the wrong end of an auditory telescope. Even the sentry's footsteps had ceased; and the endless whine of mosquitoes and the chirrup of other insects built up an obscuring fog in which other sounds were confused.

But there might have been some scuffing of wood, and the ring of a distant tramping on metal. There were voices, and a repetition of the deep steady hum that they had heard before, which drowned out the insects for a while, and then was bafflingly equal with them, and then sank away until it was lost in its turn. Then there seemed to be nothing at all but the soft swish of water against the shore and among the mangrove roots.

The owl came back and began moaning again.

But still the Saint kept silence, while minutes seemed to drag out into hours, before he felt sure enough to move.

Then light seemed to crash into the room like thunder as he flipped the switch.

They stared at him as he stood smiling, with his knife in his hand.

'I'm sorry, boys and girls,' he said, 'but I couldn't take any chances on being overheard.'

'We understand,' said Peter Quentin. 'You're so considerate that we're dazzled to look at you.'

Simon was cutting Patricia free. She kissed him as the last cord fell away, and massaged her wrists as he went over to Karen Leith.

As he freed her, she said: 'I think – I think we all thought you were loose before.'

'I was,' said the Saint.

'Of course,' said Peter Quentin, as his turn came, 'you wouldn't have cared to tell anyone.'

'I had something to do,' Simon said. He finished with Peter and went on to Hoppy. 'I knew there must be a trap-door in the floor or something, and eventually I found it. The lock was a bit awkward, but I mixed my wood-carving and my strong-man act, and sort of persuaded it. Then I had to do my worm impersonation with some wriggling and burrowing under the outside shingles – luckily the place is built on piles instead of straight foundations, and the walls don't go into the ground. Eventually I got outside and prowled here and there.'

'Boss,' said Mr Uniatz, loosening his cramped limbs, 'dijja find anyt'ing to drink?'

'There should be something left on the *March Hare*,' said the Saint, 'but I didn't investigate.'

He went to the door and opened it, standing just outside and filling his lungs with relatively fresh air, while he tamped one of the last two cigarettes from his case. Patricia joined him and took the other one. They stood with their arms linked together, looking across the anchorage where the *March Hare* still rode in darkness under the moon, but a sheet of unrippled water lay where the submarine had been.

There Peter Quentin joined them.

'I don't want to disrupt an idyll,' he observed diffidently, 'but personally I shouldn't mind being a bit further off when Friede gives his farewell broadcast.'

'You needn't worry,' said the Saint. 'I found it under the floor when I got down there – it was what I was looking for under the trap-door anyhow. A very innocent packing-case labelled "Tomato Soup". I hauled it out with me.'

'Where did you dump it?' Peter asked suspiciously.

'I parked it with a lot of other cases of canned food that the crew were ferrying out to the submarine. Or they may have been ammunition – I couldn't be sure. Anyway it was quite a difficult business, getting it out on the pier and making it look natural. But I made it, and managed to get back in time.'

Karen and Hoppy had completed the group while he talked.

And down to the south-west, where his eyes had been fixed, a pillar of jagged crimson climbed into the blue-grey sky, stamping sharp filigree out of the massed blackness of the jungle and flickering spectrally over the intent turning of their faces. Seconds later the concussion pounded upon their eardrums, mingling with a tornado rush of wind that bowed the trees and drew weird whisperings out of the scrub. It seemed like a deafened age before the shuddering earth grew still again.

'And I think Heinrich has pressed the button,' said the Saint.

Epilogue

Simon Templar was watching an errant fly that was trying to gorge itself into a drunken stupor on a drop of Ron Rey that had been spilled on the polished bar of the Dempsey-Vanderbilt. He seemed to have been watching it for a long time, and he was a little tired of making bets with himself on how much longer it would be before it keeled over – or, alternatively, whether it could keep up its ingurgitation until Karen Leith came. With a final movement of impatience he pushed his glass across to the bartender and pantomimed a refill; while the fly, which by virtue of either heredity or environment must have been a kind of insect Uniatz, took off across wind and zoomed away with only the slightest detectable wobble in its course.

Some silent-footed newcomer pulled out the adjoining stool; and the Saint turned, prepared either to bluff the seventh would be intruder out of his right to the place, or to put on an expression of long-suffering reproach if it should actually be Karen herself. But he had no chance to do either.

At his side, the lengthy funebrial form of Sheriff Newton Haskins dripped black coat-tails down the back of his perch. He looked at Simon with a fair rendition of surprise.

'Well, dang my eyes! Wheah did you come from, son?'

'I was here first,' said the Saint. 'If you remember.'

The sheriff's lean jaws champed once on nothing. As though the motion reminded him of an omission, Haskins drew one hand slowly out of a pocket and bit off a chew from a fresh length of plug.

'Waitin' for someone?' he queried conversationally.

'For youth, beauty, glamour, and red hair.' Simon's gaze was cool and impudent. 'Maybe you think you fill some of those qualifications, but to tell you the truth I hadn't noticed it.'

'Nope,' Haskins said. 'I guess that wouldn't be me. But they let all sorts o' people in heah. I happened to be out this way huntin' for a dangerous killer. I sorter worked up a thirst, like. "Newt," I says, "What better place to kill a thirst than in the nearest bar?" So in I comes. I see you heah all alone, so I jest thought you might like some company.'

'What a mind-reader you must be,' murmured the Saint.

He directed the bartender's attention with his thumb as the fresh drink he had ordered was delivered.

'Bring me a water glass,' said Haskins, 'an' a bottle o' rye.'

He pulled a bowl of pretzels closer, and munched one absently on the port side of his mouth where the traffic didn't interfere with his other chewing.

'Who was this dangerous killer?' Simon asked. 'It sounds quite exciting. Did you catch him?'

'Son—' The sheriff's mouth was slightly overloaded. He poured half a tumbler of rye into the water glass and tossed it down. 'This warn't exackly a killin'. Mo' like wholesale slaughter, you might call it. Then, it wasn't exackly in my county, neither.'

'Really?' said the Saint politely. 'Then where was it?'

'Way down in the Everglades, in a place even half the conches down theah couldn't find. But I heard tell it was shuah one helluva mess. Seems like there was almost a dozen plumb dead bodies left lyin' around. Even that feller Gallipolis we was talkin' to got himself shot down theah.'

'Did he? How extraordinary! Do you think he could have

tried to play both ends against the middle just once too often.'

'Mebbe.' The sheriff's wise old eyes held the Saint's tantalising blue ones. 'You wouldn't know nuth'n about none o' them bodies now, would you, son?'

'Corpses?' Simon protested. 'Cadavers? Lying around? . . . What a horrible thought. I always bury my dead bodies in a climate like this. It's so much more hygienic . . . Unless you leave them to drown; and then of course the barracuda take care of them.'

'Yep, that's what I thought,' Haskins said sagely. 'The Coastguard's been sorter pumpin' me, son. Gilbeck says you pulled him out of a hot spot over on Lostman's River. Seems like you was still waitin' theah when the Coastguard cutter comes nosin' around. Had one helluvan explosion offa that coast night before last, too. The Navy seems to think somebody blew up a submarine.'

The Saint sipped his drink.

'It sounds fair enough,' he remarked. 'The first time we met was on account of an explosion. There were a few small bangs in between. And now we can finish on a last big blow-up. It rounds everything out so nicely . . . Or have you got some extra professional reason for all these questions?'

Haskins reloaded his glass and repeated his remarkable feat of finding a third separate passage through his mouth. He wiped his lips with his large spotted cotton handkerchief.

'No, son,' he admitted. 'Professionally speakin', I ain't got no business to ask questions. Seems a whole lot o' big fellers come down from Washington to take charge, an' they tell all us local officers not to meddle with any of it. Seems it ain't supposed to be any concern of ours even if our respected citizen Randolph March is one o' those dead bodies out in Lostman's River. We ain't even supposed to discuss it with nobody till they get ready to issue an official report from the

State Department. But you can't blame me for bein' curious.'

'Naturally I don't blame you,' Simon agreed gravely.

Haskins rubbed the side of his long nose, hopefully at first, then with increasing depression.

'Well,' he said at last, 'that shuah is plumb understandin' of you.'

'I'm sorry,' said the Saint. 'But those guys from Washington told me the same thing too. And since they were good enough not to keep me locked up, I think I ought to play ball with them. They'll break the whole story as soon as they're set for it.'

Haskins drank again, gloomily.

'O' course,' he said, 'I don't rightly know if that covers a feller in Ochopee who's swore out a warrant agin you for assaultin' him an' stealin' his blasted car.'

'Are you going to serve it?'

'Nope,' Haskins said. 'I tore it up. I figured it warn't legal. Who the hell ever heard o' callin' a boat with ten-foot wheels on it a car?'

Simon lighted a cigarette with some care.

'Daddy,' he said softly, 'I was wondering whether you ever switched from rye whisky if a friend of yours offered to buy a quart of champagne.'

'That, son,' said the sheriff, 'is something that nobody of my acquaintance has ever offered to buy; but with the thirst I'm luggin' around today I might give anythin' a try.'

Simon caught the elusive bartender and placed the order.

'And after all,' he said, 'who ever heard of calling a mild scalp massage an assault?'

'I dunno as I'd go all that way with you,' Haskins demurred judicially. 'But seein' as this feller was workin' for Mr March, in a manner o' speakin', I figured mebbe no one would care very much.'

'You mean it was nothing but curiosity that brought you here?'

The sheriff hunched his sinewy black shoulders and stared up at the clock over the bar. He shuffled a little stiffly on the stool.

'Son,' he said, 'I told you once I had a sorter weakness for red-heads myself. This afternoon it seemed that I ought to check up on one that we both like. She was packin' bags in an almighty hurry when I got theah. Seems she had to catch a plane to somewheres in South America this evening. I reckon she just made it by now. But she took time off to write a letter an' asked me to give it to you after the plane left.'

He dragged an envelope out of an inner pocket and laid it on the bar.

Simon picked it up and opened it with hands of surgical precision.

Dear Saint:

When I made a date for tonight, I meant it. But it doesn't seem as if any of us belong to ourselves any more. And there is so little time.

I've had new orders already, to begin at once – and that means at once. I'll barely have time to pack. I can't even say good-bye to you. I had thought of calling you to meet me at the airport, but now Haskins is here and I think I'll send this note by him instead. The other would have been much harder for both of us.

I could say Thank you, Thank you, a million times, and it wouldn't mean anything. You know yourself just how much you've done, as I know it too, and as they know it by now in London as well as Washington. That should be enough for both of us. But we both know that it's still only a beginning. Both of us will have so much more to do before we can sit back in our armchairs again.

And just for myself alone, it isn't enough either. That's why I'd rather write this than have to see you again. I can't help it, darling. In spite of all the impossibilities, I still want that evening we never had.

So silly, isn't it? But if miracles happen and both of us are still alive when all this is over – we might meet somewhere. It won't ever happen, of course, but I want to think about it now.

Good-bye. I love you,

Karen.

Dry champagne frothed on the bar. Simon looked at the label on the bottle as he folded the letter slowly and put it away. Bollinger '28. That was what they had drunk when they first met. He could see her still as he had seen her then, with her pale perfect face and flaming hair, and the deep violet of her eyes. And he saw her as she had last been beside him, with his gun speaking from her hand. And so – that was the story . . .

Abruptly he raised his glass.

'Good luck,' he said.

Sheriff Haskins held him with that shrewd timeless gaze.

'I'll say that to her too, son.'

'You've been a good father to me, Daddy.' The Saint split a paper match with his thumbnail and twirled it in his glass, absently swizzling bubbles out of the wine. 'Do you mind if I'm curious too? I'm not so used to all this co-operation from the Law.'

Haskins's jutting Adam's apple took a downward journey and vanished behind his black string tie.

'Well, son, it's like this. A lot o' strange critters bed down together peaceable-like when a panther's on the prowl. Let 'em get to fightin' too much among themselves, an' the crazy cat will gollop 'em all. Take rabbits, now.' The sheriff filled his glass again and smiled ruminatively. 'I reckon if enough rabbits ganged up together an' got properly mad, they could put a bobcat on the run. Most times the folks in this country are home-lovin' an' peaceful as rabbits – but it seems to me that the time for a little gangin' up an' gettin' mad has more 'n come. You've sorter helped me straighten that out in my mind.'

Simon looked at him through the smoke of his cigarette.

'Even though I broke your sacred law?'

'There ain't no law,' Haskins declared slowly, 'when some son-of-a-bitch is tryin' to take over the whole of creation, an' usin' what laws there are to try an' make it easier for himself. Like he lets little countries believe in laws of neutrality, which means they don't begin gangin' up on him until after he's jumped on 'em. An' like he uses their laws o' liberty to sneak in his spies an' start fightin' 'em long before he comes out an' calls it a war. I done a powerful lot o' thinkin' since we had a talk the other night. Some folks are gonna blind themselves to it, an' the politicians are gonna help ball it up so they can keep gettin' votes from the people who don't want to think, but when I see a lot o' thugs drillin' right under my nose, screamin' against our kind o' government an' generally thinkin' they're bigger 'n the country they live in, I jest know the whole stinkin' business is gettin' too close to home.'

The Saint looked at him silently, a thin dowdy man against his bright butterfly background, a solemn and incongruous figure, and yet something that had been fined down to the ultimate unconquerable fibre of the land that had bred him . . .

Haskins drained his glass and set it back on the bar.

'That's right good liquor.' He dried his mouth on the back of his hand. 'I hate killin'. But there's times when things get so damn hot there ain't noth'n but a little killin' will stop a helluva sight more. I don't know, o' course, but from what

I've heard tell, you believe in back fires when things start to burn. Mebbe you've talked me round to your way o' thinkin'. Mebbe more of us have to be talked round before this fire gets too big for us. I dunno.'

He stood up, and extended one muscular brown hand.

'I got to go. But I'm hopin' more of our folks will start gangin' up before it's too late. Mebbe I just sorter like you, son.'

'Maybe it's mutual, Daddy,' said the Saint, and put out his own strong grip.

Watch for the sign of the Saint!

If you have enjoyed this Saintly adventure, look out for the other Simon Templar novels by Leslie Charteris – all available in print and ebook from Mulholland Books.

Enter the Saint
The Saint Closes the Case
The Avenging Saint
Featuring the Saint
Alias the Saint
The Saint Meets His Match
The Saint Versus Scotland Yard
The Saint's Getaway
The Saint and Mr Teal
The Brighter Buccaneer
The Saint in London
The Saint Intervenes
The Saint Goes On
The Saint in New York
Saint Overboard
The Saint in Action
The Saint Bids Diamonds
The Saint Plays with Fire
Follow the Saint
The Happy Highwayman
The Saint Goes West
The Saint Steps in
The Saint on Guard
The Saint Sees It Through
Call for the Saint
Saint Errant
The Saint in Europe
The Saint on the Spanish Main
The Saint around the World
Thanks to the Saint
Señor Saint
The Saint to the Rescue
Trust the Saint
The Saint in the Sun